Praise for *Vampires Never Cry Wolf*

"The energy is powerful and bewitching… Ms. Humphreys continues to possess the gift of storytelling and gathering the hearts and souls of her audience."

—*Night Owl Reviews*

"Fun and sexy…the chemistry is electrifying and the love scenes are smoking."

—*Fresh Fiction*

"Humorous, snarky, and totally hot, this is a terrific addition to Humphreys's Dead in the City series."

—*Booklist*

"Humphreys has outdone herself… All fans of paranormal romance need to read this book."

—*RT Book Reviews* Top Pick, 4.5 Stars

"Sara Humphreys pulls the reader into a fascinating, complex, and imaginative world of the supernatural."

—*The Reading Cafe*

"An awesome read for any reader. It had romance, passion, jealousy, betrayal, lies, and a huge twist that I never would have guessed in a million years."

—*The Romance Reviews*

Praise for *Vampire Trouble*

Praise for *Tall, Dark, and Vampire*

"Shines with fascinating new characters… Readers will not want to wait for more from the very talented Humphreys!"

—*RT Book Reviews* Top Pick of the Month, 4.5 Stars

"Engaging… Humphreys skillfully blends intrigue and romance."

—*Publishers Weekly*

"Refreshing…rousing romantic urban fantasy. The sleuthing is terrific…but it is the second chance at love that enhances this entertaining thriller."

—*Midwest Book Review*

"Riveting… I found Ms. Humphreys's writing and characters fresh and exciting."

—*Anna's Book Blog*

"Outstandingly written, it will possess the hearts of readers. A must-read for all vampire lovers."

—*Bitten by Love Reviews*

"The worldbuilding and passion will leave readers breathless."

—*The Romance Reviews*

"Mystery, action, intrigue, and hot love scenes…will literally get your blood moving."

—*BookLoons*

Also by Sara Humphreys

The Amoveo Legend

Unleashed
Untouched
Undenied (novella)
Untamed
Undone
Unclaimed
Unbound (novella)

Dead in the City

Tall, Dark, and Vampire
Vampire Trouble
Vampires Never Cry Wolf

The McGuire Brothers

Brave the Heat

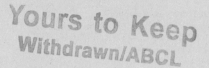

SARA HUMPHREYS

 sourcebooks
casablanca

Copyright © 2016 by Sara Humphreys
Cover and internal design © 2016 by Sourcebooks, Inc.
Cover art by John Kicksee
Cover image © Tom Tyson

Sourcebooks and the colophon are registered trademarks of Sourcebooks, Inc.

Published by Sourcebooks Casablanca, an imprint of Sourcebooks, Inc.
P.O. Box 4410, Naperville, Illinois 60567-4410
(630) 961-3900
Fax: (630) 961-2168
www.sourcebooks.com

Printed and bound in Canada
MBP 10 9 8 7 6 5 4 3 2 1

*"Forgiveness does not change the past,
but it does enlarge the future."*

—*Paul Boese*

For the badass chick inside all of us...

Chapter 1

HIDDEN WITHIN THE LUSH BRANCHES OF THE TOWER-
ing tree, Trixie crouched low to avoid hitting her head
on a dangling clump of pinecones. This had been her
usual spot ever since Chelsea moved in a year ago,
but those freaking pinecones always got tangled in her
hair. Uncomfortable as it was, this location gave her
a clear view into the kitchen and family room of the
tiny house. The thick scent of the pine needles filled
Trixie's nose as she sat motionless amid the branches,
unnoticed by the human woman inside the little white
clapboard cottage.

Trixie's throat tightened with emotion. With her
enhanced hearing, she picked up Chelsea's tuneless
hum as she washed dishes in the small sink. She seemed
content and peaceful. A combination of pride and sadness swirled inside Trixie—but not regret. That was one
emotion she never allowed herself to entertain. Everyone
made hard choices; living with the consequences of
some choices was harder than making them.

She shouldn't be here. But she couldn't manage to
stay away either. Not for long, anyway. Trixie could go
maybe two or three months without checking on the girl,
but then the nagging pull of worry would drag her back.

Was Chelsea safe? Was she happy?

Those were the only two questions that Trixie ever
wanted answered. Based on the satisfied, wistful smile

on Chelsea's sweet face, the answer to both right now was a resounding yes.

Trixie adjusted her position on the thick branch, the treads of her combat boots digging into the rough bark. It hadn't always been that way. There had been difficult times. Times when Trixie hadn't been able to stop herself from intervening. She had only wanted to give Chelsea a gift—an anonymous gift—but when Olivia found out about it, she was freaking *furious*. The vampire community did not look fondly on meddling in human lives. But that didn't matter to Trixie.

All that mattered was making sure that Chelsea was okay.

The alarm on Trixie's cell phone vibrated in the pocket of her jeans. She swore under her breath and pulled it out before quickly shutting it off. The club would be opening soon, and she had to go back to get the bar stocked and ready. She glanced at Chelsea one last time before shooting into the night sky. Maybe tomorrow after the party she would come back for another quick visit.

As long as no one found out, what could it hurt?

———

Trixie couldn't remember the last time she went to a little girl's birthday party but it certainly *wasn't* since becoming a vampire.

Olivia and Doug might be two of the world's most powerful vampires, but they had also become the first vampire parents in recorded history. Today was their daughter Emily's second birthday and they were throwing her a big old party, complete with birthday cake and balloons.

Trixie had gone back and forth all day about whether or not to attend.

Being around little Emily was bittersweet on a regular day, and the birthday celebration would only heighten Trixie's struggle. But choosing not to go would have been selfish. Trixie's personal drama wasn't Emily's fault, and she didn't want to disappoint the adorable redheaded cherub. Not only that, but Emily was Olivia's daughter, and since Olivia was Trixie's maker, that made her family.

Not showing up would have been rotten.

Olivia would have understood if Trixie bailed out; she knew her better than anyone else. But Olivia's bloodmate, Doug, wouldn't understand her absence from such a celebrated event. Neither would the other members of the coven.

Nope. Trixie decided to do what she always did. She'd put on a smile, make a wiseass comment or two, and act like nothing and nobody bothered her.

A familiar voice pulled her from her thoughts as she strode down the stone hallways of the Presidium's underground facility, buried deep beneath Fort Tryon Park and The Cloisters in New York City.

"Well, smack my ass and call me Sally."

The deep Texas drawl echoed around her, stopping Trixie dead in her tracks. A shiver of lust whispered beneath her skin as it usually did when he was nearby, but she swiftly shoved it aside.

"Okay, Sally." Trixie rolled her shoulder and fought the buzz of attraction. "But you can smack your own ass."

"What's the matter, darlin'?" Soaked with that twang,

the rumbling baritone of his voice drifted over her shoulder, but she didn't spare him a glance. Trixie continued toward Olivia and Doug's apartment door, forcing herself to put one foot in front of the other. "Don't I even get a hello?"

"Hello, Dakota," she said with a roll of her eyes.

Coming to this little gathering for Emily was difficult enough, and his arrival only ratcheted her anxiety up a notch. Damn it. Why wasn't he out on patrol? Over the past few months, the cocky and admittedly gorgeous sentry had become more and more present in her little corner of the universe.

Trixie fiddled with the box in her hands, the one she'd wrapped carefully with the pink-and-white skull-and-crossbones paper. She didn't even bother to put a card with it. Everyone would know who'd brought it. She was the only coven member with bright pink hair and a penchant for skulls and crossbones, after all.

"That your present for little Emily?" he asked. "You wrapped it real nice."

He got closer by the second.

"No." Trixie snorted. "I just like carrying around a gift-wrapped box for the hell of it. You know, for shits and giggles."

She was being a snot, but she couldn't help herself.

Trixie kept her gaze pinned to the mammoth mahogany door at the end of the hallway and tried not to notice that he'd sidled up next to her, his stride matching hers.

Dakota Shelton—the newest sentry for the Presidium, the vampire government—was not an easy man to ignore.

His six-foot, two-inch broad-shouldered frame towered over her easily, but there was something else about him that set her on edge. It was the way he carried himself. He moved effortlessly and casually, as if he was just the good old boy from Texas he claimed to be.

But Trixie knew better.

He was a sentry, a member of the elite vampire police force, and he was anything but good. Beneath that easy breezy charm lurked an executioner who could kill her, and anyone else nearby, in the blink of an eye. Dakota was deadly, stealthy, and full of swagger—and that was probably why she found him undeniably attractive.

She never could steer clear of dangerous men.

If Trixie La Roux had one talent in this shitty, crazy world, it was picking the wrong guy. As a human, her poor choices in men had constantly gotten her into trouble. When Olivia had found her in the abandoned subway tunnels of Manhattan, Trixie had just had her heart stomped on by yet another guy. He'd betrayed her and tossed her aside like she was nothing.

Men lied.

They did and said anything to get what they wanted.

They made promises that were never kept.

In the end she was always alone.

Abandoned.

Worthless.

She was powerless…until she became a vampire.

Once Trixie was turned, she slipped easily into the strength and independence that came with immortality. Being a vamp was clear and uncomplicated. There was no guesswork about how to navigate the world, and better yet, there was no addiction. She had finally been freed from the drugs that had kept her prisoner as a human.

She *refused* to be addicted to anyone or anything ever again.

"So what's in the box, darlin'?" He inched closer. "I bet it's real nice."

"Quit calling me that, would ya?"

"Why?" His grin broadened. "What would you prefer? Sweetie pie? Honeybee? Or maybe sugar?"

"As if!" Trixie snorted with a laugh. In spite of how sexist it was to call her or any woman by pet names, she found herself surprisingly amused. "How about if you try using my name? Like, I totally have one, thank you very much. Jeez, get with the program, cowboy. Don't you know that it's chauvinistic to refer to a woman by names like that?"

"Come on now." He sighed. "I'm just bein' my normal self is all, Miss Trixie."

"Not Miss Trixie," she said with waning patience. "Trixie. Okay? Like, just plain old Trixie."

"Girl," he said through a laugh, "you are anythin' but plain."

"And *you* are anything but normal." She chuckled and sent a sidelong glance in his direction. "*Sally.*"

"Why are you always lookin' to pick a fight with me?" Dakota asked, stopping in front of the czars' apartment door. "Were you this feisty as a human?"

"I guess you'll never know." Trixie stuck her tongue out at him. "I'm all vampire and being feisty is totally my thing, man."

"Damn, woman. If you ask me, Olivia should train you as a sentry and put some of that fire in your belly to work. Maybe we could get you out there and kickin' a little ass. Y'know…let you blow off a little steam."

Trixie had been about to knock on the door. Her fist stopped an inch from the mahogany surface, and irritation mixed with anxiety flickered up her spine. She dropped her hand to her side and turned slowly toward the man who was quickly becoming a total pain in the butt.

"Is that so?" she asked in a deceptively sweet voice. "You think I should kick some ass?"

He shifted his body so they were now toe to toe. Trixie's gut instinct was to step back and increase the distance between them, because getting too close to him was dangerous—for many reasons. But she held her ground even though it went against her better judgment.

Backing down wasn't her style, at least until she met this guy. He made her want to run to him and run away from him at the same time. It was more than a little confusing.

Dakota's arms hung at his sides, and even though they were always hidden beneath his long leather sentry coat, she had a hunch they were thick and well defined. His pale blue eyes, which sometimes glinted almost silver, crinkled at the corners as a grin curved his firm-looking lips. He leaned closer and his scent, a mixture of sandalwood and leather, filled the air around them.

In spite of the warning bells that went off in her head, the heat of desire pooled in her belly.

But beneath the thick scent of lust lay the pungent aroma of silver from the heavy arsenal hidden within his coat. The reminder of who he really was broke the spell.

You're playing with fire, she thought.

"Yes, ma'am." His grin widened as he looked her up and down in one slow, lazy pass, lingering briefly on her breasts before finally locking his gaze with hers again. "You look like you were made for it. In fact, if you ever wanna learn the ropes, I'd be happy to teach you a thing or two."

If Trixie didn't know better, she'd swear the man was flirting with her and egging her on. She let out a short laugh and shook her head slowly. He had no idea who he was dealing with. If Dakota wanted to play this game, he was no match for her. In the field of battle he would be the undeniable victor, but flirting was her specialty.

She shouldn't feed into his taunting, but Trixie never did know when to quit. Besides, there was something about this vampire that kept her coming back for more.

"I doubt that there's much you could teach me, cowboy." Trixie kept her voice low, barely above a whisper, and moved closer so their bodies were mere inches apart. His eyes widened slightly as she met his challenge. "And if I'm going to kick some ass…I'm totally gonna start with yours."

"That so?" Dakota pulled a lollipop out of his pocket before quickly unwrapping it and popping it into his mouth.

"What kind of vampire sucks on human candy?" Trixie arched one eyebrow. "What's with that, anyway? That is, like, way weird."

"I enjoy the way they taste. That's all."

"Yeah? Well, it's strange." She tilted her chin defiantly. "I should kick your butt for that offense alone."

"Easy there, darlin'." He slid the sucker from his lips and pointed it at her. His voice dropped to a low rumble as he leaned closer and murmured, "Your threat sounds more like a promise. If you're not careful, I'll have a mind to make you keep it."

The sweet scent of cinnamon filled her nose and mingled with the dizzying buzz of lust, which was why Trixie barely noticed that the door to the apartment had opened. She blinked and stepped back, suddenly and acutely aware of her body's intense reaction to the nearness of his. When she finally tore her gaze from Dakota's, she found Doug holding the door open and looking at her and Dakota suspiciously.

"I thought I heard you two out here." Doug stepped back and gestured for them to come in. "We were waiting for you before we brought out Emily's cake. Come on in and let's get my baby girl's party started."

"Right." Trixie cracked the knuckles on her right hand and handed him the present. "I was just about to knock."

"Uh-huh." Doug glanced back and forth between them and nodded slowly. He'd been a homicide detective in his human life, which made getting anything past him more than a little difficult. "Well, no need to knock. You two are family. Come on."

Doug took the gift and headed into the apartment. Before Trixie could force her feet to move, Dakota slipped past her and whispered, "I'd say that round goes to me. Wouldn't you?"

Trixie opened her mouth to respond but snapped it shut when her sibling Maya came running over and wrapped her up in a bouncy hug. Maya's long blond hair obscured Trixie's view as Dakota strolled casually into the apartment.

"I'm so glad you're finally here," Maya squealed.

She must have noticed how annoyed Trixie was because her giddiness faded quickly. Maya glanced over her shoulder at Dakota before stepping into the hallway and closing the door behind her. "What's going on?"

"Nothing," Trixie lied. She tried to get past Maya to the door but her sister blocked the way. "Come on, Maya. It's nothing. Let's go inside."

"Yeah, right," Maya said with a roll of her big blue eyes. "Are you gonna tell me what's happening between you and Dakota or not?"

"There is nothing happening." Trixie placed both hands on Maya's shoulders. "Other than the fact that he's freaking annoying me. Now move it."

"Mmm-hmm. I knew it." Maya's eyes narrowed and a smile curved her pink lips. "You like him," she said in a conspiratorial whisper. She poked Trixie in the chest. "Ha! I knew it. You're so full of it."

"Shut up." Trixie slapped a hand over her sister's mouth, but Maya shoved it aside. "Not so loud."

"Sorry," she said in a barely audible voice. "But you two have been flirting forever! Why don't you just sleep with the guy and get it out of your system? I mean, seriously, everyone knows you two have the hots for each other. Why not just go for it? I mean, let's be honest, it's not like you're shy. You've gotten it on with a bunch of human guys, so why not give a vamp like him a chance?" She arched one eyebrow. "You have to admit, he's a hottie."

That was an understatement. Dakota was a tall, gorgeous vampire with a naughty twinkle in his eye and a jacked body, but all Trixie said was, "*Not* gonna happen. It's too complicated."

"Why?"

"Because I can glamour a human, okay? I can't sleep with *him* once or twice and move on. He's a vampire, and you know we can't glamour another vamp. The human dudes never remember me or what happened. There's simply pleasure for everyone. No muss, no fuss, and nobody gets hurt. That is the *only* kind of sex I'm interested in."

"I think you're shortchanging yourself…and him." Maya tucked her long blond hair behind her ear before fiddling with the ends of the platinum strands. "Maybe he only wants to have fun too. Aren't you being kind of presumptuous to think he'd automatically want a relationship?"

"Maya, Dakota is a sentry, okay? The guy isn't going anywhere. He will be patrolling this city for at least the next fifty years, and since I have no intention of leaving, there is no point in risking an awkward situation for a few nights of hot sex."

And Trixie had *no doubt* it would be hot.

"Whatever," Maya said flippantly. "But I still think you're full of it."

Before Trixie could respond, her sister spun around and opened the door to the apartment.

"Let's get the party started." Maya clapped her hands excitedly. "Game on!"

Dakota captured Trixie's gaze the moment she stepped into the room and her stomach fluttered. Damn it all. He winked and that cocky grin slid across his face.

"Oh, it's on," Trixie murmured. "It's on like Donkey Kong."

And she sure as hell wasn't talking about the party.

Chapter 2

IT HAD BEEN DECADES SINCE DAKOTA HAD ATTENDED A
birthday party—and never for a vampire-human hybrid
toddler. The entire event only confirmed his feelings
about New York City.

This place was crazy.

Give him the wild plains and wide-open spaces of
Texas any day of the week. Before he'd been stationed
here a couple of years ago, everyone he met raved to
him about the Big Apple. Dakota hadn't felt at home
since he'd arrived, and the vampire-human toddler
didn't exactly put him at ease.

Vampires having a baby? Now *that* was some crazy
shit—but crazy or not, that didn't make it any less
real. These city slickers weren't exactly run-of-the-
mill vampires.

Emily, the tiny guest of honor, sat at the head of
the shiny black dining table in a white high chair. She
clapped with glee as Maya brought out the small pink-
and-white birthday cake. There was a roomful of people,
but Emily was the only one there who could actually eat
the cake.

Maya placed it on the table in front of the child as the
rest of the coven members broke into a rousing chorus
of "Happy Birthday." Even Shane Quesada, Dakota's
fellow sentry and one of the most badass soldiers Dakota
had ever met, was singing along. He stood behind his

bloodmate, Maya, with something that looked like a smile on his face. The guy rarely smiled, and when he caught Dakota's eye, his grin faltered briefly before he again stared adoringly at the curly-haired toddler.

Dakota studied the scene intently but stayed out of the way, leaning against the living room wall. They had all welcomed him. Hell, they were friendly enough. But he still wasn't one of them. Not really.

He'd watched most of his human family grow old and die. That had been difficult enough. But when Dakota lost his maker early on, he had learned the true meaning of grief. It wasn't something he ever wanted to experience again.

He liked to keep moving and, in that respect, being a sentry was a perfect fit. That, and there was nothing he loved quite as much as a good fight, the smell of blood in the air, and the freedom to put down the bad guys.

Yup. It was the perfect job for him.

Although hanging around this city-slicker coven of vampires could confuse a man. The more time he spent with them, the more he wanted to be a part of their family. They were a *really weird* family but a family all the same. Dakota stilled as Olivia hugged her little girl, and when she kissed Emily's rosy round cheek, a deep empty ache welled in his chest.

Damn it all.

The sudden and surprising swell of emotion swamped him, and he quickly pulled another cinnamon lollipop out of the pocket of his long leather sentry coat. Dakota rolled the stick between his fingers before unwrapping it and popping it into his mouth. The spicy sweet taste of the candy was a little like blood, but that's not why he liked it. Sucking on that damn lollipop was the one remnant he held on to from his previous life.

It let him recall how it felt to be human.

The czars sat on either side of their daughter, and Olivia's secretary, Suzie, was snapping pictures of the festivities with her phone. Damien, a hulking brute of a vampire, hovered behind Suzie like he usually did and waved at Emily as he sang along.

Most little ones would be frightened by a guy like Damien, but not Emily. She beamed at him with pure adoration. Besides, Dakota thought with a wry grin, the dude was wearing one of those pointy party hats and looked about as harmful as a teddy bear.

Dakota would be damned if he was going to put on a pink party hat. A cowboy hat, that he'd wear, but a pointy paper cone with sparkly ballerinas on it was not going on his head. No, sir.

"Dakota? Catch." Olivia's sharp green-eyed gaze latched on to his as she tossed him one of the dreaded paper hats. "You must have missed yours when you came in."

"Nope, I didn't miss it. I know that as czar of this district, you're my boss and all, but I'm gonna have to decline this particular request." Dakota caught it with one hand. He tilted his head in deference to the czar and winked at Emily, who rewarded him with a giggle. "Hats just aren't my style," he drawled. "Unless of course, we're talking about a Stetson."

"My mistake, but don't sweat it. It's not an order, and besides we're all off duty right now." Olivia laughed as Maya swept in and adjusted the bib around the little one's neck. "Maybe for her birthday party next year, I'll get a special cowboy birthday hat just for you."

"Thank you, ma'am." Dakota dipped his head and pulled the lollipop out of his mouth. "That would be real nice."

With a loud shriek, Emily smashed both of her pudgy little hands into the cake before giggling and eating the confection off her fingers. The entire group burst out laughing and Suzie snapped away, capturing more photos.

Everyone was having a grand old time.

Well, almost everyone.

Dakota's steady gaze shifted to the left and landed on the only individual in the room who wasn't exuding the same goofy happiness as the rest. He'd sensed her uneasiness out in the hallway before he even rounded the corner.

Aside from being the only woman who'd caught his eye in over fifty years, she was the one member of the coven that Dakota couldn't figure out. That nagged at him. He was good at getting a bead on people—human, vamp, or otherwise—but not this one. Over the past couple of years, the pink-haired spitfire of a woman had become a riddle he wanted to solve.

Trixie La Roux sat on the arm of the overstuffed brown leather chair with an expression that Dakota couldn't read. Her hair, which changed color as frequently as the wind blew, was currently streaked with variations on pink and black, and slicked back in a short stubby ponytail. Dressed in her usual ensemble of ripped-up jeans, black combat boots, and a well-worn graphic T-shirt, she looked every bit the crazy punk rock wild woman most people thought she was.

When Dakota first met Trixie, he'd expected her to be crude and rude, but no matter how hard she tried to put out that image, she was neither. Under all of that heavy black eye makeup and pink hair was a woman doing her best to hide. Her edgy appearance and saucy language were a cover, a way to hide in plain sight.

But hide from what? Or whom?

And that was what kept drawing Dakota in.

Perched on the arm of the chair, Trixie slowly swung her boot-clad feet, her pale brown eyes focused on Emily. Dakota noted an unmistakable air of sadness hidden behind a small smile. Why was she so damn melancholy? She loved Emily and the rest of the coven, so why was she acting more like she was at a funeral instead of a birthday party?

Trixie adjusted her position, her palms resting on either side of her thighs, but she froze when she caught him staring at her.

"What?" She cracked her knuckles as she did whenever she got nervous. She brushed at her shirt and pants. "Did Emily fling frosting on me or something?"

"No, ma'am. Just admiring a pretty lady, that's all." Dakota's grin grew as her cheeks pinkened. "Nothin' wrong with that."

"Right," she scoffed. "I'm no lady."

"I beg to differ," he said with a wink. "A tough one… but definitely a lady."

Clearing her throat, she hopped off the chair and moved closer to her maker, as though seeking protection.

Sticking her hands in the back pockets of her jeans, she nodded toward the table.

"Hey, Olivia. Why don't you have Emily open some of her presents?"

Dakota pushed himself away from the wall and moved in closer, giving him a clearer view of Trixie. As they pulled one present after another over to the birthday girl, Trixie's body language reeked of anxiety that grew more visible by the second.

She folded her arms over her chest and nibbled on her thumb while Olivia and Doug helped their daughter open the pile of gifts. Trixie's smile was strained and not the open, genuine smile he'd witnessed over the past couple of years. He'd been studying her closely and had grown to know her smiles—and this was her fake one. The smile that hid her sadness.

Not so tough after all and definitely not so simple.

"I left a gift for Miss Emily too. It's right there on the table." Dakota tossed the lollipop stick in the small wastebasket in the corner. "It's the one in the brown box. Just a little somethin'."

"Thanks, man," Doug said without taking his eyes off his daughter. "You didn't have to do that, but it's appreciated."

"Let's see what our resident cowboy gave you." Olivia dragged the box over. "It's not pair of chaps or something, is it?"

"No, ma'am." Dakota shook his head and let out a beleaguered sigh. "No chaps. She doesn't have a horse and gettin' her chaps now would be plain old silly. This isn't as swell as a real horse, but I hope she'll take a shine to it."

"Swell?" Trixie said with a snort. "Dude, no one says 'swell' anymore."

"I do." He clasped his hands in front of him.

"Of course you do." She rolled her eyes and muttered, "You probably say 'neat-o' too."

"Yes, ma'am." He winked at Trixie and suppressed a grin when she looked away. "Swell. Neat-o. All those words are great, and if you ask me, y'all should use 'em more often."

"As if." Trixie rolled her eyes. "I'll keep that in mind, cowboy, but if you don't update your verbiage, it won't take long for humans to figure out that something's up with you. I mean, what if Shane walked around talking like they did back in the olden days?"

"He kinda does," Dakota said with a wry smile in Shane's direction. "No offense, Quesada."

"None taken." Shane shrugged as Maya snuggled into his embrace. "I'm well aware of my outdated vernacular."

"Dude? You're totally not helping." Trixie made a face of derision. "Okay, cowboy, let's put it this way. For the decade impaired, when you talk like *that*, it makes you sound like a *real square*, man."

"Hell no." Dakota's face fell and he straightened his back. "I ain't no square, missy, and you can bet your fine-lookin' bottom on that."

Trixie flinched and an unreadable expression flickered over her features. Olivia intervened before she could respond.

"Are you two finished?" Olivia asked, looking back and forth between them with a thinly disguised smile. "I'd like to open Dakota's gift for Emily, but without the *banter*."

"By all means." Dakota made a sweeping gesture with one hand as Emily, now seated in her mother's lap, tugged at the box. "Like I was sayin', it's just a little something."

When Olivia opened the simple brown box and pulled the present from within, a squeal of delight erupted from Emily. Her small pudgy hands immediately curled around the coffee-colored wooden horse but her reaction wasn't the one that got to him. Amid the *oohs* and *ahhs* over his hand-carved creation, Trixie remained silent. Her brown-eyed gaze was fixed on Emily and her new-found prize. As the little girl hugged her present, the expression on Trixie's face went from playful to sad in a split second.

"This is beautiful, Dakota," Olivia said, admiring the handcrafted figure. "Did you make this?"

"I sure did," he said, turning his attention back to Olivia. Pride filled him along with a touch of humility. "My daddy taught me how to carve wood and, well, as y'all can imagine, I've had some years to perfect it. She's too little for a real horse, so this one will have to do for now."

"Thank you." Olivia let out soft laugh as Emily pulled at the ribbon on the table. "But I mostly thank you for not getting her a real horse."

"We both do," Doug chimed in.

"Happy to do it." Dakota nodded and slipped his hands in the pockets of his coat. "If she takes a shine to it, I'm happy to make her more. Hell, I could whittle the girl her own herd of wild horses, if you think she'd like it. Every little girl should have a horse of her own."

Before Olivia could respond, Trixie headed for the door.

"I'm kinda beat, so I'll see you guys later." She curled her hand around the apartment door and tugged it open. Her gaze met his briefly just before she slipped outside. "See you at The Coven after sundown."

The Coven was their nightclub, where Trixie and Maya tended bar every night.

"Hey," Maya called to her sister, flying to the door in a blur. "Why are you leaving? It's Sunday, the one night the club is closed. You can't tell me you're going to sleep. Why don't you and I have a good old sisters' night? Shane is going out on patrol with Dakota, and we could hang out and watch old movies."

"No, thanks." Trixie shook her head. She hugged Maya quickly before waving to the others. "I'm out. I'll see you after sundown to open the club for Monday."

"Where do you suppose she's runnin' off to?" Dakota murmured. "She's been doin' that a lot lately. Y'all notice that?"

"Trixie's private life is her own," Olivia said with a sidelong glance in Dakota's direction. "If you want to know where she's going, then you'll have to ask her."

"I dare you," Doug said with a snort of laughter.

"I second that." Shane raised his hand before gathering Maya in his arms.

"You're supposed to say I double-dog dare you," Maya said, giggling.

"What does a dog have to do with it?" Shane asked.

"Oh man, y'all are crazy." Dakota sighed heavily and pointed at Shane as he headed toward the door. "And *you* make me sound hip."

"You should go after her."

Suzie's soft hesitant voice cut through the teasing laughter in the room with more force than the shy young vampire surely intended. In the almost two years Dakota had been here, he'd probably only heard her speak twice, and that was in response to direct questions. Suzie shuffled her feet nervously and tucked a long strand of pale blond hair behind her ear.

"I-I mean if you wanted to." Lifting one shoulder, she stared at the phone in her hand. "It…it would be okay. I had one of my visions, you know. It was fuzzy, like always, but anyway…you should go after her."

Everyone shifted his or her attention to Dakota, but the knowing smile on Olivia's face gave him pause. The czar obviously knew he was attracted to Trixie, and based on the look she exchanged with Doug, so did everyone else. Shit on a shingle. Why did he suddenly feel like he was on a freaking vampire-dating game show?

"Thanks for the tip. I better be gettin' out on patrol."

Dakota tugged the door open and stilled when Trixie's sweet spicy scent, an enticing peppermint with a hint of whiskey, wafted by. Gripping the doorknob, he fought the urge to unsheath his fangs as a swell of longing rolled through him. Damn, that woman smelled like Christmas morning and conjured up images of a cozy night by a fire. For a split second he remembered what it felt like to be human—warm and alive. But the sensation was gone as swiftly as it came.

His jaw clenched and a flicker of frustration shimmied up his back.

"Damn," he whispered.

"Dakota? I think it would be wise for us to listen to Suzie." Olivia kissed Emily's head of red curls. "Why doesn't Doug go out on patrol in your territory tonight? Just for a little while. That way, you can follow Trixie and make sure everything's alright."

"Good idea." Doug rose from his chair and gave Dakota a thumbs-up. "I've got it covered, man."

"Well…" Dakota began slowly, "I *could* check on her, y'know? Make sure she's not gettin' herself into any trouble." Hands on his hips, he stared into the empty hall. "Suzie? Did you see somethin' that worries you?"

"No," she said in a barely audible voice. "N-not exactly."

"Fine then." He squared his shoulders and nodded at the well-meaning but meddlesome coven. "Happy to oblige. Once I know she's safe, I'll be right back on duty."

The door shut behind Dakota and the room fell silent, except for Emily's high-pitched babbling.

"Suzie?" Olivia placed Emily on the floor and the little girl wasted no time in starting to play with her new horse. "Is Trixie going to be okay?"

"Eventually, yes." Suzie nodded, whispering, "Dakota is her bloodmate."

"I knew it!" Maya shouted.

"Interesting," Shane murmured. He kissed the top of Maya's head and smiled as he exchanged a knowing look with his lover. "I may not be a modern man, but I do know what that poor bastard is about to go through. If you'll all excuse me, I have something I need to take care of."

"You're not going to tell him that he's her bloodmate, are you?" Suzie asked quickly. "They should figure that out for themselves…I think."

"No, I'm just going to give him some *reassurance*."

Without another word, Shane whisked out of the apartment in a blur.

"Am I crazy," Doug said slowly, "or is Quesada about to give Shelton advice on his love life?"

"You're not crazy," Olivia said with a chuckle. "But this coven sure as hell is."

Dakota stood on top of the stone wall of The Cloisters garden and wrestled with whether or not he really should follow her. Trixie sure acted like she hated him, so how would she feel if she found him spying on her?

Her form grew smaller in the distance as she flew through the night sky. He had to make a freaking decision soon or her trail would vanish. Hands on his hips, he swore under his breath. He hated feeling so damn confused.

"I suspected I'd find you here."

Shane's voice cut through the night and pulled Dakota from his thoughts. He didn't flinch but kept looking in the direction where Trixie had flown off. It would be a bad move to let Quesada know that he'd actually been able to sneak up on him.

Damn, his infatuation with this woman was makin' him crazy and sloppy.

"What are you talkin' about, old man?" Dakota settled his hands on his hips and cast a glance at Shane, who now stood on the wall beside him. "And what are you doin' out here? That party is still goin' strong."

"I'll overlook the insult about my age, given your current state."

"What state would that be?"

"Let's just say, you seem *distracted* lately."

"You sayin' that I'm not doin' my job?" Dakota

squared his shoulders. "Because if you'll recall, I was the one who took down those two drifter vamps last month. Humans didn't even get a whiff of the trouble they were causin'."

"You misunderstand me," Shane said with his typical calm. "I may be far older than you, Shelton, but it was not long ago that I was in your position."

"What are you talkin' about?" He shifted his stance to get a better look at his partner.

"I was new here as well. An outsider." He folded his hands in front of him, his expression calm but serious. "I know how odd and almost unnerving it can be to be around their family unit. It took some time for me to feel at ease here."

"So it's not just me?" Dakota ran one hand over his head and let out a sigh. "I've been a vamp for fifty years and I ain't never seen another coven like theirs. I feel like that random friend of the family that Grandma invited over for Christmas dinner, you know? I'm the guest who never left."

"Yes." Shane nodded and his mouth set in a firm line. "They're all so close that it can be a difficult group to break into. Olivia and the others welcomed me, but like you, my instinct was to keep them all at a distance. It had been so many years since I'd had any kind of family that I had all but forgotten how to be a part of one."

"What about Maya?" Dakota folded his arms over his chest and stared again out over the glittering water of the Hudson River. He didn't want to give Shane any clue about his feelings for Trixie, especially when he wasn't sure about them himself. "I mean, she's your bloodmate, right? Didn't you want to, well, *not* keep her at a distance?"

"On the contrary"—Shane let out something that almost sounded like a laugh—"I stayed away from her as much as possible, but before long I found it…I found *her*…inescapable. I did not want to be drawn to her, and I can assure you that the all-consuming urge to be near her was quite unsettling. I'd existed on this earth for almost four centuries, knowing exactly who I was and what my purpose was. And then I came here to this city and this coven…to Maya."

A gust of wind blew over them and with it came Trixie's whiskey-tinged scent. A surge of anxiety rushed through Dakota because the scent was growing weaker, and if he didn't get a move on, he could lose it all together.

"Not to be rude, Quesada, but is there a point anywhere in this little speech?" He pulled his leather gloves out of his coat pockets and tugged them on. "Trixie's got a decent head start and I'll never live it down if I lose her trail."

"Yes." Shane turned to him and slapped him on the arm. "The point is, don't allow yourself to be a stubborn fool. Life, even for a vampire, can be full of surprises. And change is inevitable for all creatures."

"Alright," Dakota said slowly. "Thanks for the pep talk, gramps."

"Anytime." Shane hopped off the wall and strode toward the entrance to The Cloisters. "And one more thing, Shelton."

"Yeah?"

"You can't fight fate."

As Shane disappeared through the doors, Dakota could swear that the son of a gun was laughing.

Chapter 3

TRIXIE KNEW SHE WAS COMING AROUND TOO OFTEN, BUT she couldn't help herself. Perched in her favorite spot among the treetops, she picked up the shrill chirp of a cell phone as it filled the air for a moment or two before Chelsea answered it. A smile bloomed on the woman's face as she spoke to whoever was on the line.

Satisfied she was both safe and happy, Trixie knew it was time to go. But when Chelsea turned and stepped away from the sink, she revealed her swollen pregnant belly. A smile curved Trixie's lips because Chelsea's tummy looked much bigger than it had a couple of weeks ago.

She was at least seven months along. Maybe more. Trixie had seen Chelsea's boyfriend several times over the past year, and he was obviously the father of her unborn child. Were they going to get married? Trixie imagined Chelsea walking down the aisle in a white wedding dress, and a pit of sadness bloomed in her chest.

Yet one more milestone in Chelsea's life that Trixie wouldn't be a part of. Trixie was a ghost, a specter lurking in the trees like a creepy, fucking Peeping Tom.

The sound of a car coming down the long gravel driveway pulled Trixie from her bout of self-pity. The blue sedan stopped in front of the house, and a few moments later, Chelsea came out. Bundled up in a warm coat to protect her from the chill in the early

November air, she opened the front passenger door and climbed in.

Trixie's stomach roiled when a faint but familiar scent wafted out of the car and a cramp racked her stomach. Gritting her teeth against the unpleasant scent, she gripped the branch above her with both hands. Her black-painted fingernails dug into the bark as she wrinkled her nose and shook her head in an effort to get rid of the stink. Chelsea's boyfriend smelled like rotten fruit or old flowers or something, and the scent actually made her a little nauseated.

"Jeez," Trixie whispered in a rush as the car backed down the long driveway. "What the hell does he do for a living that makes him smell like that? There's no way Chelsea can smell that or she'd never hang out with him." She wrinkled her nose. Having heightened senses wasn't always a blessing. "Phew."

The subtle but distinctive sound of air rushing nearby made her freeze in place. She wasn't alone. Another vampire had landed in the vicinity. Why the hell would any other vamp come to Chelsea's house in the middle of the freaking woods? Fear, panic, and an overwhelming desire to protect the young woman swelled inside her. She would be damned if any vamps would mess with this particular human—let alone feed on her.

All of her senses went on high alert, and as the headlights vanished in the distance, Trixie dropped soundlessly to the ground. Standing in a battle-ready position, her feet firmly planted on the needle-covered surface and her hands curled into fists at her side, she scanned the area for her unwelcome visitor. A gust of November wind whisked over her, rustling the fallen leaves on the

ground. With it came the all-too-familiar scent of sandalwood, cinnamon, and leather.

A potent rush of arousal and anticipation fired
through her, a feeling she had all but forgotten until
a certain vampire cowboy came to the city two years
ago and turned her world on its ear. She'd been turned
on since becoming a vamp but not like this, not in
such an uncontrolled way. Trixie had always been the
one to seek out sex as a way to scratch an itch but this
was different.

This time the itch was hunting her.

"I know you're here, Dakota," she said in a singsong
voice. He might make her feel all kinds of out of sorts,
but that didn't mean she had to let *him* know that.

Trixie stood taller. Shane had been training her to
fight and she'd discovered she had a knack for it. In
fact, she enjoyed practicing so much that she'd installed
a kickboxing stand in her apartment and spent several
afternoons beating the crap out of it.

Learning how to defend herself and her coven was
empowering and cathartic.

Her fighting skills might come in handy now, especially if old blue eyes tried to get too friendly. Wound
tight with a mixture of lust and anxiety and—she hated
to admit it—a healthy amount of curiosity, she scanned
the moonlit forest.

He was out there…watching.

"You know," she shouted, "for a sentry, you kind of
suck at sneaking up on people! What's your deal, man?
Did you come out here to take me up on my offer to kick
your ass?"

An owl hooted in the distance and a fat raccoon

waddled by quickly. Tension filled the air, and just when she thought she would scream with frustration, a tall broad-shouldered figure stepped out of the moonlit shadows of a neighboring tree. He slipped his hands in the pockets of his long leather sentry coat and leaned casually against the massive pine. Cocky as ever, he winked at her and acted like it was no big deal that he had been following her.

"Hello, darlin'," he drawled in that I'm-just-a-good-old-boy tone. "You only noticed me here because I let you. I kept my distance until the humans left."

"What are you doing out here?" Trixie demanded. She strode toward him, hands on her hips, but stopped about two feet away. Best to keep some space between them. Like it or not, he was now a part of her coven. Sort of. Flirting was one thing, but if he actually did make a move, rejecting him would make things super awkward between them. "Seriously. Why are you following me?"

"Curiosity got the better of me. You've been runnin' off every other Sunday night for the past couple months and not tellin' anybody where you're gettin' off to." He pushed himself off the tree and fished one of those damn lollipops out of his pocket before popping it in his mouth. "Not only that. Suzie said I should."

"Oh really?" Trixie folded her arms over her breasts and cocked her head. "I call bullshit on that, smart guy. Suzie barely speaks to me, her coven mate, let alone *you*, a newcomer."

"Well, she did speak to me and I ain't that new." A touch of irritation edged his voice and for a second he looked almost wounded. "In case you hadn't noticed, I've been here for two years."

"Whatever," she said as casually as possible. She had noticed. A lot. "That's new as far as vampires are concerned."

"True." He took a step closer and she held her ground. "Suzie said you might be gettin' yourself into trouble and that I should check on you. I was thinkin' you found a prime huntin' ground that was out of the way of the city, where your hunts wouldn't be noticed. Is that what this is?"

He inched nearer and his voice dropped low. He dragged the little white stick from his lips and pointed it at her. "You casin' out this house and the humans who live here for a feedin' frenzy? If so, how about lettin' me in on it? I haven't had a live feed in a long while."

Live feeds, while not illegal, were strongly discouraged because they could lead to unwanted complications. Even though she missed the buzz that came with feeding from a human, Trixie didn't miss getting the blood memories.

She hadn't fed off a living, breathing human in over a year, and the idea of anyone feeding off Chelsea was downright revolting.

"You won't touch her," Trixie hissed. She bared her fangs, grabbed the lapels of his coat, and shoved at him. He didn't move. She might be a vampire with the strength of twenty men but Dakota was bigger, older, and stronger. "She is *not* prey for me, you, or anyone else. Do you understand me? I don't want anyone in the community to know about her. Chelsea is off-limits," she said, seething. "And if you know what's good for you, you won't come here again."

Dakota towered over her, but Trixie was not going

to back down. The stench of silver from the weapons hidden in his coat scorched her nostrils, but the comforting scent of sandalwood clung to him, soothing the burn. Damn. He smelled good. Too good. Her fingers curled tighter around the smooth leather of his coat, and her knuckles met the firm, unyielding muscles of his chest. She'd long suspected the man was nothing but bone, muscle, and sinew under all that leather.

Suspicions confirmed.

Why was she attracted to a man who was as deadly as he was cocky? Glutton for punishment. That had to be it. Even as a human she never could lay off the boys who were no good for her—and look where that had gotten her.

"You lookin' to tangle with me?" Dakota leaned into her grasp and arched one eyebrow. "I'm happy to oblige."

He was trying to intimidate her into submission. Trixie wasn't easily intimidated by anyone, and she sure as hell wouldn't be by him, his weaponry, his position as a sentry, or his penetrating stare.

Dakota inched closer and pressed his firm body further into her grasp. His lips tilted, giving her a glimpse of the tip of one of his fangs. Trixie let out a strangled groan and licked her lower lip. Why was seeing only a part of his fangs such a fucking turn-on?

"If by 'tangle' you mean have *me* kick your ass?" She hoped like hell he couldn't see right through her. "Then, yeah, and for the record, I'm *not* afraid of you."

Dakota's bluish-gray eyes peered at her beneath his furrowed brow. His short-cropped dark blond hair glistened in the silvery moonlight. His hands hung at his sides and his lack of response both frustrated and confused her. He was a sentry for the Presidium and she'd basically just attacked him, but the guy did nothing. Most sentries, even Shane, wouldn't take crap from a vamp like her.

"Say something." Trixie softened her tone.

"Like what?"

Maybe she'd get a more favorable response if she wasn't so bitchy. The worst part of this whole stupid mess was that her instinct *was* to be nice to him. She liked him but she didn't *want* to want him. Not like this.

"How about," she began slowly, "if you promise me that you won't come here again. Ever."

In a surprisingly disarming move, Dakota's large hands settled on hers and he held them against his chest. A rush of warmth whisked over her skin when his flesh covered hers, and her blood hummed with awareness. She'd touched other vampires, platonically and otherwise, but none of them made her feel like this. For a human, a vamp would feel cool to the touch. To another vampire, their skin was basically room temperature or neutral.

But not Dakota.

His hands were warm, firm, and rough. They were the hands of a man who knew a hard day's work, and damn if that wasn't a turn-on. What was it about a man's man that could get a girl's blood moving? She thought of the little horse he'd carved for Emily and something inside her quivered. These hands of his could put down an enemy with swift precision, but they could also gently and painstakingly cradle a piece of wood, massaging it and whittling it carefully until it became a delicate treasure. There was more to this cowboy than met the eye.

Tender and rough. Sweet but lethal.

How would it feel to have these hands running over more sensitive parts of her anatomy?

To be cherished, cradled, and coveted?

What was she doing? Trixie blinked. He was a sentry, a soldier who dealt in death and violence. There was nothing tender about that. But still…

Pinned beneath his intense blue stare and his impossibly warm hands, she fought the surge of desire that sizzled and simmered in her blood. Her arms were crushed between their bodies, and it was impossible not to notice the subtle movements of his muscles as he inched closer.

"I'll make you a deal," he whispered, his thumb rasping lightly over her knuckles. "You tell me why you're comin' to this house in the middle of nowhere, and I'll promise to keep your secret."

"You don't know my secrets." Trixie tried to tug her hands from beneath his but he refused to release her. "Please let me go."

"Not yet." He held her in a viselike grip, cool as ice. "So you have *more* secrets than these little visits to the woods?"

"I said, let me go," she ground out.

"Why?" he asked in an almost lighthearted tone. "The sun won't be up for a few hours and you still haven't answered my questions. I *am* a sentry for the Presidium—you know, that pesky vampire government. Didn't anyone teach you to respect authority?"

"Yeah, you may be a vamp cop," she scoffed. "But your boss is my maker. *I win*."

"You are a spitfire of a woman, do you know that? You remind me of a horse that hasn't been broken yet. All skittish and full of wild energy."

"Are you for real?" Her jaw fell open. "Did you just compare me to a horse?"

"It's a compliment. You're spirited. I always preferred wild horses to the ones who'd been saddled." His eyes twinkled with mischief and flashed at her in the dark, twin pools of silver that harkened of desire and danger. "I like that in a woman. And tellin' me you have secrets is like throwin' a scented shoe in front of a hound dog. Only makes me want to find out what they are."

"Whatever secrets I have are *mine* and they're called secrets for a reason, genius. It's stuff I don't want anyone else to know about. Okay? It's personal. I don't know you well enough to tell you my favorite band, let alone my secrets."

"Alright, then. Let me guess." Dakota tilted his face toward the sky and pursed his lips together. "Give me a minute."

"Careful, you might hurt yourself with all that thinking."

"I got it," he said abruptly. He tilted his smiling face to her and looked totally satisfied with himself. "Definitely."

"What?" Panic shimmied up her back. "My secrets?"

"No. Your favorite band."

Trixie gaped at him but he didn't seem to notice.

"Now, based on that colorful hair of yours, I'm thinkin' you're a fan of that Sid Vicious fella, or maybe the Clash." His hold on her loosened and his thumb made another lazy pass along hers, sending whispers of gooseflesh up her bare arms. "Now, me? I think Johnny Cash is about the best there ever is, was, or will be. Somethin' about the way he tells a story, you know? Like he can see right inside my soul. Too bad he never got turned vamp. We'd be gettin' new songs from him forever."

Trixie was speechless. Absolutely without words.

Here they were in the middle of the woods. She had just threatened to kick his ass. And the guy was talking about Johnny Cash. Not only that, but he was right. She did love Sid Vicious and the Clash.

Damn it. How annoying. And charming. *Crap.*

"Am I right?"

"Are you going to do as I ask?" Trixie's voice wavered and she retracted her fangs. "Will you stay away from here, from Chelsea's house?"

"On one condition," he murmured. His full lips curved and he tugged her closer.

"Fine." Trixie swallowed the rising swell of desire as his firm, muscular legs brushed against hers. "What?"

"Did I get your favorite musician right?"

"Yes." She suppressed a grin because he'd hit the nail on the head. "Fine. Yes, you did. Those are my two favorites. Okay?"

"Good." Dakota abruptly dropped her hands and stepped away. The warmth from his body dissipated swiftly as the space between them increased. "Now, are you gonna tell me why you're comin' out here all the time, or what?"

"You're a piece of work." Trixie almost laughed out loud. He'd guessed her favorite musician and now wanted to know everything else? What-freaking-ever. "No. Like I said, my secrets are exactly that. Secrets. And if you know what's good for you, you won't come out here again, let alone follow me around like a creep. I don't, like, need some throwback from the fifties tailing me on my nights off. Got it?"

"Is that so?" Irritation flickered across his face. "You know, missy, I only came out here because your maker and the rest of that crazy-ass coven told me I had to check up on you. I'll be happy to let you run all over creation all by your pretty little self if that's what you—"

Dakota stopped speaking mid-sentence when a gust of wind rushed over them. It whispered over Trixie from behind, sending a tiny tornado of leaves whirling around them. A growl rumbled in Dakota's throat. His nostrils flared and he bared his fangs as he looked past her to the driveway of the house. Before she could say a word, he flew over to the gravel-covered drive and tilted his nose to the sky.

"What are you bugging out about?" Trixie flew over to him and landed on the steps of the house. There was no way she was letting him in there. "No one here but you, me, and forest creatures. Jeez, what's your damage?"

"How long you been comin' out here?" he asked as he scanned the area like the trained sentry he was. Any and all humor had vanished; he'd gone from good old boy to lethal weapon in a matter of seconds. "You run into any trouble out here on your visits? Supernatural or otherwise? Notice anythin' out of the ordinary?"

"No." She sat on the top step of the porch in a not-so-subtle attempt to block the entrance. She was getting a weird feeling in her gut, the one that warned her trouble was coming. "I've been visiting ever since she moved out of the city. Not that it's any of your business, but I like to check on the woman who lives here. That's all.

No trouble. No drama. She's just a human woman living her life."

"Right," Dakota said tightly. His jaw clenched and the muscle there flickered with tension. "Chelsea, is it?"

"Whatever." Shit. Trixie cracked her knuckles and rose to her feet. She'd let the girl's name slip. "Yeah. But she's gone now and we should be too. Let's go."

"Why is she important to you?" Dakota strode slowly toward her, the gravel crunching beneath his heavy boots. All of the sweetness was gone from his voice and his expression was tense and serious—a side she rarely saw. "Who is she? What do you know about her?"

"I know enough, and you know too much."

Before he could respond, Trixie shot up into the air and landed on top of a small pine tree. She braced her feet on the top branch and clung to the trunk with one hand. She peered down at Dakota, who remained on the ground.

"And one more thing, cowboy," she shouted down to him.

"Ma'am?"

"Keep your hands to yourself." She smirked.

"I'll try." Dakota slipped his hands in his pockets and flashed a fang-filled grin at her, his white teeth glinting in the moonlight.

"You'll *try*?" Trixie scoffed. "How about you give me your word?"

"No way, darlin'." He flew to the roof of the house and landed noiselessly in a crouching position, a cocky grin curving his firm-looking lips. "I'm not makin' any promises I don't aim to keep."

Trixie let out a sound of disgust as Dakota shot

into the moonlit night and streaked across the sky like a bullet, leaving a trail of mist in his wake. She wanted to tell him "fat chance," and no way was he gonna touch her again. But deep down, underneath the stream of protests, was a long silent voice of desire that whispered...*yes*.

Chapter 4

MONDAY AFTERNOON, DAKOTA WOKE UP BEFORE THE sun went down. He had barely slept after the run-in with Trixie, and he couldn't stop thinking about the scent he'd detected at the cabin. It had been over fifty years since he'd been exposed to that pungent aroma. It was so faint at first that he wasn't sure if he'd really smelled what he thought he did.

A gargoyle.

Eons ago they had been protectors for the humans but eventually their lust for gold took over and they abandoned humanity. As far as Dakota was concerned, gargoyles had no honor. Many in the supernatural world thought gargoyles were only a few years from extinction. Hell, some folks already thought they were. And *that* would be fine with Dakota.

He might not have smelled that scent in decades but there was no mistaking it. That particular brand of stink had been burned into his brain with painful clarity. Hell, yes. A gargoyle had definitely been at the human's cabin in the woods but the real question was why? Why would a gargoyle be hanging around a human after all this time, and why the hell was Trixie mixed up with it all?

He could go to the czars about his suspicion, but he didn't want to cause a ruckus if he could avoid it. Especially since it was connected to whatever Trixie was hiding.

Right after Dakota had been turned, he and his maker were assigned a top secret mission to eliminate as many gargoyles as possible. They were considered a danger to the entire supernatural community. Driven by greed and their obsession with gold, they exhibited risky behavior. Some had even allowed themselves to be seen by humans with increasing frequency, and that wasn't good for anyone. The top secret directive came straight from Emperor Zhao, and Dakota's maker, Jonner, had told him he was never to speak of it. *Ever.* Then Jonner got dusted, the gargoyle activity basically died out, and Dakota got himself signed up as a sentry.

If that human girl was mixed up with gargoyles, she was in a heap of trouble. They were dangerous and had no honor. Gargoyles cared for no one other than themselves and for nothing other than finding their long-lost gold.

Greedy assholes.

Dakota locked his apartment door and made his way down to the basement of the building. He passed a few other tenants, all of them human, but none of them gave him more than a cursory nod of the head. New York was not the friendliest place; moments like this made him miss the warmth of Texas.

Luckily the laundry room was empty when he got there, and he was able to slip into the utility closet without any drama.

He didn't bother turning on the light; he could see easily in the pitch-black space. As with all vampires, he had night vision. When humans saw nothing, his world was sepia-toned. He pressed the tile along the top edge of the wall and a moment later the secret door slid open, giving him access to the underground tunnel network that ran beneath the city.

Dakota flew through the narrow halls with ease. Patrol, as always, was due to start at sundown and he had to watch over his section of the city, but he needed to see Trixie first. He had to get her to trust him so that she would tell him what in the hell she was hiding. If a gargoyle was loitering in the area, then it was his duty as a sentry to put it down. His curiosity was driven by far more personal reasons.

Trixie.

The spunky vampire occupied his every waking thought, and now that he'd touched her, felt her smooth silky flesh beneath his—he wanted more. He was unreasonably drawn to her, and if he was honest with himself, he had been since his first day in the city. Hell, the gals he had dated during his time as a human were nothing like Trixie, and that's why he liked her so much. The women of his era had been prim, proper, perfectly coiffed, and soft-spoken. There was no challenge. No fire. Trixie was the exact opposite. She was…unexpected.

He rounded a sharp turn to the right, and a few minutes later he arrived at the entrance to The Coven. The vampire-run nightclub operated out of an old church in Greenwich Village, and even though the music wasn't to his taste, Dakota had to admit they ran a top-notch joint. He slipped in the entrance and made his way up the winding staircase to the door that led to the club office. He probably could have gone right in, but that still felt rude.

He rapped on the door, listening for any sign of Sadie. She was a member of Olivia's coven, the owner of the nightclub, and mated to the werewolf prince, Killian Bane. She and Bane had been in Alaska for the past few weeks visiting the Werewolf Society territory and doing their duty as senators and interracial liaisons for the Presidium. They weren't supposed to be back in New York for another week or so, but for all he knew, they'd come home early.

Vampires hookin' up with werewolves. Vampires havin' babies. And now there was a gargoyle in the area.

Weird damn coven.

"Come on in, Dakota." Damien's deep baritone came through the door before it slid open. He extended his hand and rose from the chair at the desk. "Hey, man. What are you doing here?"

"I could ask you the same question." Dakota moved into the small cozy office as the panel slid shut, and then he shook Damien's hand. "I thought you were the bouncer of this joint. The muscle."

"I am." Damien flashed a toothy white grin. "But Sadie has me run the show when she has to do her diplomat stuff in Alaska with Killian. I like it. It gives me a chance to exercise my brain and not just my brawn."

"That's a crazy thing, isn't it?"

"What?" Damien winked. "That I've got brains?"

"Nah, man. Sadie and Killian. I mean who would have thought that the heir to the Werewolf Society throne would be the bloodmate of a vampire? That's some wild business." Dakota headed for the door that led out to the club but paused for a moment and studied Damien carefully. "Next thing you know, Olivia will be welcoming gargoyles into her coven."

"Now *that* is crazy." Damien laughed and his massive

shoulders shook with each deep chuckle. "Gargoyles? Come on, man. You know they're practically extinct. Even if there are any left, they stay hidden in the shadows. No way. I think it's safe to say there won't be any gargoyles hanging around The Coven anytime soon. Besides, I heard they stink to high heaven."

"Yeah, me too." Dakota nodded and gave him a tight smile. "I best be gettin' on my way or Shane will have my hide. He's a bossy old son of a gun."

"Hey." Damien's deep baritone stopped him in the doorway. Damn. He'd almost made a clean exit. "Why are you here anyway? The club isn't open for the night yet. No bad guys to watch in there."

"It's not a guy I'm interested in." He tilted his head in deference and grinned. "I won't keep her but a minute or two."

Dakota strode down the hall to the main room of the club without waiting for a response. Music, something loud with a heavy bass beat, flowed through the cavernous space and bounced off the walls like it was trying to escape. It only took a second to find Trixie. She was behind the bar, exactly where he thought she'd be, and the woman was dancing like no one was watching. Movement to his left captured his attention. It was the DJ, Justine. The tattooed and heavily pierced vamp was up on the DJ platform waving at him, but Dakota pressed a finger to his lips as he moved silently toward the bar. She gave him a thumbs-up and kept on with her business.

Trixie was singing along with the music and dancing as she stocked the top-shelf liquors. Her body—toned, curvy, and athletic—swayed hypnotically to the beat and Dakota found himself entranced. She was clad in a black tank top and skintight black jeans, and a series of colorful rubber bracelets adorned her wrists. Her hair, which had been pink and black yesterday, was now blond with streaks of bright blue and styled in her usual messy way. Like she'd just rolled outta bed. He had the urge to run his fingers through it.

In that moment, it was crystal clear why he found her so intriguing. The women of his day had been so perfectly coiffed, with not a hair out of place. What you saw was what you got. That's how it was back then. Men were men. Women were women. Everyone knew their role and played it to perfection.

But Trixie... Well, this gal was another story altogether.

She looked like a tough girl, like she was ready for anything, but Dakota had long suspected she was nothing like the woman she pretended to be. Last night's encounter had confirmed it. The role she'd assigned herself, the badass punk rock chick, was a cover for someone far more interesting. *That* was the woman he wanted to discover.

Dakota sidled up to the bar and stood silently, waiting for her to notice his presence. He wasn't in a rush. He was having too much fun enjoying the show. Trixie bent down to grab two more bottles of booze, and when she stood up, he caught her eye in the mirror behind the bar.

The beat of the music pulsed insistently but neither of them moved.

Her pale amber gaze remained locked with his for several beats of the song. The house lights in the club dimmed, and at the same moment the lights above the dance floor flickered to life. Reds. Blues. Pinks. Greens—the space became awash in a kaleidoscope of colors, but Trixie stood out like a beacon, shining above everything else.

Then the house lights came on with a hollow click, the colors vanished, and the music fell silent. The moment broken, Trixie tore her gaze from his and shoved the bottles onto the shelf.

"AV is ready to roll," Justine shouted from her perch. "Hey, Dakota. How's it hangin', gov?"

"Fine, thanks." Dakota waved over his shoulder but kept his attention on Trixie. "Always a pleasure to see you, Miss Justine."

"Right then." Justine snorted with laughter. She flew down from her perch and headed for the office. "I'll see you two in a bit. Need to take care of somethin' b'fore the doors open."

"What are you doing here?" Trixie looked at the large black watch strapped to her wrist before grabbing the empty box. "Aren't you supposed to be on patrol or something? Y'know, protecting the city from the rando supernatural freaks who don't follow the Presidium's rules."

"Hey, Dakota!" Maya's perky voice drifted over his shoulder as she whisked past him and hopped behind the bar. She stood in front of Trixie, blocking her exit, and grabbed the edge of the box in Trixie's hands. "I'll take that out to the Dumpster. The sun just went down. Besides, that will give you time to chat with Dakota."

"I got it," Trixie said through clenched teeth. She tugged the box away and slipped around her fellow bartender. "And I don't need to *chat* with him. He has to go to work, which is what we should be doing too. I already stocked the top shelf, but you can check the beer."

"Fine," Maya huffed. "Why are you so cranky?"

Trixie mumbled something incoherent and strode toward the bright red Exit sign at the end of the dark hallway.

"I'll walk you out." Dakota followed her to the back door that led to the alley and winked at Maya. "'Night, Maya."

"Good night, Dakota," she sang. Her knowing giggle faded as he strolled down the hallway after Trixie. "Good luck."

That was weird. Why would Maya be wishin' him good luck?

"Why are you following me?" Trixie sighed without looking back at him in the dark hallway. "Don't you have a job to do? I mean one that doesn't involve bugging me. Besides, Shane and Pete will have your ass if you aren't out there by sundown," she said, referring to the two other sentries.

"I'll be out there soon enough." Dakota swept past her and opened the door to the alley for her. He held it open and stepped back into the dimly lit alley so she could pass. "But there's somethin' that's been naggin' at me all day. Woke me out of a dead sleep, as a matter of fact."

"Very funny." Trixie rolled her eyes, but he didn't miss the hint of a smile on her red lips as she swept past him and into the alley. "What is it?"

The door shut with a dull clank. Trixie tossed the box into the Dumpster before turning around and almost walking face-first into his chest. Dakota had moved in so he was only a couple of feet behind her, and a look of surprise flickered briefly over her face. She stumbled backward, but he linked his arms around her biceps in a blur of speed and tugged her compact curvy body against his before she could bump into the metal Dumpster.

He told himself that he'd done it only to stop her from hitting the dirty metal contraption, but that was a lie. He had been looking for any excuse to touch her again, to slide his hands over her and feel the comforting weight of her body against his. Last night in the woods, before the stench of gargoyle filled his head, he'd been dizzy and drunk on her. Touching her had reminded him of what it was like to be human, and that was flat-out nuts. He wasn't human. Hadn't been for over fifty years. Yet when he was with Trixie, well, that was all he could think about.

She made him feel like a man. A red-blooded, horny-as-hell *man*.

The warmth of her flesh beneath Dakota's fingers stirred his blood, and the velvety feel of it made his fangs hum. In that instant, when the smooth silky skin of her arms whispered against his palms, every animal instinct inside him went on overdrive. Her scent, the one that conjured up cozy nights by a fire, curled around him in the cool fall air and had him pulling her closer still.

"Careful, darlin'," he murmured, his thumb rushing along the curve of her bicep. "You almost hit that pretty little head."

Her hands pressed against his chest, but to his surprise, she didn't try to push him away. Those gorgeous eyes, the ones that reminded him of melted caramels, widened as her fingers curled around the lapels of his long leather coat. Hell, she was pulling him closer, almost imperceptibly. His gaze skittered over her heart-shaped face before quickly locking again on those hypnotic eyes framed perfectly by jagged wisps of bright blond hair with turquoise streaks.

For the first time since turning vamp, Dakota was swamped by lust. The kind that twisted his gut in knots and made his dick twitch. There ain't nothin' that makes a man feel more alive than white-hot desire. He hadn't been with a woman since being turned. Didn't seem right to get involved with someone when it had nowhere to go. Besides, before finding Trixie, the need for sex had paled in comparison to the desire for blood. Right this second, he'd give up live feeds for the rest of his existence for just one taste of *her*.

"What did I tell you about putting your hands on me?" Her voice was low and her meaning clear when she lifted her lip and revealed her fangs. "Let me go."

Lord have mercy, he loved a woman with moxie. And this one had bushels of it.

"Apologies." Dakota released her abruptly and took a step back, sticking his hands in the pockets of his coat. "Next time, I'll let you bump your head."

"Great." Trixie squared her shoulders and gestured for him to move. "I've been walking around all on my own for the better part of four decades. I think I can handle it."

"My mistake."

Dakota was blocking the door back into the club, but he stayed right where he was. His head might be fogged by lust, but he'd be damned if he was gonna let her leave without answering his question.

Trixie folded her arms over her bosom. "You said you had a question," she said, sighing. "What is it?"

"The birthday party."

"Okay," she said slowly, a look of confusion washing over her. "What about it?"

"Why weren't you all full of sunshine and rainbows like everybody else?"

"What are you talking about?" She cracked her knuckles before settling her hands on her hips. "Is that why you're keeping me out here in this smelly alley? To find out why I wasn't wearing a party hat? Which by the way, you weren't either."

"The only hat I'll put on my head is a Stetson." He took one step toward her. "And we aren't talkin' about me, we're talkin' about you. See, my gut tells me that there was somethin' about that party, about that little girl, that set you off and sent you runnin' back to the woods."

"You're crazy," she said through a weak laugh. Tilting her head, she met his challenging stare. She held her ground as he advanced. "I think you're starting to see things, cowboy."

"Oh, I see things, alright," he murmured. "I see the way you are around Emily." His voice dropped to almost a whisper and he stopped, his body mere inches from hers. "Even if no one else does."

"What are you talking about? I love that little girl," she whispered shakily. "She's part of my family. The only family that I've ever really had."

"Exactly and all the more reason for you to be giddy as all get-out for that sweet little baby's birthday. But you weren't. And that got me thinkin' about your secret visits out to that cabin in the woods. Why would you leave a *family* birthday party to go see some *human* woman?"

Dakota intentionally invaded Trixie's space but

refrained from touching her, even though it was the one desire that burned brightest.

He lowered his voice to a whisper and searched her eyes for answers. "Who is Chelsea? Who is she to you?"

Trixie's eyes glimmered in the dim light of the alley and her full lower lip quivered. For a split second, Dakota thought she was going to cry—or maybe haul off and deck him—but she did neither. Instead she shook her head, then slipped around him in a blur and yanked open the door to the club.

Dakota loved a challenge. Hell, the chase was the best part.

Matching her speed, he spun around and whisked to the doorway. He braced his hands along the door frame on either side of Trixie, bringing his body to within an inch of hers. The two of them remained in a virtual standoff as the music from the club echoed down the hallway.

"Funny," he said with a grin. "You don't strike me as the kind of gal to tuck tail and run from a simple question."

"I'm not running. It's time to open the club and your question isn't simple. It's nosy." She leaned closer, pressing her breasts lightly against him. Then she bared her fangs in a gesture that may have been meant as a threat but to him was seductive as all get-out. Trixie's gold-flecked eyes flashed defiantly, a slow smile spreading across her beautiful face. "And like I said before, my secrets are my own. Chelsea is someone I care about. If you care about me, or at least not pissing me off, then you'll stay away from her. Let it go, Dakota."

Before he could respond, she whisked down the

hallway to the main floor of the club and went to the large double doors to open the place for the night.

As the humans spilled in and started spreading out onto the dance floor, Dakota leaned against the wall in the dimly lit hallway and kept his steady gaze on Trixie. The vulnerable woman—the one he saw peek out briefly from behind the confident, cocky spitfire facade—was gone. Tough as nails once again, she was slinging drinks and pretending he wasn't there. But she couldn't ignore him forever, not any more than he could ignore her—*or* the secret she was hiding.

Chapter 5

A MIX OF PEBBLES AND DRY DUSTY EARTH SLID WARM AND ROUGH *beneath Trixie's bare feet. She was no longer in the massive king-size bed in her underground apartment beneath the club but standing in the middle of a grassy field. She wore the black boy shorts and tank top she had put on before she went to bed well before dawn. The last thing she remembered was lying in her bed, alone, and staring at the black-tiled ceiling with thoughts of Dakota swimming through her head.*

Where the hell am I?

Her voice sounded unbearably loud in this beautiful place that was foreign and familiar at the same time. The stone-cold silence of a vampire's sleep, the leaden shroud of utter darkness, was absent for the first time in over two decades.

Holy crap! I'm dreaming…

Gone were the bright lights of New York City and the cavalcade of sounds from the swarms of humans living there. Instead, she was surrounded by an exquisite sense of peace. It was the kind of quiet that existed only the wildest natural places on earth. Crickets and other creatures of the night scurried beneath the brush, but one noise was lacking. There were no human heartbeats filling the night air. For the first time in decades, Trixie was truly alone.

She tilted her face toward an inky black sky

blanketed by an array of luminous stars. Her grin widened. It had been years since she'd seen a night like this one. In Manhattan, she would get a glimpse of a few stars here and there, although most of them were blotted out by the artificial glow of the city's towering buildings.

But not tonight. Not here.

She knew the mountain range in the distance, past the acres of wild land, even though she hadn't laid eyes on it since she was a child. She'd been here during one of the only pleasant times during her childhood. Of all the foster families she'd lived with over the years, the Langstons had been the kindest. The year and a half that Trixie lived with them was the happiest time of her human life. If Mr. Langston hadn't died, perhaps she could have stayed there. How different would her life have been?

The dream landscape looked exactly like the isolated area in Texas where the Langstons had gone camping. It was here that she'd found her tiny treasure.

That gold disk had been her most prized possession. The unusual symbol engraved on one side looked like wings, and there was nothing but wild swirls on the other. Until Chelsea came along, Trixie had never considered letting it go. Olivia had gotten so pissed when Trixie snuck into Chelsea's bedroom and left it on the girl's pillow. Trixie had glamoured Chelsea after the visit, erasing all memory of the encounter, but that hadn't mattered. It was totally worth it.

That girl was the only one worthy of such a gift.

Trixie laughed and spun in a circle. Was she dreaming of this place because of Chelsea? Perhaps her

*overwhelming desire to protect her had Trixie walking
in the dreamscape again.*

Well, I'll be damned. *Dakota's deep voice filled the
air, playful and arrogant. The smile faded from her lips
when his Texas drawl slid through the night.*

*There it was. The real reason she'd begun to dream
again after all this time.*

Aren't you the prettiest vision I've had in a long,
long while?

Trixie's entire body stilled.

*Vampires stopped dreaming within a decade of
being turned. It was the last piece of their human life
that they relinquished. There was only one reason
that a vampire would walk in the dreamscape again.
A bloodmate.*

No freaking way, *Trixie whispered in a shaky voice
she hardly recognized.* This is not happening.

*Panic shimmied through her as her eyes fluttered
closed. Damn it. She knew it. Deep down she'd known
it the minute she'd set eyes on him two years ago, but
in typical Trixie fashion, she'd ignored it. She'd done
everything but stick her fingers in her ears to pretend
not to hear what the universe was telling her.*

*But apparently fate, much like Dakota, would not and
could not be dismissed.*

*Trixie dropped her arms to her sides and slowly
turned around to face the one vampire she would never
be able to escape. Not now. Not even in her sleep.*

*She should give him a piece of her mind, tell him that
bloodmate or not, she had no interest in hooking up with
anyone permanently—especially him. If Dakota thought
she was going to drop everything in her world and get*

with him because of some stupid legend about destiny, he had another thing coming.

But when her eyes met his, all coherent thoughts slipped from her head.

She had expected to find him standing there in his leather battle gear, all full of arrogance and ready for a fight.

Not even close. The man who stood before her was all cowboy from head to toe, and he sure as hell wore it well.

A pair of faded, worn Levi's covered his long legs, and a dark blue button-down work shirt was practically painted onto his broad-shouldered torso. It was unbuttoned almost halfway, revealing a white or used-to-be-white T-shirt underneath. Hands on his hips, scuffed cowboy boots on his feet, Dakota dipped his head and winked at her from beneath the rim of a brown Stetson.

Ma'am. *His cheeky grin broadened and his heated gaze drifted over her in one lazy stroke. If she didn't know better, she'd swear he'd touched her with more than a look.* What might you be doin' here on my ranch? And why are you wearin' so little? Not that I'm complainin'.

His ranch? What the hell was he talking about?

This is what I sleep in, and as usual, I sleep alone. I wasn't expecting anyone else to see how *little* I was wearing. *Trixie folded her arms over her breasts, suddenly feeling uncomfortable about the lack of coverage her tank and boy shorts provided.* What are you talking about anyway? We're not on your ranch, Dakota. We're in the dreamscape, cowboy. Try to keep up.

Dreamscape? *His lips curved as he strode toward*

her with slow deliberate steps. I don't know what a dreamscape is but if memory serves, this is a dream. And it's a damn fine one, if you don't mind me sayin' so.

He stopped about a foot away from her and surveyed the area. The smile faded from his eyes and his brow furrowed with confusion. Trixie studied him closely. He seemed unaware of what was really happening, and in that moment it dawned on her that while she knew the significance of sharing the dreamscape...Dakota did not.

Well, if he didn't know what was going on, she sure wasn't going to tell him. Maybe this was only a fluke after all.

Right. *She lifted one shoulder and tried to act totally nonchalant, like it wasn't a huge freaking deal that they were in the dreamscape together.* You're only having a dream that I happen to be in. No biggie.

Mmm-hmm. *He nodded and moved past her to the right, his expression serious.* But why now? I mean, why after all this time? I haven't had a dream for almost fifty years, and why the hell am I dreamin' about the ranch? *He smirked.* I know why I'd be dreamin' about you...but why *you* on *my* ranch?

Much to her dismay, her stomach flip-flopped from the suggestive tone in his voice. Right about now she was wishing like hell that she'd bothered to ask Maya or Sadie how to get out of the dreamscape once you got here.

On the other hand, since she didn't know how to leave, she might as well get as much information from Dakota as she could.

Olivia had always told her that knowledge was power.
What ranch are you referring to, exactly? All I see are wide-open spaces. *Trixie turned around, followed Dakota's gaze, and her stomach dropped. The empty wilderness was gone. Sitting in the distance, the mountains looming behind it, was the unmistakable silhouette of a house.* Where the hell did that come from?

What? *His hands settled on his hips again and he glanced at her over his shoulder.* The house? I told you. We're on my ranch. My human family's ranch, that is, and that's the house I grew up in. You know, I need to go back for a visit. It's been too long… Actually, this night is exactly like the night I was turned vamp. *He pointed to the left of the house and a low whistle slipped from his lips.* Hell, it is the night I was turned. Look over there. You see those lights, the ones flashing bright over the mountains?

Before Trixie could get out of the way, Dakota wrapped one arm around her and turned her so she could see what he was talking about. He leaned down, his face precariously close to hers, the scruff of his unshaven jaw achingly near. She had the craziest urge to touch him, to cradle his cheek with her hand and nuzzle her lips along the line of his throat. The scent of sandalwood and leather made her dizzy, the warmth of his body curling against hers in a wicked invitation.

Those are searchlights from the county fair. I'll never forget it… That night they were swinging through the sky. *His voice rumbled in his chest as he rose to his full height and draped his arm casually over her shoulder before pulling her tighter against him.* I remember watching them slice through the night like swords while

I died. Well…almost died, anyway. My maker found me lyin' out here, bleedin' and all torn up from what that animal did to me. *Anger edged his words and his muscles tensed against her as he spoke.* The last things I saw as a human were those damn lights in the sky.

B-but this wasn't here a second ago. *Trixie's voice wavered and she tried not to notice how perfect the weight of his arm around her felt. She cleared her throat and nodded toward the house.* I don't get it. When I got here it was empty. There wasn't any house or ranch or lights or anything. The mountains were here but not that house. What the hell is going on?

Trixie snapped her mouth shut. She cracked her knuckles and sensed Dakota's energy humming around her. His body stilled and she didn't have to look at him to know he was staring down at her. She'd said too much. Shit.

What do you mean, when you got here? *He shifted his tall frame so that he was facing her. She could still feel his warmth against her arm. Awareness hummed between them and his voice dropped low.* I thought this was my dream, angel. And if it is, then how you could get here before me?

Trixie shook her head, not really hearing him. Her thoughts were racing, trying to remember every scrap of information the other girls had told her. The dreams were shared by bloodmates, that much she knew. But there was more to it. What was it? Her world was changing at a breakneck pace and she was having a hell of a time keeping up. Think, damn it. But she couldn't. Staring into those gorgeous blue eyes, one thought rose above the rest.

Dakota was her bloodmate.

Sadie, Olivia, and Maya. *As the pieces came together, the words fell from Trixie's lips in a rush.* They didn't just have dreams, okay? They shared dreamscapes that were actually memories—memories of the nights that they were turned. *Fear settled in her chest. Slipping out of Dakota's embrace, Trixie scanned the suddenly ominous wilderness and backed away.* What attacked you that night, Dakota?

What the hell are—*Dakota stopped speaking and held up one hand to silence her as well. His jaw set and those steely silver-blue eyes of his narrowed, like an animal picking up the scent of its prey. The sentry was back. Every fiber of the man was coiled tight with anticipation, the tension pulsing off him in thick waves.*

She wanted to ask him what was happening but no words would come. Fear, a long-forgotten feeling, fired through her with brutal and unforgiving force, but the man in front of her was anything but afraid. Fury. Rage. Unbridled hatred simmered beneath the surface, and for the first time since she'd met him, Trixie became acutely aware of exactly how deadly Dakota could be. She'd heard about his razor-sharp focus in battle but this was the first time she was seeing it for herself.

He remained motionless in the moonlit night, all sharp edges and hard lines. Dakota looked like a rubber band that had been almost stretched to the limit. The air around them stilled and thickened, and it became obvious that she and Dakota were no longer alone.

If Trixie had any breath in her lungs, she'd be holding it.

A rock skittered along the ground, shattering the

*silence and with it, Dakota's stone-cold posture as he whispered...*Run.

Trixie opened her mouth to respond and ask just where the hell she should run to, when the pungent odor of rotting flowers filled the air. It was far stronger than before but there was no mistake. It was the same unpleasant scent she'd picked up at Chelsea's house that night. Trixie's stomach churned and an overwhelming sensation of nausea swamped her. A powerful cramp racked her gut and she doubled over in agony. She fell to her knees. She could hear Dakota shouting her name through the fog of pain, but he sounded impossibly far away.

An ungodly shriek filled the night. A shadowy, hulking figure swept in, tackling Dakota to the ground.

The darkness closed in.

Dakota catapulted out of bed with a shout and landed in a crouching position across the room by the bedroom door. His fingers pressed into soft carpet and he froze in place while regaining his bearings. He was awake and back in his apartment. There was no gargoyle, and Trixie was nowhere to be seen.

"What the hell was that about?" Dakota whispered.

Rising slowly to his feet, he pressed his hands to his bare chest. There was no blood, no gaping wounds from the gargoyle's razor-sharp claws. Only the long, bumpy, scarred skin left from the original attack rasped under his fingertips. The four slashes of raised flesh were his only physical reminder of that life-altering encounter. Until now, he'd thought the mental scars had long since healed.

Vampires stopped dreaming after about ten years of

being turned. So why now, after all this time, had he started dreaming again? He'd bet his best pair of boots it had something to do with the scent he'd detected in the woods. That girl, Chelsea, was mixed up with gargoyles. She had to be.

The two incidents had to be connected.

Frustrated and more than a little concerned, Dakota strode to the bathroom and turned on the shower. He stripped off his boxers and tossed them into the hamper before stepping into the almost painfully hot streams. He turned the dream over and over in his mind as the water poured down on him, but he kept coming back to the same conclusion.

A gargoyle was involved with a human woman. But why?

He was a sentry and he'd messed with gargoyles before. So it was up to him to find the creature and put it down like the rabid beast it was. There was almost no chance that Trixie had any idea what Chelsea was messing with, and hopefully the human wouldn't get in the way of what he knew he had to do.

Taking out a gargoyle permanently would require more than his usual arsenal. That meant he'd have to pay a visit to the local weapons master, Xavier.

A deadly smile spread across his face as he rinsed the soap from his body. He'd waited over fifty years to get more revenge; it looked like his wait was finally over.

———

"Hello, my friend!"

Xavier's enthusiastic voice boomed through the cavernous space of his workshop. He may have been small in stature but he had the biggest, most enthusiastic personality of anyone—human or vamp—that Dakota had met in all his years. A dwarf who'd been turned about a century ago, he looked like a tiny Albert Einstein. A shock of white hair stuck out from his head in a thousand directions, and a pair of wire-rimmed glasses perched precariously on the tip of his nose. Garbed in a white lab coat with a pen tucked behind each ear, he looked like the nutty professor. Brilliant, but scattered.

"Hey there, Xavier." Dakota squeezed the smaller vampire's hand and glanced at the ceiling where all kinds of weapons dangled like a macabre mobile. A moment later, a fluttering noise filled the air. A ghost, a pretty young woman with long dark hair, materialized and floated high above them. "And hello to you too, Bella."

"What can I do for you?" Xavier flew to a stool behind one of the many stainless-steel tables, all of them covered with one experiment or another. "Didn't I just give you and Shane more ammunition last week? I thought it had been quiet lately. I'm surprised you need more so soon."

"Yeah, it has." Dakota nodded and strolled slowly around the lab, surveying the different weaponry suspended overhead. "But I'm in need of something a little different. Let's say…it's for a secret project that I'm working on, and I'd be much obliged if you'd keep this little visit between us."

Xavier pushed his glasses on top of his head and nodded, not taking his keen gaze off Dakota. Dakota tried not to squirm beneath the weapon master's inspecting stare. He'd only known Xavier a couple of years, and by all accounts, the man was not only intelligent but Doug and Olivia trusted him implicitly.

"I see." Xavier slipped his pudgy hands in the pockets of his lab coat. "Is Olivia aware of this *secret project*?"

"No." Dakota stilled and met the smaller vampire's eyes. "And for now, I'd like it to stay that way. I wanna confirm my suspicions before I get everyone else's knickers in a twist." He kept his voice light and waved one hand. "No need to get the czars or the other sentries all worked up if I'm wrong."

"Are Shane and Pete aware of what's going on?"

"Not at the moment."

"I don't know about this, Dakota." Xavier shook his head. "I'm really not comfortable keeping secrets, especially from Olivia."

Xavier's agitation and nervousness were matched by the increasingly loud fluttering from the ghost girl, Bella. The sound grew louder when she floated down and hovered next to Xavier, giving Dakota a withering look. The pretty little specter might not speak English but she didn't have to. She was making her feelings perfectly clear.

"Hang on, now." Dakota held up both hands and kept his voice even. "I'm not tellin' you to lie or nothin'. If anyone comes right out and asks you about me or what I came here for, then be honest. You tell 'em that I came here for the supplies that I need to keep the community safe."

"Mmm-hmm." Xavier narrowed his eyes, his bushy white eyebrows furrowing. "How about you tell me *exactly* what you need and *then* I'll tell you if I can help you."

Dropping his hands to his side, Dakota looked from Xavier to Bella and back again. Once he asked for this particular weapon, there would be no more wondering about who or what Dakota was going to hunt. Bullets would slow a gargoyle down, send them into a dormant state while they healed, but the only way to kill 'em was by piercing their heart with a weapon made of stone. Or decapitation but that was a messy business.

"A stone dagger."

The line between Xavier's eyes deepened and he let out a short laugh, as though not quite sure he'd heard Dakota's unusual request correctly. Dakota didn't flinch. He remained resolute and Xavier's smile fell.

"A gargoyle?" he asked, his voice edged with wonder. Xavier flew to Dakota and hovered in midair, looking as excited as a kid on Christmas morning. He clapped his hands together eagerly. "You mean to tell me that you think there's a *gargoyle* in New York City? Why, that's incredible! There haven't been any confirmed gargoyle sightings in decades. I thought—I mean, we all thought—they were extinct."

"So did I." Dakota wrestled with his waning patience and the surprising response from Xavier. "They're nasty creatures, and with any luck, I'm wrong and they *are* extinct. But you can bet your ass if there is one lurking around here, I'll snuff it out so quick, it'll make your head spin."

"I don't understand." Xavier landed on the ground and peered up at Dakota curiously. "I know they weren't the most popular group in the supernatural community, and they have a reputation for being less than trustworthy, given the way they abandoned their duty of protection. But this is quite exciting and—"

"Exciting? You see this?" Dakota's eyes flashed and he tugged his shirt up, exposing his angry-looking scars. "This is what I got the last time I ran into one of those animals. It gutted me like a fish, and if it weren't for my maker, I'd have ended up food for the buzzards. So you'll forgive me if I don't share your enthusiasm for this little revelation. Make no mistake about it, Xavier. A gargoyle will just as soon kill you as look at you."

The words were barely out of his mouth before he regretted taking such a bitter tone. Xavier's expression went from wonder to empathy as his gaze skittered over the scars. Dakota swore under his breath and tucked his shirt back in, feeling stupid for such a bare display of emotion. Sentries were supposed to be calm and cool, and he had just flipped out like some hotheaded kid.

"I'm sorry, Dakota," Xavier said quietly. "I didn't know."

"Shit, man." Dakota settled his hands on his hips and started pacing around the laboratory. He couldn't look at Xavier or Bella; he was a jerk for flipping out the way he did. "I'm the one who's sorry. I don't know what my damn problem is."

"What makes you think there's a gargoyle in Manhattan?"

"It's not in the city, at least not yet." Dakota chose his words carefully. "I got a whiff of it the other night when I followed Trixie upstate. It's been a while since I got a head full of gargoyle stink, but let me tell you, that is one stench you don't forget."

"I'll take your word for it," Xavier said with a small smile. "But why were you following Trixie?"

"I was doin' Olivia a favor." Dakota tried to be casual and act like it was no big deal. "She and the others were worried about where Trixie had been gettin' off to lately."

"I see." Xavier peered at him over the rim of his glasses. "Is that the only reason?"

The jig was up. Somehow Xavier saw right through him. How long before the rest of the coven figured it out? He wanted to court Trixie, sure, but not with a damn audience.

"Ah, hell, Xavier. I don't know what it is about that woman, but I can't get her out of my head. She's the most infuriating lady I've ever known." He shook his head and pressed his fingers to his eyes. "I even dreamed about her. Can you believe that? What fifty-plus-year-old vampire *dreams*? I must be losing my damn mind." He dropped his hands and started pacing around the lab, frustration lacing every word. "Can vampires go crazy?"

A heavy silence filled the enormous space, and Dakota could feel Xavier's stare drilling a hole in his back. A flicker of foreboding skittered up his spine. When he turned around and noticed the stunned look on Xavier's face, he suspected that he had more than a gargoyle to worry about.

"What is it?" Dakota kept his voice even and fought the building sense of uneasiness. "Am I really going crazy or something?"

Xavier glanced at Bella and then flew to Dakota, hovering in midair so that the two of them were eye to eye. He placed his pudgy hands on Dakota's shoulders, a mischievous grin lighting up his face.

"You're not going crazy, my friend." He let out a short laugh and shook his head. "But it will probably feel like you are, at least for a while. That's what I've been told anyway."

"What are you talkin' about, man? I wish someone around here would give me a straight answer."

"You had a dream last night…about Trixie?" He flicked a knowing glance to Bella and the ghost fluttered louder. "Or more to the point, you were dreaming *with* her."

"Well, yeah. I guess." Dakota shifted his weight, suddenly feeling self-conscious. If his heart still beat, he'd probably be blushing like a kid caught with his father's dirty magazines. "But it wasn't anythin'…you know… Anyway, yeah, she was in it. So what?"

"That's what I suspected." Xavier patted Dakota's cheek in an almost fatherly gesture. "My dear boy, Trixie is your bloodmate."

"Bloodmate?" Dakota took a step back and held up both hands. "You mean like Olivia and Doug, or Shane and Maya? Eternal bonds, daywalking, and all that jazz?"

"Yes." Xavier chuckled and flew to the back of the lab. He pressed a button on the remote and a moment later the stainless steel wall slid open, revealing the substantial armory of the Presidium's New York office. "All that jazz."

Dakota stood there with a million thoughts swimming through his head. He barely noticed when Xavier emerged, holding a gray stone dagger with a gilded handle.

"Here you go." He hovered in midair and held the unique weapon out for Dakota. When he didn't take it, Xavier gently placed the dagger in his palm and closed Dakota's fingers over it. "One stone dagger."

Bloodmate. Trixie was his bloodmate.

As the full meaning of those words sank in, Dakota blinked. He gripped the handle of the dagger tightly before slipping it into one of the pockets hidden within his coat. Part of him wasn't all that surprised. After all, he'd been drawn to her from the minute he'd first set foot in that club two years ago. But it sure would be easier to swallow if she didn't act like she hated him most of the time. What were the odds that the one woman in the world meant to be his thought he was a dumb old square?

Xavier was still staring at him, now looking concerned, and in spite of the situation, Dakota started laughing. "You wouldn't have anything back there to help me tame a punk-rock wild child with a disdain for cowboys, would you?"

"No," Xavier said through a chuckle. "I'm afraid I don't."

"That figures." Dakota let out a sigh. "You know, all of a sudden…that gargoyle doesn't seem so dangerous."

Chapter 6

THE SOUNDS OF THE CLASH ROARED THROUGH TRIXIE'S apartment. She had the speakers on full blast, but the music still wasn't loud enough to drown out the one word that had been racing through her head since she woke up from that damned dream.

Bloodmate.

She'd woken up long before sunset, thanks to that freaking dreamscape incident with Dakota. Since falling back to sleep wasn't an option, she'd put on her sports bra and leggings and spent the better part of two hours beating the shit out of the kickboxing stand in her living room. She pulled a roundhouse kick and let out a grunt when her foot connected with the battered red leather. It was well-worn, ripped, and torn from constant use. From the looks of it, she was going to need to replace the stand again soon. This was her fifth one in as many months.

"Shit." She ran her finger over the silver duct tape that was no longer holding one of the tears together and let out a sigh. "I should make Dakota pay for it."

She grabbed the kickstand with both hands and rested her forehead against the cool leather. Squeezing her eyes shut, she let the music wash over her. Usually listening to her favorite tunes helped cure any ill, but right now nothing could wipe away the reality she was facing.

Having a bloodmate scared the hell out of her.

It meant relinquishing control over her life and her choices. And *that* was unacceptable.

The song came to an end, and in the moment of silence that followed, a light, hesitant knock sounded on the door of her apartment. She glanced at the skull-and-crossbones clock on the wall, a Christmas gift from Maya and Shane. Her brow furrowed. Who the hell would be at her door now? Sunset wasn't for another hour.

She turned off the iPod and headed for the door, but Trixie didn't have to open it to know who was on the other side. Suzie's familiar scent, a clean flowery aroma like a fresh open field, was easy to identify even with the door closed. But Suzie never visited *anyone*. The girl only went from her little apartment to the Presidium offices where she worked and then home again.

Curious and more than a little concerned, Trixie pulled the door open slowly, and sure enough, Suzie was standing there nervously. She had her long blond hair in a tight ponytail, and she was dressed in her usual conservative buttoned-up navy blue suit. Her face was free of makeup, and she looked like the skittish human that she'd been before Olivia had turned her. The girl was the only vampire that Trixie had ever known who was completely uncomfortable being a vamp.

"Hey, Suzie." Trixie gave her coven mate a smile and stepped back, gesturing for her to come in. "What a nice surprise. Come on in. I was just working out a little. You know, wouldn't want Quesada to say that I wasted all that fight training he and Pete gave us."

Suzie nodded. She dropped her gaze to the floor

before slipping past Trixie and into the apartment. She stood in the center of what had once been a living room, but was now strewn with an assortment of gym equipment. She nibbled her lower lip, hands clasped in front of her, and stared at her feet.

"I'm surprised Damien isn't with you. He's usually hovering around you like your own personal bodyguard."

"I know," she said quietly. "He's a good man."

"What's up, Suz?" Trixie pushed the door closed with her toe and took off her weighted gloves before tossing them onto the small table by the door. "I'd offer you a seat but…I don't really have one."

"It's okay," Suzie said in a barely audible voice. She glanced at Trixie briefly before looking at her interlaced fingers again. "I-I won't stay long… I have something I need to tell you."

Trixie stilled and studied the timid vampire carefully. Something was definitely up with Suzie; she'd probably had one of her wonky visions.

"Damn, did you have one of your vision thingies," Trixie whispered. She moved carefully toward Suzie, not wanting to freak her out. "Was it about me and…Dakota?"

Suzie didn't look at Trixie but nodded her head furiously, sending a long lock of pale blond hair tumbling free from her ponytail.

"Yes."

"Right." Trixie ran one hand over her hair. "So you know that we're bloodmates?"

"Uh-huh."

"Does anyone else know?"

"Yes," Suzie whispered shakily. "I kind of spilled the beans on that. Sorry."

"Awesome." Trixie cracked her knuckles but paused when Suzie flinched. "Don't sweat it. Shit happens. You might as well report to the rest of the coven that we shared the dreamscape last night; no telepathy or anything else so far. Besides, I don't think Dakota knows what's going on. *And* it doesn't really matter anyway, because I am *not* blood bonding with him. Daywalking isn't worth giving up my freedom."

"Are you angry or scared?" Suzie lifted one shoulder. "I can't tell which."

"No," Trixie said a little too quickly. "I mean, jeez, I don't know. I never really thought I'd find a bloodmate... It's kind of freaky. I see how Maya, Olivia, and Sadie are with their guys, and it's like they're addicted to each other or something. It's like there's no choice in the matter. I guess now that I'm really faced with it...yeah...I'm kind of scared and I'm a little pissed. It's like my future and my life are no longer mine to control. I don't like it. It reminds me of being human."

"Oh, I never really thought of it that way." Suzie let out a soft hesitant laugh. "I know what you mean about feeling out of control. I feel like that all the time."

Trixie's heart broke for the frightened girl. Suzie was always quiet and painfully shy, but this was the first time she'd seemed truly sad. Trixie silently scolded herself for being abrupt with the girl and immediately softened her approach. Getting pissed at Suzie wouldn't help anything. None of this was her fault.

"Is that what you wanted to talk to me about? Dakota?"

"No." Suzie's lips quivered and she started fiddling with her fingers again. "It's something else."

"Okay," Trixie said slowly. She stood in front of Suzie and gathered both of the woman's hands into hers, giving them a reassuring squeeze. "What's going on? Is it Damien? Did something happen with him?" She dipped her head, trying to get Suzie to look at her. "Because you know that boy has it bad for you, something fierce. When are you gonna put the poor man out of his misery and hook up with him? He digs you."

"I know but…" Suzie's mouth curved in a small smile and she giggled briefly. Then the smile faded, replaced by an air of sadness. "Anyway…it's not about him."

"If it's not about me and Dakota or you and Damien, then—"

"It's about the girl in the woods."

Her words were barely audible, but they hit with such force she may as well have shouted. A cold blanket of dread settled over Trixie.

"How do you know about her?" A swirl of anger and fear rippled in her gut, and she fought to keep her voice even. If Dakota had blabbed, she was going to hang him upside down on a cactus wearing nothing but those damn cowboy boots. "Suzie? *Who* told you about her?"

"Nobody told me anything. I've had visions of you *with* her before, and then tonight…I saw something else… She's in trouble." She jerked her head up to look Trixie in the eyes, and her body started to shake. "Or she's going to be. I'm sorry…I don't know when but I think it's soon."

The dizzying hand of panic grabbed Trixie by the throat. She had to push through it and keep her attention on Suzie. Freaking out wouldn't help Chelsea.

"It's okay. I was out there last week and she was fine." Trixie gently took Suzie's face in her hands and forced her to look her in the face. "I know you don't have control over these visions, and that a lot of the time it looks like a mixed-up mess…but I need you to concentrate. Chelsea is very important to me. Okay?"

"I know." Suzie nodded, her mouth set in a determined line. "That's why I'm here."

"Good girl." Trixie tucked the loose strand of hair behind Suzie's ear. "Now, tell me what you saw. Think, like, real hard, okay? Just stay calm and try to remember."

"I saw her with a baby. A girl, I think."

"Good." Trixie nodded and some of the tension that had gathered in her neck eased back. "Okay, that's good. She's still pregnant, at least she was a week ago, and I don't think she's due for a month or so. What else?"

"There's a man." She squeezed her eyes shut and wrinkled her nose. "And he smells funny, like rotten flowers."

"That's her boyfriend, I think. He stinks," Trixie said quietly. But in the dreamscape with Dakota, right before that thing attacked him, she'd smelled that same stomach-churning odor. "I picked up a scent like that the last time I saw her with him."

"I heard arguing… He wants to know where *it* is." Suzie pressed her fingers to her eyes with both hands and groaned, as though in pain. "He wants *something* but she won't give it to him or she can't," she whimpered, a pained expression covering her face. "It burns…"

Anxiety rippled through Trixie's chest.

"Stop. It's okay, Suzie." Trixie gathered her friend into her arms and held her shaking body close. Pressing a kiss to her hair, she whispered, "It's gonna be fine. I'll go out there and check on Chelsea."

"Please don't go alone." Suzie lifted her tearstained face and grabbed Trixie's shoulders tightly, her eyes wild. "I-I might be wrong. I don't want there to be trouble. Please take Dakota with you. I'd never forgive myself if something happened to you because of me."

"I'll be fine, Suzie." Trixie kissed her forehead and pulled her into a tight hug. "Chelsea hasn't had the baby yet, so we have some time, right?"

"I guess," she sniffled. "But I still don't think…"

"Stop." Trixie put an arm around Suzie and gestured to the rest of the room. "Look around you, girl. I am pretty sure I can handle a smelly human. It'll be fine. I'll fly over there tonight and look in on her. I want to see if I can find out more about this boyfriend of hers." She let out a sigh. "Shit, I was really hoping he was the good guy that I thought he was. Just goes to show you, you never know. Even the nice guys turn out to be jerks. Come on, I'll walk you back to the Presidium offices."

"No." Suzie shook her head adamantly and swiped at her teary eyes. "I'm really not the helpless mess everyone thinks I am, and besides, I have to go back to my apartment first."

"Come on, no one thinks that." Trixie knew she didn't sound as convincing as she wanted to, and Suzie's doubting expression only confirmed it. "Hey, you've only been vamp for, like, two years. You're still a baby, *and* I've never heard of another vampire with visions like yours."

"I wish I was strong like you and the other girls." Suzie bit her lip. "I feel so out of control and scared all the time. I keep waiting for it to get easier but it doesn't. It gets worse."

Trixie understood that feeling all too well. When she had been a drug-addicted human, her life was nothing but out of control and soaked in fear. Unlike for Suzie, becoming a vampire had stopped all of that. At least until recently.

"You sure you don't want me to wait and walk you over there? I have plenty of time. The club doesn't open for a couple of hours."

"I'll be fine. Besides, Damien is going to meet me at my place and walk me over like he always does."

"You're lucky, Suz." Trixie pulled the door open. "Damien's a great guy."

"He is," she agreed quietly. Suzie stepped out into the hallway and once again fixed her gaze to the floor. "But…he's not my bloodmate."

"Wait a minute. How do you—"

"Getting involved with Damien wouldn't be fair to him, and you rejecting Dakota would be equally unfair. He cares for you, Trixie, and he *is* your bloodmate. You should give him a chance… Don't punish him for someone else's sins."

Trixie opened her mouth to respond, but before she could utter a word, Suzie vanished in a blur of speed down the hall and into her apartment, the door shutting loudly behind her. A tsunami of conflicting emotions fired through Trixie as she strode toward her bedroom to get ready for the night. She wished more than ever that she still had that intimate telepathic connection with her maker and her siblings. She'd lost that when each of them found their bloodmate. A painful sense of loneliness crept into her heart, and she fought the surprising swell of tears that threatened to erupt.

She tore off her clothes and turned on the shower, needing to wash away the bundle of uncomfortable feelings. With the water pouring over her, she closed her eyes tightly and reached out with her mind in a desperate but feeble attempt to connect with her family. They wouldn't hear her—all of them had bloodmates now and could only telepath with them—but she still felt the need to try.

I miss you so much.

The silence that followed was more heartbreaking than ever. Just when she felt everything begin to unravel and she was about to go *completely* crazy, a slow, familiar drawl filled the empty spaces.

Now, that's about the finest thing I've heard in a good long while.

Trixie's eyes shot open and she looked around wildly, half expecting to find Dakota standing in the shower with her. She yanked open the curtain but found the black-and-white tiled bathroom completely empty.

She was alone…and yet…she wasn't. And only two minutes ago she had been bemoaning the fact that she couldn't telepath with anyone anymore. Trixie squeezed her eyes closed and shivered as she shut off the water. Careful what you wish for. Jeez. Time to nip this in the bud.

Get out of my head, cowboy.

You started it, missy. It's been a hell of a long time since I've been able to telepath with anyone. My maker's been gone the better part of fifty years and I have no siblings or progeny. A sound of contentment, almost a growl, rumbled through his words and sent a shiver over her wet naked flesh. *I ain't gonna lie, if this is one of the perks of bein' bloodmates, then I am all for it.*

Trixie froze. He knew. Damn it all. Her only saving grace had been that she hadn't thought he knew what was going on. So much for her having some time to figure everything out. She snagged a fluffy towel off the rack beside the sink and dried herself off with furious strokes.

You finally caught up, I see? Took you long enough.

Xavier brought me up to speed, but shame on you, Trixie. Dakota's gritty laugh rolled around her in annoyingly enticing waves. *You knew what was happening in the dream last night but you played dumb. I'll have to remember that look on your face.*

What look?

The innocent wide-eyed thing. That's your tell, darlin'. Next time I see it, I'll know you're lyin'.

Don't presume to think you know something about me because we shared a totally stupid dream.

I know you better than you think I do. I suppose the universe knew what it was doin' when it paired us up.

There is no us. There's you. There's me. And there's a bloodmate legend. That's it. We don't have to participate in it if we don't want to—and I don't want to. I am not interested in being bound to anyone or anything. I like my life. If I'm going to be with a man, it will be exactly that—because I want to be with him. Get it? Not because I have to be.

Silence filled the air and for a moment she thought that he'd broken the connection.

I couldn't agree more. His voice whispered through her head in a low seductive murmur. *I've wanted you since the first time I laid eyes on you. But if you don't want to commit to a bloodmate bond with me, then I won't make you.*

Are you serious? Trixie scoffed out loud as she got dressed. *You don't want to force the issue.*

I may be many things, darlin', but I have never forced a woman to be with me and I sure as hell won't start now. You have a nice night.

There was no mistaking it this time. When Dakota severed their mental link, an odd aching emptiness filled Trixie's chest. She rubbed at it absently, as though that physical movement would make it go away. But it was no use. Dakota wasn't going anywhere and neither was the unseen connection between them.

Luckily the club wasn't as busy as usual and Maya didn't balk when Trixie said she had to leave early. She hadn't been able to stop thinking about Chelsea or, more importantly, Suzie's vision. All of Trixie's protective instincts were on overdrive, and all she could focus on that night was getting out to the cabin to make sure Chelsea was okay.

Trixie knew she wasn't a particularly smart person. That had been evident in the choices she'd made when she was human. But she did trust her gut. Her gut— that inner voice that warned her about danger, the one that had grown loud and trustworthy as a vampire—was never ever wrong.

Her gut had told her something was up at the cabin but she'd been thrown off her game when Dakota arrived. Damn him and this stupid bloodmate legend. It was messing with her life already, and it had only just begun.

Trixie flew through the cool spring evening as fast as her powers would allow her. Maybe she should have broken the no-live-feeds rule this one time. The rush of blood from a living, breathing human always boosted her powers. As she whisked over the tall pine trees, the scent of the woods filled her head.

The lights of the little cabin twinkled in the distance and some of the tension instantly eased from her neck. When the familiar and enticing of scent of sandalwood filled the air, though, any serenity she had found was immediately gone.

Dakota.

Anxiety mixed with uncertainty shimmied through her body, and just when she was about to shout his name into the night, the son of a bitch flew up in front of her and blocked her path. She swore loudly and dove around him in midair before coming to a screeching halt. The two of them must have looked like quite the sight, hovering above the treetops, but Trixie didn't care. She didn't give a rat's ass if anyone saw them, because she was too annoyed.

"What's the matter, darlin'?" Dakota drawled. He hovered in front of her, the edges of his leather coat fluttering in the air around him. "Surprised to see me?"

Too irritated to speak, Trixie set her mouth in a tight

line as she pointed furiously toward the ground. Not watching to see if he followed, she dropped noiselessly onto the forest floor. If she was going to have it out with him, it was probably not smart to do it up in the air. He had way more battle time than she did, and she'd be able to handle him much easier if she had her feet under her.

Hands on her hips, she fought to keep her growing frustration under control, to say nothing of the unwelcome surge of desire she experienced with increasing frequency. A subtle disturbance in the air behind her, combined with Dakota's intriguing scent, let her know the cowboy had landed.

"You gonna speak to me or are you gonna stand there all night with your panties in a bunch?"

Trixie kept her gaze fixed on the little white lights in the distance that peeked out between the trees. Seeing the cottage and knowing Chelsea was close gave her some peace. But not much.

"Why did you come back here?" she asked quietly. "I told you to stay away. Not only that but stalking me is not cool either."

Trixie turned around, surprised to find Dakota mere inches away. His towering form filled the space, making the woods feel claustrophobic as the force of his presence seemed to surround her. The sharp edges and dark curves of his face were highlighted by the silvery-blue slashes of his eyes. They stood out in the moonlit shadows and stirred a flurry of sensations she'd all but forgotten.

She didn't know if she wanted to fight him or fuck him. Fear had a funny way of screwing with her senses.

The air around them hummed with awareness.

It wasn't *him* that frightened her.

Trixie was terrified of the way Dakota made her feel, the way her body responded to his, and the invisible pull that grew stronger with each encounter. Warmth. A tiny tingling at first was swiftly swelling into a tantalizing burn. A little wasn't enough. She wanted more of the delicious heat that simmered in her belly every time he was nearby.

That sensation was addictive; he would be too.

And the idea of being addicted to anyone or anything else ever again was completely terrifying.

She did not want to revert to the pathetic human girl of her past. And she'd been a mess. A pathetic drug-addled disaster who had made one bad choice after another. She refused to go back to that girl, to that way of living, ever again. Getting addicted to Dakota or the way he made her feel was not going to happen. If she was *this* attracted to him *before* a blood exchange, what the hell would she feel after one?

Dependent. Needy. Pathetic.

"Answer me." Trixie kept her hands at her side and her stance balanced, wanting to be ready for anything. "I asked you—no, scratch that—I *told* you not to come back. But here you are, bold as shit. So what gives?"

"Just followin' up on somethin'." He shrugged casually. "That's all."

"There's nothing to follow up on." She squared her shoulders and lightened her tone. "She's a regular human woman. Can't you just let it alone?"

Silence hung between them and an owl hooted in the distance.

"Why are you always lookin' to pick a fight with me?" He tilted his head and the smooth, even sound of his voice curled around her in the dark. "Look at the way you're standin'. I know a fight stance when I see one, and you shift into one almost every time I'm around. Now, why do you suppose that is?"

His expression was serious but his tone was playful, and it confused the hell out her. What was his endgame?

"Hang on." Trixie shook her head and held up both hands. "Wait just one damn minute. Stop answering my questions with another question. Okay?"

"Why?" His lips tilted and he shifted his body nearer. "Am I finally crackin' that tough shell you have wrapped around you?"

The tingling in her belly turned to throbs, and her fangs hummed as his hungry gaze met hers. Trixie had the unmistakable sense of being hunted. That's what he was doing. Dakota was sniffing around and hunting for answers to questions she didn't want to face. Ever.

The man was attracting her and repelling her at the same time, and the entire situation was making her dizzy.

"See?" She took a step back as awareness hummed through her blood. "Another question."

"Yup." He winked and kept moving toward her. "I'm full of 'em."

"You're full of something, alright."

"I never could walk away from a curious situation. My mama told me it was gonna get me in trouble some-day, and I guess she was right. After all, it was my curi-ous nature that got me turned vamp." His voice, a raspy whisper, fluttered over Trixie as a cool breeze whisked through the trees. "Who is Chelsea? Why are you so dang sad every time you look at little Emily? And *why* are you hell-bent on fightin' with me when all I want is to be your friend?"

"My friend?" She scoffed. "Not my bloodmate?"

"Yeah. What's the matter? You have so many friends you don't need one more?" He frowned. "And why do the two have to be mutually exclusive? If you ask me, the woman I'm meant to spend eternity with damn well better be my friend."

"Okay, *friend*." She held up two hands to stop him from getting any closer, but of course he kept coming. "There's not going to be any *eternity* togetherness. How about you stop with the twenty questions and answer my one."

She could have run or flown away but she didn't. She *knew* she shouldn't entertain this unhealthy attraction to Dakota, but she also couldn't resist it. God. What the hell was wrong with her?

"I told you." Dakota's hands hung at his sides but she sensed tension in his broad-shouldered frame. "I came out here to follow up on somethin' and it doesn't have to do with your friend Chelsea. Not directly anyway."

"What are you talking about?" Frustration, sexual and otherwise, shimmied up her back. At least the bloodmate revelation explained why she was ridiculously attracted to him. Unaware of what was behind her, she bumped into a tree and hit her head. "Ouch. Damn it."

She went to rub at the sore spot on her scalp, but Dakota's large warm hand cupped the back of her head with lightning speed, beating her to it. Trixie's entire body stilled and her fingers settled over Dakota's while he tenderly rubbed where the tree had left its mark. Her back pressed into the bark, her black leather jacket protecting her flesh from any further injury. She stilled when the firm planes of his leather-clad thighs brushed over hers.

The man in front of her was far more dangerous than the stupid tree, and if she allowed herself to explore the attraction, she really would get hurt. Flesh wounds knit easily but blows to the heart were another story altogether. He was picking at old scars that would never fully heal.

"Careful, now." His voice, almost a soothing as his touch, was quietly commanding in the darkness of the woods. "It'll get better in a blink, but I'm sure it stung like hell. See? Now if I could add one more perk to being a vamp, it would be no pain. I mean, it's real nice that we heal fast and all that, but gettin' shot or stabbed still hurts like a bitch. Especially silver. That sting sticks around for too damn long."

Trixie swallowed hard and dropped her hand to her side but Dakota didn't let go. His fingers threaded through her hair and fluttered along her scalp, the movement tender and seductive. Had *anyone* ever touched her with such reverence and gentleness?

The answer was a resounding no.

She'd had sex since being turned vamp and plenty of it. But it was all flesh and bone. Quickies with willing human men in the darkest corners of the city, with men who never knew her name or even cared to ask. It was about satisfying an urge, scratching an itch with quick furious strokes.

Sex in Trixie's world—human or vampire—had never been tender.

Even though she and Dakota weren't having sex right now, and they were both fully clothed, he was touching her more intimately and seductively than anyone had in her entire existence.

"It's fine," she whispered shakily. "You can let me go now."

"It's not fine." Dakota's hand slid along the nape of her neck as he shook his head slowly. "And I don't think I want to let you go. Not even a little bit. In fact, I'm just gettin' started with you."

"Why?" Her voice trembled as a storm of confusion swirled inside her. "What do you want from me, Dakota?"

"I'm not entirely sure." He cupped her face gently and swept his thumb along her cheek. "But let's start with gettin' to know each other. I've been here for almost two years, and until a couple of weeks ago, you'd barely said three words to me. And now that we know we're...you know..."

"Don't say the *B* word. Please, this whole situation has me totally freaked out." Trixie studied him closely, looking for any sign of deception, trying to see if he really was the good guy he claimed to be. "I-I'm not good with men. My track record sucks."

"Mmm-hmm." He ran his thumb over her lower lip and the whisper of friction sent a shiver up her spine. "I had a hunch that was the case. You strike me as a woman who's been burned more than once. But lucky for you I'm stubborn as a mule. I want to know you, Trixie. I want to know who you are...who you *really* are. Is that so bad? Forget the bloodmate stuff for now and let's just get to know each other."

When Dakota's mouth covered hers, the world

around her erupted in an explosion of color and light. His lips, warm and firm, melded over hers and his tongue gently but persistently sought hers. Trixie moaned and opened to him, her hands instinctively curling around his leather coat, tugging him hard against her.

He tasted like cinnamon, sweet and hot. It was those lollipops he was always sucking on. It had to be. No one could just *taste* like this. Or maybe *he* could. Damn. Whatever the reason, Trixie didn't care. All she could think about was getting more.

He grasped her face with both hands and groaned as he tilted her head, deepening the kiss, taking full control. His tongue lashed along hers, the intensity growing with each passing second. And with her body crushed between him and the tree, every nerve ending beneath her skin flared to life.

It was like being hooked up to an electrical current.

No live feed or any drug she'd taken as a human could compare to the taste and feel of this man. She held him against her, matching his greedy kiss with her own, and when the hard evidence of his desire dug into her hip, Trixie's fangs burst free.

"I can't get enough of you," Dakota murmured against her lips. He lifted his head but kept her pinned against the tree. "You taste like summertime in Texas. Sweet and hot. Damn, girl. If I still breathed, I'd be suffocated by how much I want you."

Trixie stilled. There was something in the tone of his voice. Gentleness? Emotion? Whatever it was, it made her nervous. If he wanted to get physical, that was one thing, but anything more than that was not happening.

Sex? That she could do.

Intimacy? Nope.

"Then why are you stopping?" She nipped at his lip. "Let's keep this going. As long as we don't do a blood exchange, we can avoid the full mate bonding. We can still fool around." She pressed her breasts into the hard planes of his chest and grasped the buckle of his pants.

"What's your hurry?" He brushed his lips over her forehead and covered her hands with his, stopping her from going any further. "I said that I want to get to know you and I meant it."

"That's what I'm trying to do," she said before popping up on her toes and flicking her tongue over his lip. "Come on. Saddle up, cowboy."

"No."

"No?" Trixie said with more than a little incredulity. "You don't want me?"

"That's not what I said," he murmured. "And I believe I've made it plain that I want you."

"Great. Then let's go." She tried to unbuckle his belt, but Dakota tightened his grip over her hands. Trixie fought the tickle of panic that flickered in her chest and let out a flippant laugh that didn't even convince her. "Well, it would be easier to do this if you didn't have clothes on."

"That's true, but gettin' to know you doesn't involve gettin' naked." His cocky grin widened. "At least, not yet."

What. The. Hell. He was turning her down?

Anger and embarrassment flashed hard and fast as she yanked her hands away from his belt. Shoving him away from her, Trixie pushed her hair off her forehead, then folded her arms over her breasts. She couldn't think of the last time, or any time, a man had rejected her for sex.

"I should've known you wouldn't be able to seal the deal. All that swagger of yours is bullshit."

Dakota didn't move but kept his narrowed steely gaze on her, studying her like some damn bug under a microscope. She knew that look. She'd been on the receiving end of the judgmental well-aren't-you-a-slut look plenty of times as a human.

"What's the matter? Didn't the women from your time have sexual freedom? You think I'm a slut because I want to fuck you without having a freaking conversation first?"

"This isn't about sex. Not by a long shot." Hands on his hips, he looked her up and down. "And, no, I don't think you're a slut but I do think you're scared. And I sure as hell want to find out why." He winked and said, "You can add that to my list of questions."

She opened her mouth to tell him what he could do with his list. Before she could respond, a woman's scream pierced the night. Fear bloomed bright in Trixie's chest.

Chelsea.

Trixie's frightened voice shot into Dakota's mind as she bolted into the air like a bullet. The surprise of hearing her voice in his head, the sweet beauty of it, set him off balance for a split second—just long enough for Trixie to get ahead of him. Dakota swore under his breath and took off after her. It took only a few moments for him to catch up and match her speed, but he suspected that she barely noticed. The fierce, determined expression carved into her features spoke volumes as they zipped above the tree line and seared through the air side by side toward the cabin.

You watch your pretty little ass. He touched her mind with his, praying she'd heed his warning. *I think your friend is mixed up with some—*

She's a good girl. Trixie shot back. Anger and fear laced her voice but she didn't take her eyes off the cabin. *You don't know anything about her.*

Maybe not but you don't know as much as you think you do.

Damn it. Suzie warned me about this. I'll never forgive myself if I'm too late.

The gargoyle's scent grew stronger as they approached and Dakota scanned the area with his heightened senses. The same car from the other night was in the driveway but the area was hauntingly quiet. Too quiet.

Only death brought silence like this.

Movement in the air to his left captured his attention as they dived down to the gravel driveway. Dakota whipped out the stone dagger as he landed solidly on the ground and carefully surveyed the area. The door to the porch stood open, and golden light spilled out into the darkness. No further sounds came from inside. That could easily mean that the worst had already happened. Trixie landed silently beside him, but he grabbed her arm, preventing her from going any farther.

Let me go. She tugged but he held fast. *I have to get in there.*

Wait. He shook his head slowly. *The scent is strong and it could still be here.*

What are you talking about? The blood? That's her blood, Dakota. I know it. Trixie's brow furrowed. *I have to get to her... She's hurt. Oh my God. I can hear her heartbeat, Dakota. It's fading.* Her voice shook and tears filled her eyes. *Please let me go. I have to help her. Damn it all. This is your fault. If I hadn't been out there wasting time with you, she wouldn't have gotten hurt.*

Fine. Her words stung like hell but he didn't flinch. *But I'm a sentry and you damn well better do as I tell you. Besides, you don't know what you're messin' with.* He pulled her closer and scanned the area around them intently, his enhanced vision revealing who or what could be hiding in the woods. The gargoyle's pungent aroma was fading and the trail was off to the west of them, toward the main road, which was probably where the coward ran. *You're gonna get yourself killed.*

You don't understand. Tears spilled down her cheeks and tugged at Dakota's withered excuse of a heart. *She's my daughter.*

Stunned by her admission, Dakota loosened his grip just enough for Trixie to yank her arm from his grasp. As she disappeared inside the house in a blur of speed, a renewed surge of hatred for gargoyles bubbled up. He closed his eyes and refocused his attention, immediately picking up on the gargoyle's scent. He snapped his head to the left and a growl rumbled in his chest as he leaped into the air, following the bastard's trail.

Chapter 7

THE SMELL OF BLOOD OVERWHELMED TRIXIE THE instant she stepped inside the tiny cabin, but it was the first time in decades that it made her stomach turn. This wasn't just any human's blood…it was Chelsea's.

She'd been too late.

Clutching her belly with one hand, Trixie stood in the living room and tried to calm her quaking body, but it was useless. A sense of dread filled her as she moved through the house, surveying the wreckage. The sweetly decorated home, the one that Chelsea had worked so hard to maintain, was completely destroyed in the wake of what must have been an epic battle.

Trixie made her way toward the bedroom at the back of the cabin, following the horrifying sound of Chelsea's fading heartbeat. She wanted to run, to fly. But her body wouldn't cooperate. Fear and disbelief had her in their viselike grip and made her feel as though she was walking through a river of molasses.

She was rendered practically immobile by the idea of what she might find in that bedroom. Blood smeared the wooden floor of the hallway, and the sight turned Trixie's stomach. Mingled with the familiar scent of blood was the aroma of rotten flowers.

Trixie pushed the door open and let out a strangled cry. Chelsea was on the floor, unconscious and bleeding from several wounds to her chest. The white nightgown she wore was stained red and torn from whoever had attacked her, but amid the damage, it was evident she was no longer pregnant.

On the ground nearby lay the body of a creature Trixie had never seen before. It was covered in greenish-gray scaly flesh, its body contorted in death, its face frozen in mid-wail. It looked like something that hovered between man and animal. A high forehead gave way to long pointed ears. It had a flat nose, a mouthful of sharp-looking teeth, and large pair of leathery wings that were curled around the body in a macabre embrace. Long, daggerlike claws curled out from the bony, blood-covered hands.

Chelsea's blood.

Whatever that thing was, it was dead.

Dakota! She screamed his name, praying he would hear her. *I need your help!*

After what she'd said to him, basically blaming him for Chelsea getting hurt, she wouldn't be shocked if he didn't respond. Trixie launched herself across the room and knelt down next to her daughter. She pushed the matted, bloodied strands of hair from Chelsea's sweet face, gently lifting the girl's wounded body into her lap. Tears spilled down, blurring her vision. She glanced around the room frantically and spotted an empty cradle.

There was no sign of the baby anywhere.

"H-he took her," Chelsea whispered in a shaky brittle voice. "He took Rebecca."

Trixie stilled, and for the first time since the day Chelsea was born, she found herself staring into the beautiful brown eyes of her daughter. Trixie was no longer a ghost lurking in the shadows, but a mother holding her baby girl. Why had she waited? Why had she stayed away and listened to the stupid Presidium rules? If she hadn't, maybe none of this would have happened.

This wasn't Dakota's fault. It was entirely hers.

"I'm so sorry I wasn't here sooner," Trixie murmured. She cradled Chelsea in her lap and pressed a hand to her cheek. "I'm sorry."

"I...I know you." A flicker of recognition whispered across Chelsea's face. She licked her dry lips and between labored breaths she whispered, "You're the angel lady."

"No." Trixie's brow furrowed with confusion and she shook her head. "I'm no angel, Chelsea."

"I-I saw you." Her voice was weak and barely audible as her blood-spattered fingers went to the gold chain around her neck. "You gave me this and said you'd watch over me."

"But I glamoured you," Trixie said with a strangled sob. "You remember that night?"

"Yes." She curled her hand around the necklace chain as another wave of pain racked her ravaged body. "He tried... It burned..."

"Shh." Trixie held her tighter and gently moved the shredded nightgown so she could inspect the wounds. "Don't try to talk. It's going to be okay, but I need you to save your strength. We're going to take you some place safe and then I'm going to find your baby."

"He...took her... Rebecca..." The words died on Chelsea's lips and her eyes rolled back in her head as she lost consciousness.

Trixie was about to scream for Dakota again when

he appeared in the doorway. His towering frame filled the small space, making him seem even bigger than he was. Eyes wild and weapons drawn, he looked like death incarnate. Without a word, he went to the body of the creature, knelt down, and turned the body so its contorted, twisted face was turned toward the ceiling. Fury carved into his features, Dakota pressed one hand to the beast's chest and raised the other high. A gray dagger curled in his fist, he whispered, "Payback's a bitch, but I always settle my debts."

"It's already dead, Dakota."

"No it's not." He seethed as he drove the dagger down and into the chest of the fallen creature.

Trixie held her daughter close and let out a shivering sound of awe as the body of the beast crackled and turned to gray stone before her eyes.

"*Now* it's dead." He sheathed the knife beneath his coat. "It was in hibernation, trying to heal itself. The other one got away. I lost the trail about a half mile from the cabin, out on the main road. I think it had the baby with it, but I can't be sure. The scent of that thing was too strong."

"We have to get Chelsea back to the Presidium."

Trixie didn't have any clue what that *thing* was, but whatever *it* was had almost killed her daughter. She glanced out the window at the sky. The inky blackness of night was beginning to give way to the impending dawn, and panic clawed at her like the vicious self-defeating nightmare it was.

Sunrise was coming and their odds of making it back to the city before that were dwindling.

"She's in bad shape, Trixie." Dakota squatted down

next to them. Gone was the vicious sentry. The man across from her stared at her with empathy-filled eyes, and gentleness edged the deep timbre of his voice. "She's not gonna make it back to the city. You're gonna have to turn her now."

"No." Trixie shook her head furiously and held Chelsea tighter. "We can just give her some blood… It will heal her."

"She's too far gone, baby." Dakota shook his head. "Turnin' her is her only chance."

"I-I can't do it. We have to get her back to the city. Xavier can help without turning her. He can heal her. I know he can." Her lips quivered as she stroked Chelsea's cheek with one quivering finger. "Damn it all. I want her to have a normal human life. I wanted her to have what I never did."

"She was mixed up with gargoyles." Dakota settled his large warm hand over her arm reassuringly. "I'd say she's well past a normal human life."

"Gargoyles? That's what that thing was?" Trixie flicked a glance at the hunk of stone in the middle of the room and a shiver whisked up her back. She'd heard about those creatures, about their viciousness and traitorous behavior, but she thought they were extinct. "What the hell was Chelsea doing hanging around with gargoyles? And why do you know so much about them?"

"She may not have known what they were. They look human when they want to." He sent a furious glare at the stone creature at the center of the room. "That's how I knew it wasn't dead. They shift to human form when they die, unless that dagger or the sun gets 'em first. That one was in hibernation tryin' to heal itself."

Trixie sniffled and shook her head with her eyes squeezed shut, sending streaks of her mascara streaming down her cheeks.

"I could do it," Dakota said quietly. His serious silvery gaze met hers. "I've never turned anyone before but I know what to do. She should be in the transition sleep for at least two days. We can start the process now, stay here until sundown, and then get her back to the Presidium to let her ride it out." Trixie was about to argue with him but his mouth set in a firm line before he whispered, "It's her only chance, Trix."

Trixie pressed a hand to the bloody wound on Chelsea's chest and grief welled. The beat of the girl's heart weakened with every passing second. Dakota was right. Time was about to run out. She had to make a decision. Either let Chelsea die here and now, or turn her into a vampire, something she might not want. Olivia had given Trixie a choice that night in the tunnels all those years ago and Trixie hadn't even hesitated. But not everyone embraced the life of a vampire with such enthusiasm.

"Don't you think she'll want to watch her baby grow up?" Dakota's voice drifted over Trixie like a warm blanket. "Would you give up the time you've had with *her*? It may not have been the way you wanted it but it was somethin'. You should allow Chelsea the same opportunity."

"You're right. I wouldn't trade one minute of watching her grow up," Trixie whispered.

While Dakota cleared off the bed to make room for Chelsea, Trixie leaned down and pressed a kiss to her daughter's forehead. She slipped the necklace over Chelsea's head and quickly put it on herself.

"I love you, Chelsea." The weight of the coin settled between her breasts, instantly putting her at ease to have this piece of her daughter with her. Somehow, some way, she knew it was all going to be okay. "I'll give this back to you when you wake up."

"We'll do it in here. There's only the one set of windows to cover, and the hallway is long enough to keep out direct sunlight from the living room." Dakota slipped his arms gently beneath Chelsea's body and rose to his feet with the unconscious woman cradled against him like a child. He strode to the bed and laid her out carefully before settling her hands on her belly. "Those drapes aren't heavy enough. We're gonna need to cover up the windows as much as we can. She'll be especially vulnerable during the transition."

Trixie nodded her understanding but didn't move. Her feet felt like they were nailed to the floor and she didn't take her eyes off Chelsea. Anxiety and uncertainty fired through her but one thought rose above her flood of concerns. Trixie could not let her daughter die.

Dakota sat on the edge of the bed and gingerly lifted Chelsea's arm to his mouth. Trixie was completely fixated as he bared his fangs, pierced the soft flesh on Chelsea's wrist, and drank. After a few moments, when her heart had almost stopped beating, he licked the wound closed and laid her hand on her belly before using his fangs to make an incision on his own wrist.

With heartbreaking gentleness, he cradled her neck and lifted her head from the bed, bringing his wrist to her lips. His life-giving blood dripped into her partially open mouth. Nothing happened; was there a chance it wasn't going to work? But after a few seconds, Chelsea's lips closed over his wrist and she began to drink. He must have determined that she'd had enough and pulled his wrist away. Dakota laid her head back on the pillow and rose from the bed.

"Now we wait." He pulled his sleeve down, the wound on his wrist already healed. "We'll take her back to the city after sundown."

"That's it?" Trixie asked nervously. She went to Chelsea's side and found her stone still and totally lifeless—the sleep state of a vampire. "I've never seen anyone turned before. I mean, I saw Maya in the transition sleep but I didn't see the actual blood exchange. It was…" Words escaped her as her gaze fell over her daughter's motionless form. A dull ache bloomed in her chest and fresh tears welled when the full weight of Dakota's gift sank in. "Thank you for saving her, Dakota."

Silence filled the room and he was gone.

She gathered one of Chelsea's hands in hers before stretching out on the bed next to her. How many times had she dreamed of sleeping by her daughter's side, of being there to kiss away the nightmares? Her feeling of happiness was short-lived though. What might happen when Chelsea woke up? There would be confusion. There always was, even for vamps that knew what they had been through. But Chelsea was completely unaware of the choice Trixie had made for her.

Would she thank Trixie for bringing her into the vampires' world, or would she hate her for it?

"Found what we need." A moment later, Dakota reappeared with some black garbage bags and a roll of duct tape in hand. "None too soon, either. It's almost sunrise."

Trixie swiped at her tear-stained face while Dakota covered the windows. Silently and swiftly he made sure the room would be free of sunlight, but there was something different about him. A shift in his demeanor that gave her pause, as well as the way he seemed to avoid looking at her.

"What is it, Dakota?" She studied him closely. "I feel like there's something you're not telling me."

"I'm not sure if she knew." He secured the edges of the garbage bags with the duct tape and nodded toward the stone creature on the floor. "About the gargoyles, I mean. Poor girl got the shock of her life today when that one came after her."

"How do you—" Trixie stopped mid-sentence and nodded as she realized how he could know such information. "Right. Her blood memories."

"They weren't clear, at least not as clear as with most humans. It's probably because she'd already lost so much blood, but hell if I know. My vampire training wasn't exactly regular, but I promise, as her maker, I'll do right by Chelsea," he said quickly. "Plus, she'll have that whole crazy coven helpin' her out. Hell, Maya will probably want to give her a vampire makeover."

"Right." Embarrassment and a flicker of jealously fired through Trixie. Dakota now knew her daughter better than she did. Now that he was Chelsea's maker, this was only the beginning. "Thanks again for what you did. You didn't have to do it. I mean, I know that being a maker is a big responsibility…and…you two will have a special bond now."

Trixie stilled when his eyes met hers and something in her belly fluttered with awareness. There was so much she wanted to say to him but all of the words were jumbled in her weary brain. Dakota picked up the stone gargoyle, hoisted it effortlessly onto his shoulder, and strode to the door. He paused for a moment in the open doorway before glancing over his shoulder at Chelsea.

"You're her mama, Trix," Dakota said quietly. "There's no bond on earth more special than that."

His tall form disappeared down the hallway and around the corner, leaving Trixie alone with her daughter once again. Lying by Chelsea's side, she couldn't help but wonder—perhaps there was one other bond worth exploring in her increasingly crazy life.

Bloodmate?

No. Trixie squeezed her eyes shut. That was the last thing she should be thinking about now. All that mattered was Chelsea's transition and finding the baby. They were her family—her real family. Her gaze skittered over the tattered and bloodied nightgown, and a fresh wave of fury bloomed in her chest. It was going to be challenging enough for Chelsea to adapt to the change when she woke up. How awful would it be for her to awaken covered in bloody clothing?

Trixie hopped off the bed and to the dresser in search of something clean. She settled on a pair of pink satin pajamas and then went to the little bathroom next door to get a towel so she could clean the blood from her daughter's healing body.

"Dakota," she shouted from the doorway. "I'm going to clean Chelsea up and change her clothes, so give me a couple minutes. Okay?"

No need to shout, darlin'. His sweet sexy drawl filled her head. *I have to finish off our ugly friend here and then I'll stand watch.*

Right. It's been a while since I could telepath with anyone. It'll take some getting used to, I guess. Trixie suppressed a laugh as she closed the door. *What do you mean, you have to finish him off? I thought it was dead.*

A gunshot fired through the woods, and the shock of it sent Trixie to her daughter's side in a flash.

What the hell is going on, Dakota?

Standing in front of the bed in a battle-ready stance, she was about ready to scream when Dakota's voice once again slipped into her mind like a warm breeze.

Now it's dead as dirt. He laughed, a low gritty sound that tickled her from the inside out. *Well, he's more like a heap of gravel. Leave the bedroom door open so I'll know when it's safe to come back in. Then I think you should lie down there with your baby girl and get some shut-eye. I'll stand watch in case the other fella comes back.*

Do you think it will?

Maybe, but I doubt it. They don't get dusted by sunlight like we do, but it does turn 'em to stone, so I suspect he won't be a problem for now. But, if it comes back at any point, I'll kill it. The steady, resolute tone in his voice instantly put her at ease. She had no doubt Dakota could and would protect them. *You'll be safe. Both of you. You have my word.*

The baby. Tears clogged her throat and the cold hand

of fear curled around her heart. *The other one...it has Rebecca, doesn't it?*

Silence stretched out, seconds feeling like minutes, before he finally responded.

Yes. But I swear to you, Trixie, we will get that baby back. Besides, if it wanted to kill her, it could have done that here.

Why would it take her? Trixie cringed at the thought and went to her daughter's side. *What good would she be to them?*

Ransom, maybe? Chelsea had somethin' they wanted but it beats the hell out of me what it was. His voice was edged with obvious frustration. *I wish her blood memories weren't so damn foggy. I only got a peek at what happened in here tonight. I didn't see anythin' about her life before today.*

Trixie's blood ran cold and she curled her fingers around the coin. Chelsea said that the gargoyle tried to take the coin but it burned him. Trixie nibbled her lower lip and debated whether or not to tell Dakota about it. Not now. She was too tired and all she wanted to do was protect her girl. When they got back to the city and Chelsea woke up, then they could hash it all out.

I'm sure she'll tell us when she wakes up. Brushing a strand of hair off Chelsea's face, Trixie touched Dakota's mind once more. Saying thank you and swallowing her pride were two things she wasn't really good at, but there was no doubt that this guy was due both. *I don't know if I can ever repay you for this.*

I'm sure we'll come up with somethin'. A hint of humor laced his words and Trixie couldn't help but smile. The sound of his voice in her head was becoming positively normal, and she had to admit she was beginning to enjoy his teasing. *But for now, you just worry about tendin' to your baby girl. You and I will have plenty of time later to...settle up.*

Chapter 8

DAKOTA STOOD IN THE BEDROOM DOORWAY ALL DAY, his senses alert and his gaze almost always pinned to the two sleeping women in the bed. Not just any women. One was his bloodmate and the other his new progeny—who was also his bloodmate's biological daughter.

Fate was a funny thing. For a guy who never wanted to be tied down, he'd gone and gotten himself a family overnight.

He shook his head and let out a short laugh. It looked like he was beginning to fit right in with this weird city coven. He'd never considered becoming a maker. It was too much responsibility. A maker and its progeny were tied for the first one hundred years of the new vampire's life. He'd never wanted to be beholden to anyone else in that way. But then he'd seen the heartbroken expression on Trixie's face…and none of that mattered.

All he could think about was easing her pain. It wasn't even a choice, not really. Turning Chelsea was simply what he had to do to ensure Trixie's happiness. Seeing Trixie in such distress was worse than anything he'd endured in his life—vampire or human. Hell, Dakota would rather get shot with silver ten times over than see her upset like that ever again.

He moved closer to the bed, his gaze sliding over the faces of Trixie and her daughter. Spooned together, with Chelsea in the loving embrace of her mother, they looked so much alike. They had almost the same profile. The same upturned button nose, high cheekbones, and determined chin.

Granted, they looked more like sisters than mother and daughter, but there was no denying the family resemblance. A smile played at his lips because he sure as hell had gone and gotten himself saddled. For the first time in decades, he could actually build a home somewhere.

He'd never thought his home would be in New York City.

A dull throb in his gut told him the sun had begun its leisurely descent and night had started to yawn into existence. They'd made it through the day without any further sign of the gargoyle but he didn't want to linger around here any longer than necessary. He was going to fly Chelsea back to the Presidium as soon as the sun was down.

Trixie's question nagged at him though. Why *would* that gargoyle run off with the baby? The only answer he could imagine was that it wanted a hostage to use as a bargaining chip. But for what? What could Chelsea possibly have that those two creatures were after?

He surveyed the room, taking in as much as he could about his new progeny. She had simple tastes, and based on the way the house was decorated, she was frugal. They obviously weren't coming out here to rob the woman. She didn't have much to speak of. Even her blood memories showed little. Chelsea was a loner by all accounts, and other than images of the attack, he only saw memories of her boyfriend and her baby.

Looking around the room, he realized there were no pictures of family or friends. Come to think of it, he didn't recall seeing any out in the living room either.

His brow furrowed.

That was odd, wasn't it? Especially in this age of the selfie when most humans recorded every waking moment with their camera phones, it seemed strange that a woman with a new baby wouldn't have photos around. Combine that with her foggy blood memories, and all of the alarm bells started to go off. Hands at his sides, he scanned the wreckage in the bedroom. He had to be wrong about that. The woman had to have pictures somewhere.

That was when he spotted a pink frame facedown on the floor by the closet near a pile of clothes that had been torn from their hangers. Dakota scooped up the frame and turned it over, broken pieces clinking onto the wood floor.

Behind the shards of glass was a photo of Chelsea, smiling broadly and wrapped in the embrace of a man who was obviously her boyfriend. His hands were settled protectively over her swollen belly, and the guy looked as happy as one would expect him to be. It was exactly the kind of photo Dakota had hoped to find—but then again, it wasn't. As Dakota recalled one of the last images Chelsea saw before she lost consciousness, the smile fell from his lips.

Had he seen this picture earlier, he never would have offered to turn her.

Because if he was right, if Dakota did what he knew he would absolutely *have* to do as a sentry, he and Trixie would be over before they'd had a chance to begin. She'd hate his guts and he wouldn't blame her.

Fate was one sick, twisted bitch.

"Hey." Trixie's sleepy voice cut through the room and yanked his gaze from the photo in his hands. He slipped it quickly into the pocket of his coat. "Have you been up all night?"

Dakota nodded but said nothing.

Trixie stretched her curvy, nimble body, reminding him of a cat working out the kinks of sleep. Desire stirred as she arched her back, the movement making her breasts heave toward him, teasing him with what he now knew he could never have. There was no way she'd want him once she knew about the task he was going to have to carry out.

He must have had a funny look on his face, because she arched one brow and said, "What's going on? You seem totally freaked out." Worry flickered across her heart-shaped face. "Did something happen while we were sleeping?"

"No." He set his mouth in a tight line and shook his head, her pale brown gaze locked with his. Unable to look her in the eye, and with the ugly truth clawing at him from the inside out, he strode toward the door. "Sun's down and it's time to go. We gotta move. I'll do a quick sweep of the area. You stay here with Chelsea."

"Hey, hang on." Rising to her feet, she glanced at Chelsea briefly before closing the distance between them. "Why do I feel like you're not telling me something? You're acting weird." Her hand curled over his, stopping him dead in his tracks. She pulled him toward her, dropping her voice to that low smoky tone he loved so much. Her body wavered achingly close, so that her breasts brushed over his arm with painful brevity. "I mean weirder than usual."

Dakota's guts twisted in knots. He had to tell her the truth—and he would. But not yet. He couldn't bring himself to spoil the long-awaited reunion with her daughter. No. He'd hold off and give Trixie at least a day or two of happiness. Besides, there was still a small chance he was wrong, and waiting would give him time to sort it all out.

Once he got them both back to the safety of the Presidium, then he could break the news to her if he had to. His chest ached as he noted that the hard edges of her face had softened. That wall, the one he so desperately wanted to knock down, had finally started to fall. She was doing exactly what he'd hoped and opening up to him. His jaw clenched and he bit back the surge of rage that threatened to bubble up at the injustice of the situation.

"We have to leave in five minutes," he bit out.

"I know we should get going," she purred, pressing the soft flesh of her body against his and fitting against him with painful perfection. She laced her fingers through his and peered up at him from beneath a fan of dark lashes with an unmistakable look of invitation. "But we do have a little time. Remember all that getting-to-know-you stuff we started out in the woods?"

Dakota bit back the growl of lust and frustration as his body hardened to the point of pain. Damn it all to hell. He had been a total fool for thinking that he could have some kind of a normal life. How in the world could he have allowed himself to believe, even for one second, that he could have a family?

He was a sentry. A killer. An executioner.

This coven of theirs might be able to operate outside the usual vampire community rules, but he couldn't. A sentry didn't have that kind of luxury.

In that moment, Dakota faced the cold, hard reality of the life he'd chosen. He couldn't pursue this bloodmate thing between him and Trixie any further. Not when she would surely hate him before the next sunrise.

"No time for that now." He slipped easily from her grasp but didn't miss the flicker of hurt and confusion in her eyes. "You better pack up whatever you think she'll want to take with her, because she can't come back here until I hunt down the other one. I also want to bring her laptop with us. There could be something on there to help us figure out what they were after."

"Sure." The word slid between her lips on a hiss, and any softness in her features vanished in a blink. Trixie ran both hands through her blond-and-blue-streaked hair before cracking her knuckles loudly. "Whatever you say, cowboy. You know…for a minute there, I almost forgot that you're a sentry."

"Me too." Dakota squared his shoulders and nodded curtly. "But I won't be makin' that mistake again."

They made it back to the Presidium offices in record time and in stone-cold silence. Neither of them said a word, which was fine with Trixie. She'd never been so humiliated or confused in her entire miserable life. One minute Dakota had been a caring, self-sacrificing wiseass with a clear desire to get in her pants and the next he was cold, distant, and with a sudden urge for celibacy.

She didn't know which end was up, and that was not a feeling she enjoyed.

Still in the transition sleep, Chelsea lay motionless in the examination room bed. The makeshift hospital room was adjacent to Xavier's lab, and up until today, it hadn't ever been used. The scientist flew back and forth between the lab and the exam room, taking blood samples from Chelsea and hooking her up to monitors. As much as Trixie hated the idea of her daughter waking up here instead of in her apartment, it was for the best. If the turn went bad, Chelsea would be in a safe place where they could handle it.

Trixie sat on the edge of the bed holding her daughter's hand and doing her best to ignore Dakota. He stood silently off to the right. She didn't have to look at him to know he was staring at her; she could feel his steely gaze. The wiseass cowboy was gone and had been replaced by a stone-cold emotionless sentry.

At least he'd had the decency to fill everyone in on what had happened and spared Trixie from having to relive it.

"I'm sorry, Olivia," Trixie said in an almost audible voice. "I know I should've stayed away from her but I—"

"Stop it." Olivia's hand curled over Trixie's shoulder and squeezed gently. "She's your daughter, and truth be told, I feel like an asshole because I made you follow the stupid outdated laws of the Presidium." Her voice dropped to just above a whisper. "I can't imagine staying away from Emily for one day, let alone years. I'm the one who's sorry, Trixie. I hope you can forgive me."

"It's okay." Trixie fought the tears and nodded. "I know you were doing what you thought was best."

"Damn, girl." Doug let out a low whistle. "You sure can keep a secret. I cannot believe you didn't tell the rest of us that you had a daughter."

"I wanted to protect her," Trixie said quietly. "Not from our coven but from the others. I figured that it was safer for Chelsea if no one else in the community knew she existed."

"And it wasn't my secret to tell." Olivia gave Trixie a familiar and reassuring smile. "But you are gonna have a lot of explaining to do with your sisters."

"I know." Trixie swiped at her eyes. "Maya is gonna go totally nuts."

Olivia directed her attention back to Dakota. "Do we have cleanup to do in terms of the humans? What kind of evidence was left at the scene?"

"It's clean," Dakota said curtly. "No evidence of the supernatural left behind. Any human who finds the place will likely assume she was abducted. The only blood at the cottage was Chelsea's. There was none from the creature, and right now it's a pile of gravel in the driveway."

"What a shit show." Olivia's weary voice sounded behind Trixie's shoulder. "Gargoyles? They were the least trustworthy of all the supernaturals. Even the demons didn't want to deal with those guys. What the hell was she doing hanging around with them?"

"Chelsea didn't know what they were. At least I don't think she did. Her blood memories were foggy." Dakota took one step toward the bed but stopped when Trixie glared at him. He held up both hands. "I don't believe she's a sympathizer, is all I'm sayin'. Xavier has her laptop, and he and Pete are going through it."

"Still"—Olivia let out a weary sigh—"this could be a really messy turn if Chelsea doesn't know about the supernatural world. Not only that, but we've got at least one pissed-off gargoyle to contend with. For all we know there could be more of them out there."

"Can someone clue me in?" Doug interjected. "I may be a czar but I'm still kind of new to supernatural craziness. What was the deal with these guys? I thought they were extinct."

"So did I, babe. So did everyone." Olivia pulled her cell phone out of the pocket of her black suit jacket and shot Dakota a narrow-eyed glance. "I'm wondering how our newest sentry has so much working knowledge about gargoyles."

"That's classified," Dakota said quickly. "With all due respect, Emperor Zhao is the only person I can discuss it with."

"Oh really?" Olivia let out a curt laugh and folded her arms over her breasts. "Care to elaborate?"

"Not particularly," he drawled. "Let's just say I've tangled with these assholes before."

"There was one incapacitated when you got to the cottage?" Doug asked. "Not much tangling then."

"It was." Dakota flicked his icy gaze to Trixie briefly. "I meant before yesterday."

"That's what I saw in the dream, isn't it?" Memories of the dreamscape came flooding back. "You were attacked by a gargoyle the night you were turned. *That's* what your maker saved you from. Why didn't you tell me, Dakota? That smell…oh my God! You *knew* a gargoyle had been at Chelsea's place!"

"Yes. But in my defense I had no reason to think it would be back. For all I knew, a lone rogue had only passed through the area. They have no territory, no home, and are basically wanderers. Have been for centuries." The angles and edges of his handsome face seemed sharper at the mention of that night. "I'd been attacked by one out on our ranch. My maker, Jonner, found me and turned me. In return, I was assigned to help him with his mission and I was only too happy to oblige."

Anger and confusion shimmied through Trixie. The son of a bitch knew a gargoyle had been in the area. That's why he kept going out there. He didn't care about her or her daughter.

"So this was all about revenge?" Trixie seethed. "You were only after the gargoyle. You weren't there to help me or Chelsea."

"Woman"—Dakota's expression darkened—"you are so wrong it's scary. I knew she was in danger. You too, for that matter. This isn't about revenge. I'm a sentry for the Presidium and it is my job to keep this community safe."

"Maybe next time you could try being honest," Trixie shot back. "If you had, then Chelsea might not even be in this mess."

"You wanna blame someone, darlin'?" He strode toward her but stopped short and pointed at her. "You can start with that thing that attacked her. It was after somethin' that your daughter had."

Trixie's hand went to the coin hidden beneath her shirt and her face heated.

"Dakota is on to something," Xavier shouted as he flew in from the lab. He landed on the floor next to Olivia and Doug. "Seems that our friend Chelsea was an avid numismatist—a collector. According to her Facebook page, she collects rare coins. Fascinating stuff. She had a photo album there full of the various coins she's gathered over the years."

"Valuable?" Olivia asked.

"Definitely." Xavier nodded and looked from Trixie to Dakota. "Did you find anything like that when you were there?"

Trixie opened her mouth to respond but Dakota spoke up first.

"The place was trashed, but I'll go back and have another look around." He nodded curtly and turned his attention back to Olivia and Doug. "I would venture to say that if she had a collection like that, it would be in a bank or somethin'. The one other fact I can tell you about gargoyles is that their viciousness is matched only by their greed. Jonner stressed that above all. If Chelsea had a treasure trove of coins, you can be sure the gargoyles would want it."

"Interesting," Xavier said. "Perhaps other collectors in the area have been attacked. I'll have a peek into the human police database and see if there are any similar cases."

"Good idea," Dakota said firmly.

"I didn't know Jonner but I'd heard about him. He was known for being something of a loner." Olivia's brow furrowed. "I remember hearing that he died not long after you were turned, correct?"

"Yes, ma'am, down in Texas. Jonner was a hell of a fighter and tough as they come, but even he couldn't escape a silver bullet to the heart. He got dusted a year after I was turned. We were out on a hunt and got separated."

"Gargoyle?" Olivia asked.

"Unlikely. Jonner was shot with silver, and in my experience, gargoyles like to use their claws."

"Ah, yes," Xavier exclaimed. He pushed his glasses onto his head. "They have a poison on their claws. It has the same effect on us as silver—on the wolves too, for that matter. It can be lethal if it hits the bloodstream."

"Don't do much for humans either," Dakota said flatly. "Their poison may not affect humans, but the claws work just fine."

"It makes sense," Xavier murmured. "After all, the gargoyles *were* charged with protecting humans. Humans have typically been prey for our kind and even for the wolves, especially during, shall we say, less-than-civilized times."

"These sons of bitches are anythin' but civilized." Dakota's hands curled into fists. "I've never seen 'em do anythin' other than cause damage. Besides, from what I heard, a bunch of 'em murdered their own royal family to get their stash of gold."

"I remember that story." Olivia ran both hands through her red curls and made a snort of derision. "The royal family was slaughtered and the gold stolen. That was the beginning of the end for them. The gold vanished along with the culprits. According to legend, the gold was the source of much of the gargoyles' power. Without it, their community completely dissolved into chaos."

"They killed their own kind and shirked their duties as protectors. You ask me, they deserve to be extinct." Dakota clasped his hands in front of him, his expression cold. "Anyway, after Jonner was killed, there was no more trouble with these bastards around here. Until now."

As annoyed as Trixie was with Dakota for keeping his suspicions to himself, a pang of sympathy burned in her chest when Dakota spoke of his maker. She couldn't imagine how horrible that must have been for him to be left alone so early in his vampire life. How could she not have known he'd suffered such a loss? She didn't know much about the man who was supposed to be her bloodmate.

Maybe he wasn't wrong about that whole getting-to-know-each-other stuff.

"That all happened around the last time there'd been a confirmed sighting," Olivia said quietly. "I'm sorry, Dakota. Losing your maker is never easy."

Olivia wasn't simply saying it for the sake of saying it. She'd lost her own maker a couple of years ago, and even though Victor had been a stodgy old coot, it had still hurt Olivia deeply.

"I managed." Dakota squared his shoulders. "All I found was his sentry dagger in a pile of dust. When I got sworn in as a sentry, I asked to keep his instead of gettin' one of my own. Seemed like the right thing to do."

"Sorry, man." Doug slipped his arm around Olivia's waist. "That must've been tough."

"That's ancient history," Dakota said evenly. He shifted his weight, clearly uncomfortable with the attention on him and his past. "Ma'am, if everyone thinks these things are extinct, I think it might be better if we left it that way. Keep the buzz to a minimum. I don't want the one that got away to know the Presidium is lookin' for it. Odds are that it has no idea I'm a sentry or that I'm on to it."

Olivia and Doug exchanged a look Trixie had seen before, and she could tell that they were telepathing with each other. A twinge of jealousy wiggled under the surface. Part of her wanted to reach out to Dakota but he'd been so cold and distant that the idea of letting him into her head wasn't appealing. It was bad enough to get rejected face-to-face; why risk an intimate telepathic connection? Getting shut down that way would sting twice as badly.

"Okay." Olivia nodded and slipped her phone back in her pocket. "Given your past experience with the gargoyles, I'll hold off on calling Zhao."

"Thank you, ma'am."

"Please, stop with the 'ma'am' stuff." She gave him a weary smile. "I've told you a hundred times to call me Olivia. One week, Dakota. That's it. Believe me, I'd much rather call him and tell him the situation has already been handled, but we can't risk a bigger mess than we already have. You've got a week to find the gargoyle and get Chelsea's baby back. If you don't find it by then, I'm going to have to call the emperor."

"No problem." Dakota nodded curtly. "I'll put it down the minute I find it."

Panic fired through Trixie when she thought of that tiny baby in the midst of a battle between Dakota and a gargoyle.

"You're going to kill it? Hang on. That thing has Chelsea's baby." She hopped to her feet and shot Dakota a withering look. "You are not going to go at it with guns and fangs blazing, cowboy. Not when it has my granddaughter."

Dakota's hard expression faltered. For a split second Trixie saw empathy but it vanished as swiftly as it came. Arms at his sides, Dakota stared her down in silence. Fury buzzed in her chest, and she stalked around the bed toward him.

"Did you hear me?" she seethed. Hands curled into fists at her sides, she moved in so she was mere inches from him. "You will not put that baby girl in danger."

"It's too late," he whispered. "She's already there."

Tension rippled between them and throbbed through the room. Trixie didn't back down.

"Fine." She poked him in the chest. "Then I'm going with you. Because if you think I'm gonna let you risk that baby's life, then you've got another thing coming, bucko!"

The *Happy Days* reference probably sounded stupid, but she hoped the big jerk would get the point. His silvery-blue eyes flashed. His stubble-covered square jaw clenched as he leaned in, swallowing what little distance was left between them.

"That so?" His voice dropped to a growl. "And if *you* think I'm going to let you put yourself in danger, then all that dye in your hair has gotten to your brain. You aren't gettin' within a mile of one of

those things ever again. You're gonna stay right here
with Chelsea."

"You're not the boss of me," Trixie insisted. "This is
not *Leave It to Beaver* land, dude. And if you'd let me
speak, then I would have told you that—"

"Maybe not." He poked her in the chest, cutting her
off again. His narrowed gaze drifted over her face and
down to her breasts, which both turned her on and pissed
her off. "But I am not only a sentry, I am your bloodmate *and* your daughter is *my* progeny and—" Dakota
stopped mid-sentence, his finger sliding lower along the
curve of her breast.

For a second she thought the guy was actually going
to try to cop a feel in the middle of their fight. But
he didn't. Relief mixed with disappointment rippled
through her as he reached between her breasts and
pulled the coin from its rightful home.

He held the gold disk in his thumb and forefinger and
swore under his breath, staring at the damn thing with
nothing short of total shock. Too quickly, his expression
of wonder shifted to one of fury. The dark, dangerous
look in his eyes made her take a step back.

A tense heavy silence fell over the room and no one
moved a muscle. Even the czars remained quiet.

"Is this the necklace you took off Chelsea before I
turned her?" Dakota rasped. Frustration fired through
her as Trixie stared into his angry face. "Answer me,
damn it! Where did you get this coin?"

"I found it years ago, when I was human." She
snatched it from his hand and crossed back to Chelsea's
bedside. "It was the only possession I had that ever
meant something to me. I gave it to Chelsea when

she was little." Trixie couldn't bring herself to look at Olivia. "I know I wasn't supposed to, but I wanted her to have a piece of me with her."

"Where did you find it?" Dakota asked in a quiet, almost deadly tone.

"I was on a camping trip down south with one of my foster families. I found it wedged between a couple of boulders. I was freaking nauseated almost the whole time. I guess I'm not a camping kind of girl."

"Where were you camping?" His voice was barely audible and the color drained from his face. "Was it in Texas by any chance?"

Trixie nodded wordlessly and rubbed the cool gold disk between her fingers. Her thoughts went to the dreamscape. When she first got there it had reminded her of the place where she'd found the coin, but when Dakota arrived, it had changed to his family's ranch. Both places were in Texas…

A tickle of uneasiness whispered up her spine, and she remained pinned beneath the weight of his steely stare.

"Dakota?" Olivia said slowly. "What is going on?"

"Looks like our fates were tied together long before either one of us turned vampire," he murmured.

"What are you talking about?" Olivia asked, her patience waning.

"That coin," he whispered. "I've seen it before. It was only in a picture but I'd never forget that symbol. Jonner showed it to me."

Uneasiness filtered around them like smoke, and Trixie thought she might actually choke on it. She sat on the edge of the bed and gathered Chelsea's hand in hers, wanting to protect her from whatever was coming.

"No wonder they came after Chelsea," he said in a quiet, almost reverent tone. Dakota flicked his fierce gaze to hers briefly before turning to the czars. "That isn't just any coin. Chelsea had a piece of the gargoyles' gold."

Chapter 9

DAKOTA COULDN'T TAKE HIS EYES OFF TRIXIE. SHE WAS sitting on the edge of Chelsea's bed fiddling with the chain of her necklace and holding her daughter's hand, looking as nervous as he had ever seen her. Not that he could blame her. The world they knew—and the one they were only beginning to know with each other—had blown up in a big, fat way.

He had wondered on more than one occasion over the past few weeks how two polar opposites like them could be paired up. But now it made sense. His fate had been intertwined with Trixie's decades before either of them had known about the existence of vampires. He'd bet his boots that she'd found that coin in or around Fredricksville, Texas, the same place he'd been attacked and where he and his maker had hunted down the other gargoyles.

"Do you remember the name of the town?" he asked gently. If he pushed too hard, she might shatter. The vulnerable woman under that hard-as-nails facade was now plainly evident. "Trix?"

"I don't know." She sniffled and swiped at her eyes with the back of her hand before straightening her back defiantly. "It was something that started with an *F*... kind of like a guy's name."

Dakota's gut clenched. "Like Fredricksville?"

"Maybe." She lifted one shoulder. "I'm not sure. That

sounds like it could be right. We were camping at some big state park. I remember the town nearby had a really cool building at the center of it. The town hall had been converted out of—"

"An old barn," Dakota finished for her. "Yeah. It was originally the stable for the sheriff and his deputies."

Her brown eyes met his and he felt the contact deep in his gut. Trixie hadn't even touched him, but she didn't have to. She was a part of him. They were tied. Their lives and destinies had been intermingled from day one.

He looked at Chelsea briefly. They were his family. Both of them. And if there was one thing Dakota always did, it was protect his family.

"Looks like you two are going to Texas," Olivia said, tearing him from his thoughts. "If that is a piece of the gargoyles' gold, then it should be put back wherever Trixie found it."

"Hell no." Dakota scoffed audibly and folded his arms over his chest. "She's not going anywhere near any more gargoyles."

"Wait, what?" Trixie shook her head and looked at Olivia like she'd lost her mind. "Not that Bossy Boots over here has any say in where I go or what I do, but why do you want us to go and put this back? And what about Rebecca? We have to find her."

"It's the logical choice." Olivia started pacing the room. "Before last night, the last time any gargoyles were sighted was down in Texas. We now know that they're looking for the gold—gold that you found in that same area, Trixie. They obviously attacked Chelsea to get that coin." Olivia stopped at the foot of the bed and leveled a concerned look at the two women. "Maybe that's why it took the baby. It wouldn't surprise me if they try to use her to find out where the rest of the gold is. I say we give it back to them."

"Makes sense," Doug said evenly. "They probably figure that if Chelsea has one piece of their gold, then she knows where the rest is. That other gargoyle probably split with the baby because it got wind you were close by. Taking on a human woman is one thing, but facing two vampires is a different story. How the hell did they even know she had it?"

"I'll check the coin album she posted online," Xavier interjected. He flew out of the room and shouted, "Perhaps she put it on there and one of them spotted it."

"Why didn't it take that piece?" Olivia asked quietly. "The one that got away with the baby… Why didn't he take the coin?"

"I think it burned him," Trixie said quietly. "Before she passed out, Chelsea said, 'It burned him.' I wasn't sure what she was talking about, but now it makes sense."

"That must be why the injured gargoyle went into hibernation," Dakota said with his gaze pinned to Trixie.

"Why would it burn him?" Doug ran one hand over his head and let out a growl of frustration. "Shit. My guess is that other one is gonna hang on to the baby until they get what they want without getting burned. What do you think, Liv?"

Dakota had a damn good idea why that thing took the baby. No more stalling. He had to tell them, tell *Trixie*, what he'd discovered.

"I don't think that's why he took the baby," Dakota said, immediately silencing everyone else in the room.

All eyes were on him, but Trixie's reaction was the only one he really cared about.

He slipped his hand in the pocket of his coat and curled his fingers around the framed photo before pulling it out and handing it to Trixie. Steeling his resolve and knowing there was no way around the truth, he threw a prayer to the universe before finally coming clean.

"Is this guy in the photo Chelsea's boyfriend *and* Rebecca's daddy?"

Trixie rose to her feet with the frame clutched tightly in her ring-studded hands and studied the picture intently.

"Yes. That's him. That's Gatlin." She nodded slowly, a wistful smile curving her full pink lips. "Chelsea looks so happy here… They both do. I didn't see her with him very often, but whenever he was around, she always had a smile on her face."

"That's what I was afraid of," Dakota murmured.

"Why?"

"I'm sorry, Trix, but I saw *him* in Chelsea's blood memories." Dakota clenched his jaw and took a moment before forcing himself to tell Trixie the truth. "That man isn't a man at all. Gatlin is a gargoyle, and if he's the baby's father…"

"What? No way!" Trixie shook her head furiously and shoved the frame into Dakota's hands. She backed up and pointed at him accusingly, her voice thick with the tears he knew she was fighting. "That's *bullshit*. That can't be true because that would mean…"

Heavy silence, swollen with the unfinished statement, flooded the room and no one moved. Dakota's chest clenched and something inside him broke as tears streamed down Trixie's face. All the heavy makeup had long since been cried away, revealing the youthful face she hid beneath it.

How old had she been when she was turned? Eighteen? Twenty? Whatever it was, it was too young. All he wanted to do was make the hurt go away, to protect her, and yet he seemed to be making it worse at every turn.

"The baby is a hybrid," Olivia said with pure awe. "She's half-gargoyle and half-human."

"I'd say that complicates things," Doug murmured. "Especially if it's the Presidium's policy to put down gargoyles."

"We don't have a policy on gargoyles," Olivia said wearily. "They weren't well liked and they kept to themselves. We thought they were pretty much extinct. Therefore, a non-threat and no standing policy."

"Well, not exactly," Dakota said evenly. Orders or not, the cat was out of the bag. "How do y'all think they got that way? Jonner's mission was to wipe out any that he encountered."

"You're telling us that Emperor Zhao ordered the slaughter of the remaining gargoyles?" Olivia asked quietly. "That was your top secret mission?"

"Yes. It was highly classified." Dakota nodded and finally admitted the truth. "That's what Jonner was training me for before he died. Even the czar of that district didn't know about it. Only Emperor Zhao was read in, and I was instructed to *only* discuss it with him. Given everythin' that's happened…well…looks like it's no longer classified."

Olivia and Doug exchanged a look of confusion right before Trixie pounced.

"You're not going to hurt her!" Trixie shouted. Fangs bared, eyes wild, she flew across the room and grabbed the lapels of Dakota's coat. "You won't harm one hair on her head, do you hear me? I don't care if Rebecca is a fucking fairy-werewolf-demon-gargoyle-freak or descended from a line of vampire hunters. She is *my granddaughter*."

Trixie pounded on his chest in a fit of rage and screamed through her tears, fury and frustration lacing every blow. Dakota stood there and let her attack him. She needed to get it out, to expel her outrage at the injustice of it all. Olivia and Doug made a move toward them to stop her, but he held up one hand and shook his head.

"You can't kill her," she wept and pleaded with him. Trixie sobbed and buried her face against his chest, her body sagging against his. He could feel her anger shifting to utter despair. "Please, Dakota," she said through her tears. "She's just a baby and she's my family."

"I know." Uncaring that the czars were a few feet away, Dakota wrapped her in his embrace and held her quaking body firmly against his, wanting to calm the storm. "And that makes her my family too, darlin'."

To his great relief, she curled her arms around his waist and clung tightly, sobbing quietly against his chest. Pressing his lips against her hair, he touched her mind with his. The moment he did, it was like getting water after a drought. Orders or not, there was no way he was going to do anything to put that child in danger.

I'm not going to hurt her, Trixie, but I am gonna find her and bring her home to you. I promise.

"Do you swear?" Trixie sniffled and pulled back enough so she could look him in the eye.

"Yes, ma'am." Dakota cradled her cheek and swiped at the tears with his thumb. "I gave you my word, didn't I? And I told you before that I only make promises I can keep."

"I guess the telepathy kicked in." Doug wagged his eyebrows. "Just wait, dude. The bloodmate thing? It gets better."

"Amen to that." Olivia winked as Doug pulled her into his arms. "Trixie, no one is going to hurt the baby. First of all, I don't toss out execution orders at the drop of a hat. You should know me better than that. Besides, if Gatlin is her father, it's unlikely he's going to hurt her. The more I think about it, the more it seems unlikely he took her hostage to get at the gold."

Relief fired through Dakota and he tilted his head in gratitude. Hell, he would have dropped to his knees and kissed the woman's feet, but he was trying to maintain some kind of dignity. He'd never been happier to be part of such an unorthodox coven in his whole damn vampire life.

"I know." Trixie sniffled and shifted in his embrace. "But if she's a gargoyle hybrid…"

"Hey, this coven isn't exactly standard issue." Olivia let out soft laugh and shook her head. "Doug has an angel bloodline and Sadie is bloodmated to a werewolf prince. What's a little gargoyle thrown into the mix? Let's take this one step at a time. All we know now is that Chelsea's daughter has been taken and we have to get her back. After all, Chelsea isn't only your daughter but part of our coven now. That makes her family."

Olivia pulled her cell phone from her pocket and started punching buttons. "If we can make nice with the werewolves and the Amoveo shifters, why not with a few lone gargoyles? I know that you said you were the only one to know about this, but I think it's time I call Emperor Zhao."

"With all due respect, ma'am, are you sure that's a fine idea?" Dakota didn't like challenging the czar, but he was wary about taking this to Zhao. "What if he isn't as understandin' about the little girl's bloodline? After all, he's the one who ordered their execution."

"I know, and that's what confuses me. I've known and worked with him for over two centuries, and an order like this seems way out of character." Olivia raised one eyebrow. "This is the same Emperor Zhao who approved the mating of a vampire and a werewolf. I think it's safe to say that he's gotten more open-minded recently.

"Anyway, I was a sentry for over a hundred years, served in several districts, and I *never* heard about any gargoyle hit squad. And I was privy to some shit that would curl your toes. If there was some kind of secret gargoyle task force that is obviously no longer in service, then I'm sure Zhao will want to know what's going on. And you don't survive as long as he has if you can't keep a secret. Trust me, he'll keep a lid on it."

Dakota held Trixie a little tighter.

"And no matter what, I would never let anything happen to a member of my coven. Regardless of her parentage, Rebecca is now a part of our family."

Dakota nodded his agreement but a tickle of wariness crawled up his back. If Olivia, a czar and seasoned sentry, had never even heard of the gargoyle project, maybe he should have kept his mouth shut. But the horse was already out of the barn. Besides that, he had a baby to find. Playing nice with politicians was no longer on his priority list.

"I'll run a quick background check on the boyfriend." Dakota kept Trixie's body tightly against his and noted how perfectly she fit in his arms. "It's doubtful that Gatlin went back to his old place, but it might give us something else to go on. We'll see what else Pete and Xavier found on Chelsea's computer that might help."

"Fair enough." Olivia's brow furrowed as she hit Send. "*Then* I think we should follow the Texas lead and get that coin back where Trixie found it."

"But…I can't remember where I found it," Trixie said quietly. All eyes turned to her and she lifted one shoulder. "It was a long time ago and I was so freaking sick the whole time. Plus, most of my human life is a blur."

"Well, all the more reason for you to get down there and figure it out," Olivia said firmly. "That gold has to go back where it belongs, and it sure as hell doesn't belong here with us. We should check out the rest of her collection, if we can find it, and make sure there aren't any more of those particular coins."

"But what about Chelsea?" Trixie asked. "She's going to wake up from the transition in a day or so. She's probably going to be frightened."

"She'll be fine." Dakota tapped Trixie's nose with

one finger. "She'll have you here to greet her when she wakes up."

"Are you high?" Trixie slipped out of his arms, the tough, edgy exterior back in full force. "I'm going with you."

"Hell's bells, woman." He settled his hands on his hips and let out a growl of frustration. "You haven't been listenin' to a damn thing. I told you that you aren't goin' anywhere near them gargoyles. You'll stay here and that's the end of it."

"As if!" Trixie let out a loud curt laugh. "I'm going with you to that cabin to see what else we can find."

"No, you are not," he seethed. "I'm goin' alone. Then you can give me the coin and I'll go figure out where you found it."

"Oh, and how do you plan on doing that?" Trixie shot back.

Dakota glared at her because he didn't have a damn answer. She was right. He'd never be able to figure it out without her help.

"Hang on." Olivia held up both hands and shot the two of them a scolding look. "You aren't going anywhere for at least a day or so. You'll still be in town when Chelsea wakes up tomorrow."

"But she won't wake up tomorrow." Suzie's tentative, shaky voice drifted through the room and everyone fell silent. She stood in the doorway looking like her usual skittish self, but Dakota hardly paid her any mind. He was too busy being pissed at Trixie.

Would the woman ever listen?

"Where's Emily?" Olivia asked, her voice edged with a hint of concern.

"She's sleeping in the apartment. Maya is with her."

"Hang on." Olivia waved her in but kept her concerned gaze on Trixie and Dakota. "What do you mean Chelsea won't wake up tomorrow?"

Everyone in the room turned their attention to the shy young vampire. Dressed simply in a long-sleeved shirt and dark slacks, she looked as scared as ever.

"It's going to take her longer to turn, like it did with Maya. I came here to tell you that *and* that I can stay with Chelsea while Dakota and Trixie go to Texas."

"How do you—" Doug began before stopping and answering his own question. "You had a vision or something, didn't you?"

"Sort of." Suzie flicked her blue eyes toward the floor as she inched her way closer to Chelsea's bed. She quickly sat down in the chair next to Dakota's sleeping progeny, her pale blond hair tumbling loose over her shoulders. "The visions are getting stronger lately. Anyway, I know how scary it is to be turned and not know anything about this world. I-I can help her make the transition more easily."

"Are you sure?" Dakota asked warily. "I mean, no offense, sweet pea, but you aren't the toughest vampire gal on the block."

"I know," she said through a soft laugh. "I'll stay with her… It will be okay. Trust me. Besides, I think you'll be back in time."

Between the innocence in her eyes and the earnest tone of her voice, Dakota was convinced she was being truthful on every level. He didn't think that girl could lie even if she wanted to.

"That's great. Thank you." Dakota smirked before

adding, "Your visions wouldn't happen to tell you where the baby is, would they?"

"No." Suzie shook her head and flushed pink with embarrassment. "I'm sorry but I don't really have any control over what I see. It comes and goes. But I don't think she's in danger."

"That's fine, sweet pea." Dakota nodded curtly. "I do appreciate your help but you don't have to stick so close." He placed a kiss on Trixie's head and slipped from her embrace. Steeling his resolve, he strode to the door and winked at the others. "Trixie will be stayin' here too."

"The hell I will!" Trixie shouted. "Hey, don't you walk away from me. I'm talking to you."

"No, you're not. You're yellin' at me and not listenin' to a damn word I say." Dakota spun around and glared furiously in her direction. "I'm goin' back to the cottage to see what else I can find out about Gatlin and then hopefully get over to his place before the sun comes up. I don't know what I'm gonna run into. Damn, woman. We don't know if there are two more gargoyles or twenty. We *think* he's not gonna hurt the baby but we don't *know*. And who knows where in the hell I could get stuck when the sun comes up. There are too many unanswered questions. You are stayin' right here."

"He's right," Doug said flatly. "You don't have as much experience in fighting as he does, and it's safe to say you have *none* fighting gargoyles."

"Neither do you," she shot back.

"Yeah," Doug scoffed. "But I'm stronger than you are, a better fighter, and a trained homicide detective. I win."

Trixie flipped the czar the bird, and Olivia smirked.

"Please, Trixie," Dakota rasped. "You have too many people countin' on you to risk your safety. You are stayin' right here and that's all there is to it. I'm not only a sentry, but whether you like it or not, I'm your bloodmate and your safety is my top priority. The discussion is over."

With Trixie shouting after him, Dakota flew down the halls and headed for the tunnels. He could feel her mind reaching out to his but he put up a mental barrier, preventing any further contact. Having Trixie pissed off and safe was better than happy and dusted.

Chapter 10

DAKOTA WHISKED THROUGH THE TUNNELS OF THE Presidium before reaching the secret entrance that led into The Cloisters above. He pulled the iron lever, and a second later, the door hidden within the massive fireplace swung open. He knew Trixie was furious with him for being an old-fashioned misogynist, but right about now he didn't give a shit.

All he cared about was keeping her safe.

He stepped into the cavernous room of the museum and stood motionless as the fireplace shut behind him with a dull *thunk*. The only other sound was the faint steady heartbeat of the night watchman in the front hall. Based on the slow cadence of it, the man was sleeping.

"I glamoured him." Trixie's sassy voice cut through the room and instantly sent a ripple of anger through Dakota, along with a hint of surprise. "He'll be out until sunrise."

"Son of a bitch," Dakota seethed. "How did you beat me up here?"

"I guess you haven't found all of the shortcuts yet."

Trixie stepped out of from around the corner of a stone archway with a smug smirk on her beautiful face. Dakota's hands curled into fists at his sides and a growl rumbled in his chest as she strolled toward him, her arms swinging like she was about to take a casual walk in the park.

"What are you doin' here, woman?" He closed the distance between them but refrained from touching her. If he did, he would end up either shaking some sense into her or kissing the life out of her. He wasn't entirely sure which. "You aren't comin' with me. Your little stunt is holdin' me up. In case you've forgotten, a gargoyle has your grandbaby."

"No, I haven't forgotten. Besides, Gatlin is not going to hurt her," she said firmly. "I know it. I saw the way he was with Chelsea, and gargoyle or not, he loves her. If he didn't and was only after that coin, don't you think he could have figured out a way to get it already? *And* he loves that baby. Let me ask you something else, cowboy. If vampires have a history of hunting down gargoyles, what makes you think he didn't take her to save *her* from *you*?"

Dakota stilled. That had never occurred to him. What if Trixie was right and the creature only took the child to protect it? Maybe the gold had nothing to do with it.

"Alright, I'll agree that could be possible," Dakota said slowly, a wide grin sliding over his face. "But you still aren't comin' with me."

"Yes, I am." She cocked her head to one side, her blond-and-blue hair glinting in the moonlight that streamed through the arched leaded-glass windows. "I may not be as experienced a fighter as you, but I do know a thing or two *and* I've been practicing."

"Oh yeah? Like what?" he groused. Hands on his hips, he leaned closer, hoping to get her to back down, but the stubborn beauty wouldn't give an inch. "How to get yourself dusted?"

"No." Hands behind her back, she swayed nearer and

her voice dropped to that low, husky whisper that lit a fire in his belly. "Like the secret tunnels in the Presidium that *you* didn't know about. Not to mention different places to hide out, both in and around the city. You may be older but I've lived in this area way longer and know it like the back of my skull-ring-covered hand."

Dakota opened his mouth to argue with her, but she wiggled her fingers in his face.

"Stop it." He grabbed her wrist and tugged her close, pinning their arms between their bodies. Someone was shaking and he wasn't sure which one of them it was. Could have been both. What was she doing to him? "I mean it, Trix."

"Why?" she whispered. Trixie slipped one leg between his and applied pressure to his quickly hardening cock. "What are you gonna do to me if I don't?"

Desire slammed into Dakota as she issued her challenge, and all coherent thoughts went out the window. A wicked twinkle glimmered in Trixie's eyes and he knew he was a goner. He couldn't think straight, let alone tell her why she couldn't be with him. He never wanted to be without her.

Ever.

Dakota's gaze flicked down to her full pink lips, the ones that reminded him of rosebuds, and all he could think about was getting another taste of them. Licking and suckling them until the sun came up.

On a curse, he closed the distance and captured her mouth. Trixie opened to him immediately and swept her tongue along his, seeking him out as eagerly as he sought her. She moaned with pleasure and the sound reverberated against his lips. He wanted to hold back, to savor every second, but it would have been like trying to slow the tide.

Dakota's fangs emerged when Trixie hooked one leg around his and pressed her thigh harder against him. The movement sent a pulse of lust streaming through his blood. His mind and body were completely fogged by stark raging need, and he was blinded by the driving desire to devour her. He was completely spellbound by the all-consuming urge to strip her naked and lick every wicked inch of that curvy, taut little body.

That was probably why she was able to use the full weight of her supernatural strength to yank his foot out from under him and throw him to the ground.

It happened in a split second.

One minute he was standing there necking with the prettiest little woman he'd ever had the pleasure to know, and the next, he was on his back on the cold stone floor with her straddling him and sitting firmly on his crotch.

Trixie had his arms pinned to the ground on either side of his head and her breasts, barely contained by her T-shirt and bra, swayed enticingly close to his face. Fangs bared and with a satisfied grin covering that heart-shaped face, she wiggled her hips against the hard length of him.

"Like I've been telling you," she whispered. "I can handle myself. By the looks of it, I can handle you too, cowboy."

"That so?"

Trixie opened her mouth to respond, but in a blur of speed and strength, Dakota sat up, linked his arm around her waist, and spun her to the ground so she was splayed out beneath him with both arms pinned over her head. He gathered her slim wrists in one hand and held her there easily as he trailed the other down the length of her arm. Trixie shivered and arched her back, eagerly seeking more of his touch. A whimper of need escaped her luscious mouth when his hand slid lower and covered her breast.

"I'd say we're about even on that front," he murmured. Dakota dipped his head and brushed his lips lightly over hers, achingly close to the tip of her fangs. "Looks like I can handle you too, darlin'. No matter how stubborn you are."

"Dakota," she rasped. Trixie hooked one leg over his and tilted her hips, the combined movement pressing the rigid length of his cock deeper into the heat between her jean-clad legs. "Shut up and kiss me."

"Yes, ma'am," he growled before covering her mouth with his. He pushed his tongue deeper, desperately seeking more of her taste.

Hunger.

That word thundered though his head as he devoured her, licking and suckling at her lips like a man who'd been starving. And until he met Trixie, that's exactly what he had been. His body had been sated by blood, but until he'd found her, his spirit had been empty and hollow, shriveling up until it had practically vanished altogether. Trixie's feisty nature and her need to shout at the world made a fire that fed his soul. All these years, he'd wandered the earth, looking for something to make him feel human again, to make him feel alive. It wasn't until she came into his life that Dakota finally *lived*.

From the moment he'd set eyes on her, he had hungered for her. He'd been desperate for her to give him just a *taste* of the electric energy that flickered off her so effortlessly. He longed for her touch, her scent, and everything in between. In that moment, with her body rising seductively beneath his, the entire world fell away and all he could see or feel was *her*.

Dakota broke the kiss and trailed his tongue down her throat. His hand slid over the curve of her hip before settling on her ass. He groaned when the soft flesh of her bottom filled his palm, and he silently cursed the thin fabric that separated them.

So close and yet so far.

Dakota nuzzled her throat, flicking his tongue over the soft tender spot of her neck, the one with the thick vein beneath it. She let out a tiny moan of pleasure when he tilted his hips and pressed his cock, which had hardened almost to the point of pain, along the tempting heat of her sex. He rocked against her slowly and intentionally so she would know exactly what she did to him. Dakota brushed his hand along her leg before hooking it under her knee and hiking it higher, giving him better access to the heated apex of her thighs.

He licked a trail along her collarbone and lifted his head long enough to see the look of pleasure on her face, which was bathed in soft moonlight. Eyes closed, her lips parted, she gasped as he rocked against her once again, harder this time. He loosened his hold on her wrists but kept her hands above her head. Damn. He would never *ever* get tired of seeing that look on her face. In that instant, all he could think about was making her come.

That's what he wanted to see: all of her walls crumble. He desired nothing more than to see her exposed for him—and only him. If she would allow him inside and show him the part of herself she'd hidden away for so many years. That was the treasure he was searching for...the real Trixie. Could there be anything more priceless than that?

"Does that feel good, darlin'?" Dakota dipped his head and murmured against the smooth, sensitive flesh of her throat. He rocked his hips again, rubbing his hard length against her core, the slow deep strokes punctuating his words and making his intent clear. "You've got me all fired up but I want more from you, Trix. I want what you won't give to anyone else... I want everythin' you hide... Give it all to me. Give me your pain...your secrets. Show me."

"Yes," she rasped. Trixie arched her back and tilted her head, offering herself to him. Her hips bucked beneath him, wriggling seductively and seeking more of what he was offering. "Take it. Please, take it all."

A growl rumbled in his chest as his fangs unsheathed. Lifting his lip, he scraped the tips lightly along the side of her throat, wanting to be sure that she knew exactly what he planned on taking. Trixie let out a cry of pleasure and hooked both legs over his, rocking her hips up to meet him.

"I need more," she whimpered and arched her back. "Take off your clothes. I want you inside me."

"Not yet, darlin'," Dakota rasped. "First, I want *you* inside *me*."

His fingers tightened around her wrists as his hips moved faster before he dipped his head and dove deep.

The moment his fangs pierced her flesh and Trixie's blood bathed his tongue, light and color exploded behind his eyes. Pleasure shot through him. It rushed through his flesh like an electric current, while Trixie's blood memories flooded his mind in a cavalcade of images and sounds. Dakota pumped his hips furiously and Trixie cried out, an orgasm ripping through her body, just before his own pleasure reached its peak.

Amid the white-hot climax, Trixie's hidden secrets were revealed, one after the other in all their raw painful glory.

A little girl. Sitting alone in the corner of a dark room as a man approached. Screaming and berating her for some unknown indiscretion.

Fear. Anger. Abandonment.

A warm Texas summer. A glint of gold in the rocks. Joy. Peace. The face of a kind, loving woman, smiling and pulling Trixie into a warm embrace.

Cold. The city at night. Music pulsing wildly around her. A crowd of humans thrashing and shouting. Needles. Drugs. A young man whispering words of love but with a lie lingering beneath them.

Desperation. Need. Craving.

A heartbeat. Soft at first. Once. Twice.

A baby's cry vanishing in the distance, tangling with Trixie's sobs of grief. A stone-cold blanket of loneliness hanging over her like a death shroud.

She's alone. Lying on the cold, filthy concrete floor of a subway tunnel. Her clenched fist unfurls and a needle rolls from her limp fingers before tumbling to the ground.

Trixie's voice, drenched with regret, whispers around him in a swirl of sorrow... Leave me here... I deserve to die... Besides...who would care?

Trixie thought she could handle Dakota, flirt dangerously along the edges of desire—but she'd been dead wrong. The pleasure washed over her completely, swiftly and without mercy, leaving her unable to form a coherent thought or keep her defenses up. If she'd had her wits about her, she never would have let him drink from her, but the orgasm came over her with such ferocious intensity that she was swallowed up by it.

No one, human or otherwise, had ever lit her up and turned her on the way Dakota did. The only time she'd come close to feeling that kind of bliss was when she was high, and the similarity between the two sensations terrified her. As the delicious fog of pleasure began to ebb and her limbs sagged with exhaustion, her brain finally started registering other sensations.

The cold stone floor beneath her back and the delicious heat of Dakota's body covering her front created a tantalizing contrast for her senses. A smile curved her lips as his long, strong fingers loosened their grasp on her wrist. They still had all of their clothes on, but the guy had given her the best orgasm of her life.

But there was something else, something...dangerous. His mouth was clamped tightly over her throat. She felt him deep inside...touching her...tasting her.

"No!" Trixie shouted and with all of her supernatural strength she tore her hands from his grip and shoved at his shoulders. "Stop, Dakota. Right now."

He tore his mouth from her neck. Underneath the slightly dazed drunken expression, a haunted gleam of awareness lingered in his eyes. That was all she needed to see to know. He had seen too much.

Panic shimmied through her flesh. She wiggled out from under him and hopped to her feet. She backed up, pointing at him accusingly as he rose to his full height and licked a trickle of blood from the corner of his lips. Lips that only moments ago been had been worshipping her body with almost painful reverence.

The man standing before her was kind, gentle, and good. He might be a killing machine for the Presidium but he'd shown her and her daughter nothing but kindness. Why would a man like that want to be with someone like her?

Bloodmates or not, he didn't deserve this. He didn't deserve *her*. She was a hot mess. Trixie was damaged goods, a sad, pathetic girl who had given away her baby because she was too weak to contradict the social workers at the hospital.

A coward who had tried to take her own life.

An addict. A junkie. Trash. Broken.

Shadows and moonlight might have obscured all the sharp edges and rough angles of Dakota's handsome face, but nothing could hide the look of pity lingering there. He moved slowly toward her, and Trixie's gut clenched. There was nowhere else to hide.

Unable to face him, she flew out of the room and pushed open the enormous, ornately carved wooden doors that led out to the gardens. The crisp, cool air of the late November night slammed into her like a wall as she fought the tears, but it was no use. Her vision blurred as the floodgates opened. Her chest ached with regret, fear, and shame. She could no longer hide the ugliness from him.

She wanted to fly. To get the hell away from him and from the knowledge that he could no longer be tricked into thinking she was something that she wasn't. For the first time since she was turned vamp, Trixie wished she could get high. She wanted to fall into the sweet oblivion of the heroin rush and be cradled in its forgiving embrace. The drugs didn't judge or accuse. They provided the ultimate escape from the truth of who she was and what she'd done.

Before she reached the edge of the wall, a pair of strong warm hands curled around her biceps and pulled her gently backward. Trixie let out a shuddering sob when Dakota's tall firm body sidled up behind her. He held her there in his unyielding embrace. He dipped his head and pressed a kiss against her cheek, his scruffy jaw rasping over her flesh with delicious friction.

"Please don't run away from me," he whispered. Dakota linked his arms around her waist and pulled her against him. He nestled his mouth against her ear. "I'm sorry. I'm so sorry for everythin' you had to go through all by yourself. But you are not alone, darlin'. Not anymore."

"I'm so ashamed. I don't deserve to call myself her mother." Trixie squeezed her eyes shut and covered her face with both hands, shaking her head. "I gave her away. I told myself it was because I wanted her to have a better life but I think that was a lie. I didn't do it for her. I did it for me. I was afraid," she said, her voice full of pain.

"Of course, the adults that surrounded me at the hospital—nurses, social workers, all of them—told me I couldn't handle it and that I would ruin her life. They told me I had to give her away... I wasn't good enough to be her mother. They were right, you know. Then after I got out of the hospital, Chelsea's father was gone and I was alone. Again. But do you know what never abandoned me?"

Dakota held her tighter. "Tell me."

"Drugs...booze." The words were barely above a whisper. "Those lovers were always there. That's why I love being a vampire. From the moment Olivia turned me, the need for drugs and booze was gone. It was the kindest gift anyone had ever given me. She freed me."

It was the first time she'd openly admitted to another person that her one true love had been drugs. As her maker, Olivia had known but they'd never discussed it. Trixie finally and completely let out the horrible truth she'd carried with her for so many years.

"I was sixteen when I first used. Darryl, that's Chelsea's real father, he got me hooked. That first high? It was pure bliss. I just remember thinking that was what love must feel like. Over the years, no matter what else happened, the hazy highs were always there. They became my constant, something I could count on." Her voice shuddered and cracked with shame. "When I was human, all I cared about was getting another fix... I gave away my daughter. What kind of mother does that?"

The tears fell freely now, but contrary to what she expected, Dakota didn't let her go or push her away, revolted. The man hung on and rocked her gently, the

way a mother might rock her baby. The hitching sobs
slowed as he continued his tender, hypnotic movement.

"Trix?"

Dakota turned her gently so she was facing him
and cradled her face in both hands. He wiped her tears
away with his thumbs before pressing his lips to hers
in an almost reverent gesture and resting his forehead
against hers.

"You are one hell of a woman. I saw what you went
through, baby. No family. No one to love you or show
you how to love. But you know what? In spite of all
of that, you *do* know how to love." His Texas drawl
swirled through the night air, his presence covering her
like a blanket, the steady dependable force that was
Dakota Shelton. "You're a fighter. Don't you think for
one second that what you did was wrong. Givin' Chelsea
up for adoption was the best thing you could have done
for her at that point. You gave that girl a good life, and
that makes you a damn good mother."

"You really believe that?" Trixie shook her head
and pulled back, looking at him with nothing short of
astonishment. "You aren't disgusted by who I was and
what I did?"

"Not a chance." He shook his head and tilted her chin
with his thumb, forcing her to look him in the eyes. "I'm
just glad I finally got to see what you've been hidin'.
This is part of that gettin'-to-know-you stuff I've been
talkin' about. After all, we are bloodmates."

Silence hung between them for a few seconds, filled
with weight of that word.

"Right." Trixie nodded as he held her close and she
grabbed the front of his shirt. The all-too-familiar feeling

of panic threatened to rise, but she stuffed it down and forced herself to remain in the moment. "Can we take it slow? One step at a time, okay?"

"Yes, ma'am." Dakota dipped his head and pressed his lips to hers in a slow, sweet kiss. "Now, I hate to kiss and run, but I have to be gettin' on my way to the cabin. And you need to stop kissin' on me, or I'll never get there."

Trixie was about to argue with him when the cell phone in his pocket buzzed. Dakota let out a groan of discontent.

"It's fine." Trixie slipped from his arms, suddenly self-conscious about her unusual display of emotion. Before today, Olivia had been the only one who had ever seen her cry. "You better see who it's from."

She swiped at her eyes and hopped up onto the stone ledge. Trixie allowed the cool air to wash over her. She stared out over the Hudson River. It glinted in the darkness as the water ebbed and flowed. It was so peaceful up here at this time of night that it was almost easy to forget she was in the middle of the big bad city.

"Change of plans," Dakota said abruptly. He stepped up onto the ledge next to her. "Xavier said there were no other gargoyle coins in the collection, and from what he can tell, she kept 'em all in a safety deposit box in the bank. Except for that one." He pointed at the necklace. "Doug ran a background check on Gatlin, and it looks like we have an address in Queens and one in…"

"Let me guess," Trixie said slowly. "Fredricksville, Texas?"

"Yes, ma'am." Dakota's lips set in a tight line and he

ran his hand over his jaw. "Chances are he didn't stick around, but Shane and I are going to have a look at his place in Queens to see what we can dig up."

"Great." Trixie cracked her knuckles. "Let's go."

"Last time I checked, your name wasn't Shane." Dakota let out a beleaguered sigh and settled his hands on his hips. He kept his gaze on the river, not looking at her. "Woman, are you gonna make me fight with you again?"

The muscles of his jaw clenched, and as Trixie studied his strong profile with the glow of the moon washing over it, a pang of guilt struck her. It was her turn to do something kind for him.

"Never mind," she said quickly. "I've got some stuff to take care of at the club anyway. Suzie's with Chelsea, and Sadie's gonna be back from Alaska in a couple days. She'll be super pissed at how messy the bar has gotten and it's closed tonight. I should make good use of the time."

"Are you sure?" Dakota narrowed his gaze and studied her intently. "I'm not gonna find you followin' me to Queens, am I?"

"No, it's cool. I'll go to the club." Trixie spoke firmly and succinctly, trying to convince herself more than him. "I can't just sit around and do nothing. That will drive me crazy." She spun to her right and grabbed the lapels of his leather coat. "But you better promise that you'll keep me posted. And if we do have to go to Texas or if you get any sign of that baby, you'll let me know right away and—"

Before she could say another word, Dakota silenced her with a hot demanding kiss that stole any further arguments from her mind. As he swept her up in his arms and deepened the kiss, his gruff whisper rushed into her mind. *Darlin', you can count on it.*

Chapter 11

It had been years since Trixie had felt this exposed and vulnerable.

She sat alone on the roof of the nightclub, her knees pulled to her chest and her chin resting on top. How exactly had the world been turned upside down and inside out so quickly? She closed her eyes and let the sounds of the city drift over her, surrounding her with their familiar comforting hum. It was close to four in the morning—Trixie's favorite time because the city was *almost* quiet. There was still life to be heard, cars whizzing by and human heartbeats in the air, but there was calmness to it that she found soothing.

When Dakota read her blood memories, he had stripped her of her defenses. To her surprise, she was actually okay with it. She knew, deep in her gut, that he wouldn't exploit that vulnerability. That knowledge alone was what kept her from spinning into the abyss.

Somehow it would all work itself out.

We're on our way back, darlin'. As if on cue, Dakota's seductive drawl drifted into her mind, soothing like the breeze. *No sign of Gatlin or the baby but someone else had already been there. His place was completely trashed. Seems we aren't the only ones who are lookin' for this fella. There was also a message written on the bathroom mirror.*

A message? The cold finger of dread tickled the

back of her neck, making her sit up straighter. *What did it say?*

See you in Texas.

Oh my God. Fear laced her voice, in spite of her best efforts to sound calm. *We have to find her, Dakota.*

Then you better pack your bags, because we're leavin' as soon as possible.

We? Hope and uncertainty fired through her. *You want me to go with you?*

Well, you don't think I'm gonna go away with Quesada for a few days do you? A low laugh rumbled through her mind and tickled her from the inside out. *Besides, how am I ever gonna find the spot where you found the coin?*

Trixie squeezed her eyes shut as a fresh flood of tears threatened to run. A funny feeling of melancholy washed over her when his mind withdrew from hers. The connection between them had deepened significantly since he'd tasted her blood. The way he touched her mind now was almost seamless, as though he'd been communicating with her that way forever.

It was startling how easy it was…how *right*.

How much more connected would they be once she completed the bloodmate bond and drank from him? Once that was done, would she still be Trixie, or would she become someone else? Would she become dependent upon him? A shiver ran over her, and she hugged her knees tighter.

That was the big bad question that hung over her head, more frightening than anything else. How much of herself would she have to give up to be Dakota's bloodmate?

"You okay?" Damien's deep voice sounded behind Trixie as he landed on the roof. "I was worried about you."

"What tipped you off?" Trixie said with a laugh. "That my daughter is turning vamp, my granddaughter is missing, or that Dakota is my bloodmate and my life might not be mine anymore?"

"None of the above." He elbowed her as he sat down next to her, his hulking frame a welcome and familiar presence. "The only other time I've seen the bar that clean was when Olivia was in labor with Emily."

"Very funny." Trixie rolled her eyes but couldn't conceal her smile. Damien was like the brother she'd never had. He always could put her at ease with his good-natured teasing. "I never could get anything past you, could I?"

"Nope."

They sat for a few minutes in comfortable silence, the kind that could be shared between true friends. But as the sky began to ebb purple and the tug in her gut warned her of the approaching sunrise, Trixie knew this moment of peace couldn't last too much longer.

"We should go in." Trixie patted Damien on the leg and rose to her feet. She brushed off her butt, ridding herself of the grit from the rooftop. "The sun's coming up. And unlike most of our coven mates, you and I are not daywalkers."

She extended her hand to him and yanked the big lug to his feet. His toothy white grin practically gleamed in the brightening night, and she couldn't help but smile back.

"You will be soon enough though. I heard through the grapevine that you and Dakota have started to telepath."

"Jeez. There is, like, totally no privacy around here."

"Truth." He elbowed her playfully. "Come on, girl. You remember what it was like when the other girls hooked up with their men. It's exciting. So tell me, are the rumors true?"

"Yeah, we have telepathed." Her face heated with embarrassment. "Among other stuff."

"What's it like to hear someone else in your mind?" His voice softened with almost childlike inquisitiveness. "I was turned by Pete, and since he's mated to Marianna, an Amoveo, I've never been able to telepath with him. I'm the only one he ever turned, so no siblings. I get the feeling that it would be pretty cool to be able to speak to someone else with your mind, especially someone you care about."

Trixie was caught off guard by the question. She and Damien had always shared a playful relationship, one full of good-natured teasing. This was probably the most personal question he'd ever asked her. She paused for a moment, not sure how honest she should be. Staring into his sweet face though... He deserved the truth.

"Telepathing with Dakota is the most intimate, freaky, amazing, and wild sensation I've ever experienced." She folded her arms over her breasts and looked out over the twinkling lights of the city. "It's different than it was with Olivia and the girls. Kinda like he can touch my soul with one word...a whisper. I know that sounds dopey," she added quickly.

"No," he said wistfully. "It sounds awesome." The look of surprise on her face elicited a belly laugh from Damien. "Girl, you know my deal. I was a street kid, and until Olivia found me, I didn't even have a family.

Not really. I love all this coven drama. I tell you, if the supernaturals ever come out of the closet, you girls need your own reality show. *The Real Bloodmate Housewives of New York City.*"

"You are too much," she said with a laugh. Trixie ran her hands through her hair and laced her fingers behind her head. "Olivia and Sadie were the first real family I've ever had too. Olivia was the *only* person who knew everything about me and still…" Trixie let the words die on her lips as she dropped her hands to her sides. "Anyway…the telepathing is cool."

"Dakota's a good guy, Trixie. I know, I know, he's kind of a dork, with all his outdated slang and his lollipops, but he's solid. Y'know? You're lucky that you've got a bloodmate."

"I guess. But it's scary, Damien. To have someone else see inside you and get past all of the bullshit." Trixie walked to the edge of the roof and peered over the side to the alley below. "Besides, I haven't decided if I wanna commit to the whole bloodmate deal. Y'know?"

"No, actually," Damien said flatly, "I don't."

Surprised by his admission and unusually serious tone, Trixie turned to him. An air of sadness clung to her friend, and the smile that was almost always crinkling at the corners of his eyes was gone.

"I love you, Trixie. You're that wacky baby sister I never had. But if you squander this gift—and that's exactly having a bloodmate is—then you really are crazy, girl."

She opened her mouth to argue with him but he held up both hands, immediately silencing her. Damien rarely spoke to her with such seriousness and she wasn't sure how to react.

"I know, you're gonna tell me that you don't care about daywalking and all that shit, but that's not the gift I'm talking about." He placed his hands on her shoulders and peered at her with earnest intensity. "That man cares for you, Trixie. No matter how much you want to deny it. I know that you dig him too. He would do anything for you. Think about how special that is. Love, any kind of love, should be cherished and appreciated. Trust me. Until Olivia came into my life, I didn't even know what it felt like."

Trixie was rendered speechless. He was right. She was being foolish. How many nights in her human life had she wished for someone to love, to really truly love her? And now that the possibility was in front of her, she was wary of it.

"Jeez." Trixie let out a laugh and cracked her knuckles before punching him in the arm. "You sure do tell it like it is, don't you?"

"Hey"—he shrugged his massive shoulders—"I gotta look out for you. That's what family is for. Right?"

"Right," Trixie said wistfully. She linked her fingers around her chain and pulled the coin out from under her T-shirt. "But our family won't be complete until we get that baby girl back here with her mama."

"Yeah, well, something tells me that Dakota will move heaven and earth to find her." He slung his arm over her shoulder and started leading her toward the hidden entrance into the building. "The sun's coming up. Let's get inside and go check on Chelsea."

"Hmmm." Trixie bumped her hip playfully against

him. "Your desire to check on Chelsea wouldn't have to do with the fact that Suzie is with her, would it?"

"Maybe."

Damien's shoulders shook as his deep baritone chuckle rumbled through the night. Trixie smiled and was about to open the hidden panel when the sickening familiar scent of rotten flowers drifted through the air. Without even realizing what she was doing, Trixie reached out and touched Dakota's mind with hers... *Dakota, the gargoyles are here at the club!*

Trixie's fangs unsheathed. A powerful cramp racked her stomach and she fought to stay on her feet, the pain stabbing through her body in unrelenting waves.

"Damien, we have to get inside right now," she bit the words out through clenched teeth, but it was already too late. "Gargoyles. That smell...it's them."

"Where?" Damien glanced around warily. "I don't see anything."

"They're coming..." she said, barely able to get the words out.

"It's okay. I got you."

Damien grabbed her arm as she stumbled to her knees, but her body wouldn't cooperate. Somewhere through the red haze of agony and the debilitating fear, she heard her friend's concerned voice call her name.

She peeled her eyes open and struggled to get back on her feet. That was when she saw them. Like something out of a nightmare, the two massive creatures swept down from the skies, a pair of dark hideous silhouettes with glowing eyes, descending like death incarnate. Their screeches, high pitched and ragged, reminded her of the sound a subway train makes as it comes to a grinding halt. That sound filled the air as they swooped in, claws extended and yellow eyes glowing in the night. Damien pushed Trixie out of the way just before a pair of silvery talons could slash her arms.

Pain blinding her and their hideous scent fogging her brain, Trixie rolled down the slanted slate roof and tumbled toward the alley below. She landed on the pavement and bounced against the metal Dumpster, and as the pain racked her body, the screeches of the beasts above filled the city night.

Dakota had never flown that fast in his whole damn life.

The instant that Trixie's frightened voice filled his mind, Dakota knew true fear. The knowledge that she was in danger and those creatures could get to her was almost more than he could bear. What if he lost her?

No. That was not an option.

Would the fates be that cruel? Would they finally give him the one woman he was meant to be with only to take her away? He'd tried to connect with her since she called to him but had been met with gut-wrenching silence.

The sounds of the creature's shrieks, their battle cries, the ones he hadn't heard for years, rippled through the early morning sky as he and Shane swept onto the scene.

Dakota scanned the area wildly, but it didn't take long to find Trixie. She was in the alley with one of the creatures hunched over her. She wasn't moving. The gold coin glinted against the pale flesh of her throat as the gargoyle, its wings outstretched, shuffled around her. It looked like it was to figure out how to get the gold without getting burned.

"Oh, dear God," Shane murmured as he flew next to Dakota. "Damien…"

Fury, pure and unadulterated, bloomed in Dakota's chest when he saw his woman at the mercy of one of those *things*. Trixie was obviously wounded—if anyone would stand up and fight, it would be her.

In that moment he understood the expression "blind with rage."

He sliced through the air like a bullet, pulling the stone dagger from the sheath in his belt. He landed on the creature's back, slinging his arm around its throat. It fought and thrashed wildly, desperately trying to take flight, but Dakota clenched his legs down, pinning the creature's leathery wings to its sides. The gargoyle bucked and screamed, shaking him like a bull at the rodeo. There was no chance Dakota was gettin' thrown off this time around.

He grinned wickedly and clenched his powerful thighs and tightened his noose-like grip around its neck. Then he raised the knife high in the air.

The gargoyle spun around and threw itself backward, slamming Dakota into the brick wall of the building. He hung on with a viselike grip—for Trixie. Clinging to the creature with all of his strength, Dakota drove the knife down and into the chest of the gargoyle with one powerful thrust.

Within seconds the beast stilled. A crackling sound filled the air as it turned to stone. Dakota scrambled off the creature, sheathed the dagger, and immediately ran to Trixie's side. He knelt down and pulled her gently into his lap before noticing the ever-brightening sky.

They had to get inside.

"I-I couldn't help him," Trixie sputtered. "I couldn't do anything."

"Shh." Dakota stroked her hair and whispered, "Stay still."

"Hey, man." A pair of drunken humans stumbled across the entrance of the alley. The club was closed and the city mostly quiet, but there was no escaping the presence of humans. "That was some crazy shit. What is that thing, dude?"

Dakota was about to tell them to piss off when Shane Quesada landed silently behind them. He took them both by the shoulders, spun them around, and started whispering to them. Once he was there, Dakota barely paid them any mind. When he looked back down at Trixie, she was staring up at him with wide, frightened eyes. He helped her sit up a bit, but she winced with obvious pain.

"Take it easy, darlin'." He bit his wrist and offered it to her. "You definitely broke some ribs. Drink this. You'll heal faster and then we have to get you inside."

Trixie took his hand and started to bring it to her mouth but stopped, shook her head, and pushed his arm gently away.

"No." She forced herself to a sitting position and artfully avoided his gaze. "I-I'm fine. Let's just get inside. I want to see Damien."

Dakota tried not to think about how much her rejection stung, especially with everything going on and in front of Quesada. She didn't want to take his blood because that would mean completing the bloodmate bond. Even after everything he'd said and done…she still wasn't ready.

"Where's Damien?" Her voice cracked and tears glimmered in those gorgeous brown eyes that were edged with pain. Rising to her feet, she used the side of the building for support and refused the hand he offered. "Is he…?"

Shane moved toward them, and the question died on her lips. The saddened expression on his face gave them the answer neither of them wanted.

Trixie shook her head wildly, a harsh sob tearing from her throat. Dakota reached out to pull her into his arms and comfort her, but she resisted. He stood there helplessly as she limped away weeping. Trixie tugged open the alleyway entrance to The Coven before disappearing inside.

"Is it dead?" Shane asked quietly.

Filled with rage and frustration, Dakota slowly rose to his feet, then turned to the hideous stone creature behind him. These beasts had stolen everything from him. First they took his human life, and now they were hell-bent on stealing his one chance at happiness. Growling in fury, Dakota picked the stone creature up and hurled it against the back alley wall, shattering it into a thousand pieces.

"It is now," Dakota growled, then followed Trixie inside.

<center>~~~</center>

"They're both dead?" Olivia asked flatly. Still and virtually lifeless, Damien lay on a bed next to Chelsea, an IV blood drip attached to his arm. Olivia stared at Damien's hulking form, her green eyes filled with tears. Doug held her in his arms as she shook with grief, trying to soothe her pain. "You're sure?"

"Yes." Shane nodded, his expression grim. "I shot the one that attacked Damien. Looks like silver bullets work if you shoot them in the head. It shifted to its human form and Dakota tells me that indicates a true death. Xavier has the body in his lab." He arched one dark eyebrow and glanced at Dakota. "The other is currently a pile of rocks out in the alley. Therefore, also dead."

"Good," she bit out.

"It's lucky for Damien that you were the one who turned him, Pete." Doug nodded toward the other sentry, currently standing at the foot of Damien's bed. Pete's eyes glowed red, a side effect of his demon heritage. "If he didn't have your suped-up vampire-demon blood, he probably wouldn't have survived that attack."

"True, but it doesn't make me feel much better." Pete nodded slowly. "I reached out to Asmodeus to see if my dear old dad knew anything about these creatures or the gold, but he wasn't much help. Some bullshit about the demons in the Brotherhood not wanting to open old wounds or something. He did have one bit of information that was helpful."

"What's that?" Dakota asked.

"Dakota, you said that Trixie gets pain or cramps or something when these things come around?"

"Yeah, but I think tonight was worse than ever before." Anger bubbled up when he recalled the way the gargoyle had loomed over her in the alley. "She was incapacitated. She couldn't fight back or fly."

"And that is not like Trixie," Doug said with a touch

of irony. "That girl has been feisty and ready for a fight since I met her."

"You said it," Dakota murmured.

"Asmodeus said that Trixie must have something funky in her bloodline. He thinks she *could* be descended from witches, and that's why she gets those weird cramps when the gargoyles are around. It's some kind of biological warning bell. I don't know. He's a cryptic son of a bitch."

"Then her daughter could have it too." Dakota stilled and flicked his attention to Chelsea, still deep in the transition sleep. "That might be why her turn is taking so long and her blood memories were foggy."

"Our little coven sure is full of surprises. A witch bloodline?" Olivia said absently. "I didn't pick up on anything like that when I turned Trixie, and her turn was completely normal."

"Who knows? Maybe Chelsea has a different percentage of witch genes or whatever." Pete let out a growl of frustration and folded his arms over his broad chest. "I went through my entire human life not knowing I had demon blood. Anyway, Asmodeus said it could be way back in her family history. The kind of thing that might not have been noticed until these guys showed up from supposed extinction. You know, their presence woke up her dormant genetics."

"Not so extinct after all," Olivia murmured.

"No." Dakota clasped his hands in front of himself and fought to keep his anger in check. "And neither of the two that attacked us tonight was the one from the cabin. The scents are different. Not only that, but I detected something strange about one of the scents I picked up at Gatlin's apartment. I can't put my finger on it…but it was…off."

"You're sure?" Doug asked.

"Absolutely." Dakota nodded. "The differences between their scents are subtle but they're there. What's worse is that we have no idea how many more of them might be out there and lookin' to come at us." He set his mouth in a tight line. "The game has changed. We're not talkin' about one rogue. This is organized and calculated. They want that gold back."

"Where is Trixie?" Olivia swiped at her eyes and sat down on the edge of Damien's bed. "Dakota, did you give her the blood she needs to get her strength back? She was pretty banged up from that fall."

"She's with Maya," Shane interjected. "And is on the mend."

Shane cleared his throat and flicked an apologetic glance at Dakota. He had been there. He'd seen Trixie reject Dakota's offer. Shane may be a stodgy old son of a bitch, but Dakota could have kissed him for sparing him the humiliation of explaining *that*.

"I should have seen this," Suzie whispered. She sat between the two beds, one hand holding Chelsea's and the other linked with Damien's. "Why didn't I see this coming?"

"It's not your fault," Dakota said. "It's those things. They came here lookin' for their damn gold, and they aren't gonna stop until they get it—or we do."

"How did they even know Chelsea had that gold piece?" Doug asked.

"Xavier said she posted about it on one of them blog things. She did that with several of her unusual coins, looking for their origins and value," Dakota murmured. "The damn Internet was how they found her. Hell, she led 'em straight to that coin."

"And it brought them here to the city," Olivia fumed. "To my front door."

"Yes." Dakota cast a grave look at the czar. "They aren't going to stop until they get the coin."

"You want to go to Texas, don't you?" Olivia asked quietly.

"That's where it all started. The way I see it, that's where we finish it." Dakota pulled his leather gloves out of his pocket and tugged them on. "We know Gatlin has an address there."

"He's on the run with a baby," Doug interjected. "He's going to want to go somewhere familiar."

"Yes." Dakota nodded. "We also know that other gargoyles are lookin' for him and for this gold. That message scrawled on the mirror in his apartment—*See you in Texas*—that was for Gatlin. So I say we go find the gold before they do. Trixie found one piece down there, so it goes to follow that's where the rest of it is."

"I haven't heard back from Zhao, and that's not making me feel any better about this. His assistant said he's *indisposed*," Olivia said. "You and Trixie will go to Texas and figure out where she found that coin. I want that gold as far away from our people as possible. I know she wants to find the baby, but as far as we know, that little girl was taken by her father and isn't in any danger.

"I love Trixie, but I have to think about the good of the entire coven and our people as a whole. If the gargoyles blatantly attacked two of my coven members in the middle of New York City, what else will they do? I'm a czar and I don't have the luxury of making choices based solely on my personal feelings. That gold goes back as soon as possible. I'm sorry to say this, but the baby has to be a secondary consideration."

"No, ma'am." Dakota shook his head and the room fell silent. "With all due respect, she is not and we'll be doin' it a different way."

"Oh really?" Olivia rose slowly to her feet, the fire in her gaze leveled at Dakota. "Care to tell me why you are blatantly defying my orders, Sentry Shelton?"

All eyes were on him and the expressions on their faces ranged from curious to furious. Dakota didn't give a shit.

"Because I love her," he shouted.

Olivia's eyebrows rose but she said nothing.

"That's right." Dakota settled his hands on his hips, not quite believing he'd actually admitted that out loud. Hell, he hadn't even admitted it to himself. "I love her. Trixie is my bloodmate, but that don't even matter. Even if she doesn't bond with me, I love that crazy woman and I'm not lettin' her out of my sight for one damn minute. We'll get the gold back where it belongs, but I am also going to help her find that baby girl. And if she's got some kind of gargoyle alarm hooked up inside her, then maybe she can learn how to find these things. Or at the very least, warn us if they're comin' around."

"How is she supposed to learn how to do that?"

"Well, I don't know but—"

"I do," Pete said in a matter-of-fact tone. "My old man has a friend who lives out west who can help. Her name is Isadora. She's a witch, older than dirt and smart as a whip. If anyone can teach Trixie how to get her witch on, it's that woman. I can put you in touch with her."

"I'd be much obliged," Dakota said firmly. "We'll find her grandbaby and the damn gold."

"You want to find all of it and use it to help you get the baby back, don't you?" Olivia kept her serious gaze locked with his.

"Damn straight. Those sons of bitches can have every ounce of it for all I care, but I'm not givin' them one piece until we find that little girl safe and sound. Like I said. I love Trixie, and I am gonna find that baby if it's the last thing I do."

Before anyone could argue with him, Dakota turned to head for the door and found himself staring into a pair of gorgeous brown eyes.

Based on the stunned expression on her face, Trixie had heard it all.

"I guess all those times that Damien said I was being a bitch…he wasn't too far off the mark." Trixie's teary gaze met Dakota's, and the pain and confusion he saw there made his gut clench. "I'll get my stuff and meet you at the entrance to the tunnels, Dakota."

She vanished from the doorway in a blur.

"Keep us posted on Damien and Chelsea," Dakota said quietly without taking his gaze off the empty doorway. "I have a safe place we can stay in Fredricksville. That's where we'll be headed, and I'll text you when we get there."

"Dakota?" Olivia's voice, edged with concern, stopped him before he stepped out the door. He didn't turn around. "Don't let her get hurt. She's my family."

"Not a chance," he said curtly. "She's mine too."

With the chatter of the others fading, Dakota went into Xavier's lab to stock up on weapons and ammunition. As he strode through the massive storage room and carefully selected exactly what he wanted, he couldn't help but wonder if he was the one who would get hurt. A vampire's physical injuries healed swiftly and left no trace behind.

A vampire's heart didn't beat and Dakota was no different.

His heart was a shriveled-up husk inside his chest, a remnant of a life no longer lived. With no heartbeat, he should be impervious to love—free of the heartbreak suffered by humans who lived and breathed. Dakota was a vampire, and therefore he had no heart to wound.

If that was true, then why did it hurt so fucking bad?

Chapter 12

TRIXIE AND DAKOTA BARELY SAID TWO WORDS TO EACH other on the entire trip down to Texas. They traveled through the extensive underground tunnel system by day, and once the sun went down, they flew side by side the rest of the way to Fredricksville. Whenever Dakota looked at Trixie he found that same grim but determined expression on her face. It was a combination of fury, guilt, and sadness, and Dakota had had about enough. Before they got to the ranch, there was a conversation they needed to have.

Without a word, he pointed to the winding creek below that cut through the ranch. Trixie simply nodded and followed him to the water's edge, landing noiselessly beside him. She adjusted the black backpack she was carrying and hooked her thumbs behind the straps, avoiding his stare all the while.

"Where are we?" she asked, looking around them. Looking anywhere but at him. "I thought we were staying at some ranch or something."

"This is it. The Circle S has almost a thousand acres to it. Used to be more, but we sold land off over the years. Most of it is part of the state park now, back that way. My family's ranch sits right along the edge of it." He snagged the strap of the duffel bag he had slung across his chest, pulled it over his head, and tossed it onto the ground. "The main house and cottage are just over that hill," he said, nodding to his left.

"Then why'd we land over here?"

"You and me need to get a couple things straight before we invade the peace and quiet of Hector and Addie's lives."

"Hector and Addie?" Trixie's brow furrowed. "Who are they? Familiars?"

"Sort of." Dakota moved closer but Trixie didn't move. She kept her gaze on the horizon. "They're my family. They live in the main house but keep the cottage available for me when I come back this way to visit."

"What do you mean, your family?" Her head snapped toward him, her eyes wide in total surprise, but she recovered quickly. "I never met a vampire with a human family that was still…"

"Alive?"

"Well, yeah," she said with a small smile. "It's not exactly a regular thing. Most vamps leave their human family behind, and then they eventually die off."

"Well, like you, I wasn't turned all that long ago. Hector is my nephew, my brother's only kid, and Addie is his wife." He smirked and settled his hands on his hips. "He ain't much of a kid anymore. Hell, he was a baby when I was turned, but the man is in his sixties now. Anyway, he and Addie never had any kids, so they're all that's left of my *human* family."

"Okay," Trixie said slowly. "So…they know what you are?"

"They surely do." He let out a sigh. "After Jonner died, I was kinda lost. No maker. No siblings. He was the only other vampire I had any contact with, because that gargoyle hunt was top secret. I decided to go home. I'd stayed away for over a year, and tellin' 'em all the truth seemed a lot easier than makin' up some big old lie."

"Wow…they must have really loved you."

"I suppose they did… Especially my mama. Anyway, I hung around for a couple years, and let's just say I didn't exactly fit in. Eventually, I went to the local czars and enlisted as a sentry. I come home from time to time. They know what I am, but I wouldn't say they *embrace* it. In fact, Addie refers to it as a lifestyle choice."

"Holy shit." Trixie gaped at him. "Does the Presidium know about this?"

"Maybe. I haven't given it much thought. I work for them, Trix. They don't own me." He took one step closer so their bodies were mere inches apart, her sweet scent filling his senses. It was tempting and wicked, daring him to touch her. But he didn't. "If you had taken my blood last night to heal those broken ribs, you'd already know all of this—and then some."

She stilled and nibbled on her lower lip, but she wouldn't look at him. Dakota linked his hand around her slim bicep and turned her gently so she was facing him. He tipped her chin up with his other hand and ran his thumb over her mouth.

"Care to tell me why you wouldn't take my blood?" Dakota dropped both hands to his sides, the hurt and pain from that moment rushing back. "That wasn't *too* humiliating with Quesada standin' right there," he said sarcastically. "I mean, damn, woman, everyone knows we're bloodmates. What was the big deal?"

"What was the *big deal*? You really can be dense

sometimes." Trixie's eyes narrowed and a familiar glint of anger flickered over her face "Everything you know about women wouldn't fill up the strip of paper in a fortune cookie."

"Is that so?" He leaned forward. "Why don't you enlighten me."

"Okay, cowboy," she said. "Let's set aside the fact that I thought Damien was dead up on that roof. Did it ever occur to you that the freaking reason I didn't want to drink from you—*for the first time ever*—was because we had a damn audience watching the whole thing? Taking your blood, whether it's for healing purposes or not, isn't like drinking from anyone else.

"Come on, man. I have no idea what's going to happen when I taste your blood, Dakota. I don't know what I'll see, what I'll feel, or how the fuck my body will react. I mean, for all I know, I could've lost my damn mind and stripped you naked in the middle of that alley, or had some kind of mind-blowing orgasm. Oh sure. Awesome plan." Trixie gave him a double thumbs-up and took a step back.

"But excuse the hell out of me for bruising your big, fat male ego," she shouted. "I am *so* sorry that I totally didn't want to share an intimate moment like that in the middle of a dirty alley in front of Shane I'm-a-total-stick-in-the-mud Quesada!"

It wasn't often that Dakota found himself speechless, but this was one of those times. She was absolutely right. None of that had occurred to him and he felt like a total ass. All this time, he'd been thinking that he was putting her needs first and worrying about her comfort and happiness, but that wasn't true at all. He'd been so caught up in his own wounded ego that he didn't stop to think what their bloodmate bond meant for her.

Dakota recalled a moment in his childhood when another boy in class had to wear the dunce cap and sit in the corner. He was pretty sure he needed one of those hats right about now.

"I'm sorry," Dakota said quietly. "And you're right. I don't know squat about women or love or bloodmates. I'm just tryin' to figure it all out and keep us from gettin' killed in the meanwhile."

Trixie tore off her backpack and threw it to the ground, as though the weight of it was too much. Most likely, the bag wasn't what was weighing on her. Trixie kicked at a rock, then squatted down, resting her elbows on her knees. She stared into the moonlit creek, an air of guilt hanging over her like a shroud.

"It wasn't only because of that. I was disgusted with myself. I freaked out when those gargoyles showed up," she whispered. "Nothing worked, Dakota. It's like my body totally betrayed me for the first time since I became a vampire."

"What happened to Damien was not your fault." He spoke softly and with as much tenderness as he could muster, but she still flinched. "I know that Olivia and everyone else already told you that, but I thought you needed to hear it again. Besides, he's gonna recover."

"Yeah, but no thanks to me." She cracked her knuckles. He moved closer, but she refused to look at him. "I'm a damn disaster area—a former drug addict vampire, apparently with witch's blood in her veins and a massive inferiority complex. What a mess."

"But a beautiful one, and thanks to Pete, we've got that Isadora woman comin' to meet you tomorrow night. Hopefully, she can help you with this witch stuff."

He bent at the knees next to her and picked up a smooth gray stone. He tossed it into the creek and smiled as it skipped four times before finally disappearing into the water.

"What do you say we get on over to the house and get ourselves settled. Besides"—he rose to his feet and extended a hand to her—"I'd like you to meet Hector and Addie. They know we're comin' and they might have gotten up extra early to greet us."

Trixie flicked her gaze to his hand and hesitated for a moment before tangling her soft fingers with his. Dakota squeezed them gently and swallowed the sudden lump in his throat. He'd never been a particularly mushy guy, but Trixie seemed to have a direct line to his heart. She stood up slowly, a smile curving those full rosebud lips. When she inched closer, he linked his other hand with hers. A surge of desire pulsed in him as that lush womanly body wavered inches from his.

"I'm sorry that you felt rejected or embarrassed," she said quietly. Her tongue flicked out, moistening her lower lip, and she pulled him almost imperceptibly toward her. "I'm not going to lie to you, Dakota. I am freaked out by the whole bloodmate bond."

"Why?" He rasped his thumb over the top of her hand before bringing it to his lips and pressing a soft kiss there. "Would it really be so bad to get saddled with a good old boy like me?"

"No, it's not you…it's me," she said through a laugh. Trixie rolled her eyes and tossed her head back with a playful growl of frustration. "Jeez. I know that sounded lame. Just give me some time, okay?"

She popped up on her toes and kissed his cheek quickly, then let go, grabbed her backpack, and pulled it on. The gold from the necklace glinted along her throat in the moonlight as she moved. It probably wasn't wise to be standing out here exposed.

"Well, if there's one thing us vampires have plenty of, it's time," he groused, slinging the duffel bag over his head. "But promise me somethin'."

"What?" Trixie eyed him suspiciously but a smile lingered beneath it. "You're not gonna try and get me to go line dancing, are you?"

"I might." He winked.

"As if!" Trixie let out a short laugh and gestured to her torn jeans, skull-and-crossbones shirt, and colorful hair. "Do I look like the line dancing type to you? A mosh pit? Definitely. Two-steppin'? I don't think so."

"Well, smarty pants, that ain't it." He grabbed her hand and held it tight. "No more hidin'. Not from me. Not from your feelin's. And when you're ready, I wanna hear about what it is exactly that 'freaks you out,'" he said, making air quotes with his free hand. "Deal?"

Trixie's mouth set in a tight line and she studied him closely, as though weighing her options, before finally nodding her head. "Deal."

"Alright then." Dakota grinned wickedly as he released her hand and whispered, "Last one to the house is a rotten egg."

With Trixie laughing and cursing right behind him, Dakota flew through the warm Texas evening. For the first time since this whole mess had begun, he had the one thing he'd been missing.

Hope.

———

Trixie stood in the large airy living room of the expansive ranch house and did her best not to fidget. This *little* ranch house was nothing like she'd expected. It was freaking huge. The sprawling one-level home was absolutely beautiful. The vaulted, exposed beam ceilings gave it a cathedral-like feeling, and the white-washed brick hearth that went all the way up to the roof stood at the center of it all. To the left was a giant kitchen with top-of-the-line everything, and to the right was a huge family room full of lush furniture and a bank of huge windows that made it seem even bigger than it was.

In all her life, Trixie had never been inside a fancy home like this.

She'd never been so nervous in her whole stupid existence, and she was wishing she'd worn something nicer than the T-shirt, jeans, and combat boots she currently had on.

What a dummy.

Here she was meeting Dakota's human family, practically the Holy Grail in the vampire world, and she looked like she'd just rolled outta bed. Awesome. What had she been thinking? The answer? Not much. She'd had her head up her butt ever since the whole bloodmate debacle started. Her wardrobe certainly hadn't taken up much of her thoughts over the past couple of days.

Hector and Addie were perfectly pleasant, but she didn't miss the look they exchanged after being introduced to her. Addie, in particular, looked her up and down with thinly veiled horror. It was probably a safe bet that there weren't many blue-haired punk rockers in this tiny Texas town.

"Thanks again for waitin' up to see us," Dakota said, after releasing Addie from a big hug. "I can't believe it's been almost five years."

"Of course, sweetheart." Addie giggled. She was wearing a floral robe over her soft round form, and her short gray hair was tucked behind her ears. With her ruddy complexion and a wide smile, the woman looked like a grandmother from one of those sitcoms. "You're family and, well, I suppose you are too, Trixie. After all, you must be special to Dakota if he brought you here. You're part of the same *lifestyle* that our Dakota is?"

"Uh, yeah." Trixie smiled and lifted one shoulder, not sure what else to say. She was still trying to figure it all out, so good luck explaining it to anyone else. "I am, I guess. Thanks for getting up so early to meet us."

"Honey, this is a horse ranch," Addie said with big smile. "We're up before the sun on most days."

"We don't have too many visitors out this way." Hector hitched up his faded jeans and swiped at his round, bald head with a handkerchief. The guy was sweating like a pig. Unlike Addie, he was not wearing his pajamas. Hector looked like he'd already done a full day's work. "Just us and the horses. And Miguel, of course."

"Miguel?" Trixie asked, inching a little closer to Dakota. "More family?"

"No. Well, not exactly." Dakota laughed and slung his arm over Trixie's shoulder in a casual and familiar way. A day or two ago, a gesture like that might have annoyed her, but not tonight. Right now, she was more than happy to stick close to him. Hector made her nervous. "Miguel is a local fella. He's been a ranch hand out here for well over twenty years, and he's a familiar."

"Oh, cool." Trixie nodded. "I hope I get to meet him too."

An awkward silence fell over the group, between the stares and smiles. Trixie gently elbowed Dakota in the ribs. *I'm super uncomfortable... Addie looks like she wants to take me to her hairdresser's, and Hector is eyeing me like I'm gonna drink him dry. Can we go to the cottage now, please?*

"We're gonna get settled over at the cottage," Dakota said, finally breaking the quiet. His voice echoed through the huge room, which only made it more awkward. "We'll see y'all after sundown tomorrow. Trix and I are lookin' forward to a little R and R. If I have my way, I'm gonna get her on a horse and ridin' like a pro in no time."

"Ride a horse?" Trixie gaped at him. "You never said anything about that."

"You know me, darlin'." Dakota winked. "I'm full of surprises. Good night, y'all."

Dakota took her by the hand and walked her to the door, but Hector's voice stopped them before they could make a clean getaway.

"I'm surprised you two would want to take a vacation here." Hector pulled some chewing tobacco from a tin in his pocket and deposited it in his cheek. "I thought your kind liked the big cities. Not much to do around these parts. No real nightlife."

They don't know about the gargoyles or the gold or any other supernatural stuff. Just vamps. Dakota tightened his grip on her hand. *Sorry, I shoulda mentioned that.*

"And it ain't like you're comin' here for the sun." Hector snorted with laughter, obviously feeling proud of himself for the clever joke. "Y'all give 'sunburnt' a whole new meanin'!"

The mortified expression on Dakota's face was priceless. Apparently, being a vampire didn't rule out the experience of being embarrassed by family.

"Oh, hush." Addie slapped Hector playfully on the arm and gave Trixie a sympathetic smile. "Don't pay him any mind, sweetheart. You two lovebirds go on ahead. The place is all ready for you."

Hand in hand, they trotted down the steps from the wide porch and made their way toward the cottage. The clean country air smelled of hay and horses, and mingled in with it, rising above everything else, was Dakota's leather and sandalwood.

But something was missing. Cinnamon. Those damn lollipops that he'd always been eating, ever since she'd met him two years ago, were noticeably absent. Her brow furrowed. Come to think of it, she couldn't remember seeing him with one for a few days.

"After we check out Gatlin's address tomorrow night, I wanna see if we can jog your memory about exactly where you were when you found that gold. The rest of it has got to be nearby."

"It was somewhere in the state park." Trixie growled with frustration and kicked a rock out of their path. "We were camping and I found it when I was out poking around by myself."

"Well, that park is over a thousand acres. It would help if you could remember somethin' specific about the area."

"Sorry." Trixie shrugged. "My human memories are kinda foggy, especially from when I was a kid. I only remember seeing the gold glinting between two rocks. I'm a city girl." She waved one hand in a broad stroke. "This all looks the same to me."

"Now that is somethin' I'm gonna have to remedy at some point." Dakota squeezed her hand. "But I know you're not *that* much of a city girl. From what I saw, you spent most of your childhood in the Southwest. Seems to me you didn't have the right kind of experiences out here. You have got to learn to appreciate nature."

"Right." Trixie snorted with laughter. "Central Park is about as natural as I like to get."

"There it is." Dakota lifted their joined hands and pointed at the tiny log cabin in the distance. "Home, sweet home. No windows and totally safe."

The deep inky blackness of night was beginning to give way to a dark purple as the sun began to announce its impending arrival. They walked in silence until they reached the front door of the cottage. Without warning, Dakota scooped her up in his arms, and Trixie shrieked in surprise.

"What are you doing?" She laughed loudly and linked her arms around his neck. "I am perfectly capable of walking, dude."

"I know that." Dakota nodded to the door. "It would seem that I have my hands full. Would you mind openin' the door, ma'am?"

"Sure." Trixie giggled before leaning over and turning the knob. "There you go. But why are you carrying me?"

Dakota tapped the door open with his foot but didn't go inside. He stood there with Trixie in his arms, those silvery-blue eyes studying her intently. She suddenly became acutely aware of every place his body touched hers. His fingertips dug into her flesh gently but insistently, and her hip pressed into his firm torso as he held her tighter. The swarm of butterflies in her stomach fluttered to life, those firm lips of his curving at the corners.

"Well, bein' bloodmates is about as close to bein' married as vampires can get," he said with a smile. "I figured, what the hell? I'm carryin' my woman over the threshold."

Chapter 13

WITH HIS FOREHEAD PRESSED TO HERS AND THE SWEET old-fashioned sentiment lingering, Trixie did the only thing she could. She cradled his cheeks with both hands, the rough unshaven flesh rasping deliciously beneath her palms, and closed her eyes. She pressed her mouth to his.

The kiss was slow at first, soft and almost tentative as he opened, then tangled his tongue with hers. Trixie reached out cautiously and touched his mind. *Make love to me, Dakota.* Her voice trembled, the same way her body did when he tightened his grip, clutching her like he would never let her go.

Trixie had chosen those words carefully. She had always referred to sex as "fucking" or "getting laid" before. "Making love" sounded goofy. It seemed so over-the-top that anytime she heard it in a movie, she'd roll her eyes. Who could really believe in that silly phrase?

But cradled in Dakota's protective embrace, their minds and hearts mingled, she knew how wrong she had been. She did love him. Even if she wasn't ready to say it out loud, she would damn well show him.

For now, that would have to be enough.

Trixie suckled his bottom lip and broke the kiss. She pulled back and captured his fierce, hungry stare with her own. Their bodies were wound tight with desire and only the sounds of nature filled the air. Had she said the wrong thing? But before she could talk herself off the ledge, the gaping precipice of uncertainty, he was on her.

Dakota's mouth covered hers and a growl rumbled in his throat. Kissing her deeply, he carried her over the threshold into the cottage. He kicked the door closed as Trixie threaded her fingers through his hair. She licked and nibbled at him all the while, knowing she'd never get enough.

Even without the candy he tasted like cinnamon. Hot and sweet.

She squirmed and hopped out of his embrace, her boot-clad feet hitting the wooden floor with a loud thunk. Breaking the kiss briefly, Dakota and Trixie tore off their bags and threw them to the floor with little care to where they landed. Dakota grabbed her around the waist and tugged her toward him but Trixie grinned wickedly. She wiggled out of his grasp, wagging a finger at him.

"Where do you think you're goin'?" he rasped, stripping off his leather sentry coat and throwing it to the floor. The weapons hidden inside landed with a muffled thud. "There's only one big room, aside from the bathroom. What do you have in mind, darlin'?"

Trixie hooked her fingers beneath the edge of her shirt as she walked slowly backwards. Dakota leaned against the door and devoured her with his hungry gaze as she removed the shirt and tossed it aside. She shivered under the heat of his stare, but continued to kick off her boots, peel her jeans from her body, and step out of them completely. Everything was too tight and she'd never wanted to be naked so much in her life.

No one had ever looked at her this way.

It wasn't merely lust carved into his features, making that handsome face look even more feral and dangerous than ever before. It was the glint in his eyes. There was hunger there, desire and need, but there was also something else, something she'd never seen from a man.

Love.

Underneath the flesh and bone, behind the carnal whisper of lust, she could feel his soul calling out to hers.

She stood before him shivering, but it wasn't from cold. It was the nearness of him and the knowledge that at any moment, his hands would be on her—touching, stroking, and bringing her to life.

Standing in only her bra and a thong, Trixie ran her fingers lightly over her belly, up along the curve of her breasts and then her neck. Dakota watched, unmoving, the entire time. Trixie smoothed her hair back with both hands, then spread her arms out to the sides and took one more step back. She stopped when her legs hit the end of the bed.

Nowhere else to go.

"I want you to touch me, Dakota." Trixie reached behind her back and unhooked her bra, allowing it fall to the floor. She cupped her breasts and tweaked her nipples, all while holding his hooded gaze. "Please, put your hands on me."

"Take off your panties," he rasped. "I like watchin' you. I'll be touchin' you soon enough but right now... I'm enjoyin' the show."

A moan escaped her lips at the commanding tone in his voice, the deep rumble filled with wicked promise. Trixie did as he asked and slipped the lace thong over her hips. The fabric slid down her legs to the floor, creating a delicious friction over her sensitized skin. She was burning with desire and anticipation. One move in the wrong direction might make her shatter into a million tiny pieces.

Broken. That's what she'd been for as long as she could remember. Trixie was a woman desperately trying to hide the scars and imperfections, the creases and lines left from her lifetime of bad choices. Until Dakota came into her world, it never occurred to her that perhaps, if she allowed someone else to see those blemishes, he wouldn't judge her.

All Dakota had ever done was attempt to help her soothe those wounds.

She smiled softly as Dakota strode toward her, slowly closing the distance between them. Even if she did come apart, he'd be there to help put her back together.

Could someone do that? Hold her so closely and love her so deeply that all of those broken pieces could be mended? As Dakota moved in, his body achingly near to hers, she knew the answer.

He stopped, his clothed body mere inches from her naked one, but he still didn't touch her. She was about to ask him what he was waiting for, when Dakota trailed one fingertip up her arm, over her shoulder, and along her collarbone. The long slow stroke was a whisper-like caress over her needy flesh, and the gentleness of it almost broke her heart.

Trixie's eyes fluttered closed and the movement sent

one fat teardrop down her cheek. His hand cradled her face and she leaned into it, wanting and needing more of his touch—but at the same time, she didn't want to rush it. Trixie's body was on fire, and once they got started, she wasn't going to last long.

She was greedy for him.

Her fangs unsheathed on a sigh when his other hand cupped her breast. He dipped his head and took her nipple into the wet heat of his mouth. She tangled her fingers in his hair and let out a cry of pleasure. He suckled and nipped at the sensitive bud until she sagged against him, her head falling back. The heat in her belly swirled as he continued his merciless assault on first one breast and then the other.

"You are wearing way too many clothes," Trixie murmured.

Tearing her hands from his hair, she grabbed the edge of his shirt and tugged upward. They laughed between kisses as he helped her pull off the tight shirt, but the smile faded from her eyes when she caught sight of his bare torso. The muscles in his chest were dusted with dark blond hair and as well sculpted and beautifully defined as she'd expected. But there was something else she was definitely not prepared for.

Letting out a small cry of distress, Trixie brought her fingers up to the series of red angry-looking scars that streaked over Dakota's chest and stomach. The four rough, raised lines went from just below his left nipple all the way across to his right hip. She traced the ropy scars gently as he stood still beneath her inspection, his hands at his sides. Her tears flowed freely as she thought about the pain and suffering he must have endured that night.

"You got these the night you were turned, didn't you?" she whispered, her voice small. As Trixie glanced quickly at him, his silvery blue eyes, which glittered in the dark, narrowed in response and his body tensed beneath her touch. "A gargoyle did this? It practically gutted you."

"Yeah, it did," he said in a gravelly whisper. Dakota linked his hands gently around her wrists before tangling his fingers with hers. "We all have our scars, Trix. Mine just happen to be where you can see 'em."

"You're beautiful," she murmured. "I never thought I'd say that to a man, but it's true."

Trixie pulled her hands from his, popped up on her toes, and nipped his lips lightly, careful not to cut him with her fangs. She undid his belt while he slipped his hands around and cupped her bottom. She slid his zipper down, releasing him from the confines of his leather pants. Trixie swore against his lips when she was met only with hot, hard flesh—he had nothing on underneath. She shoved the pants down his hips and he quickly stepped out of them and his boots, kicking all of it aside.

Now there was nothing between them. They stood in each other's arms. Exposed. Vulnerable. Two people holding each other's broken pieces together.

Dakota kissed her deeply and she moaned into his mouth, taking the full, heavy weight of his cock in her hand. She linked one arm around his neck while massaging him, taking note of the way her breasts crushed against his chest. The combination of rough and smooth as his chest hair tickled her nipples added to her pleasure, fueling the fire in her gut.

Dakota tightened his hands in her hair, tilting her head to deepen the kiss, which intensified with every stroke of Trixie's hand up and down his shaft. She ran her thumb over the wetness on the swollen head, and the slickness of it made her sex tighten with anticipation. Her tongue tangled with his before she finally broke the kiss and slid down his body, dropping to her knees and trailing hot kisses over his chest along the way.

She knelt before him and settled her hands on his narrow hips. The steely length of his cock seared along her throat as she took her time and lavished gentle kisses over the scarred lines on his belly. He cupped the back of her head, and when she peered up at him and their eyes met, Trixie knew what he wanted. And she wanted nothing more than to give it to him.

"Put me in your mouth." His voice, gruff and filled with need, rumbled around her in the dark. "I want to see you wrap those sweet lips around me. Please, baby."

"You mean, like this?" Trixie asked innocently.

She curled her hand around the base of his shaft and brought the swollen purple head to her mouth before slowly, achingly brushing the slick flesh over her lower lip. He stilled and let out a low deep groan. She swirled her tongue around the tip of his cock in long slow strokes, but refrained from taking him in. Holding his heated stare, she ran her tongue up his shaft in one long lazy pass before lapping at the head and blowing softly on it.

"You know I love it when you tease me, darlin'." Dakota shuddered and tightened his grip on her hair. "But remember, payback's a bitch."

"I'm counting on it," Trixie whispered.

She'd made him suffer enough. Trixie wrapped her lips around the head. She massaged his balls and squeezed the base of his cock while taking him in and out with wickedly languid passes. His hips pumped with her, slowly at first, but it wasn't long before the pace picked up and she knew he was getting close to the edge. She would have kept going and let him reach his peak just like this, but apparently Dakota had other plans.

Stop. He linked his hands around her biceps and pulled her to her feet. Pleasure ran warm under her skin as his mind touched hers. He kissed her deeply. *I want to come with you...not alone.*

With their lips mingling and bodies pressed together, Trixie lifted one leg and hooked it over his hip. She cried out when his fingers dipped between her thighs and slipped into her slick folds. She clung to his shoulders and tossed her head back as he massaged her clit with swift, deft strokes. His other arm was clamped around her waist, the only thing keeping her upright because her legs had turned to jelly.

When Dakota pushed two fingers deep into her channel, Trixie shouted his name and pumped her hips. But it wasn't enough. She needed more. More of him. More of his touch.

She linked her arms around his neck and hopped up, wrapping both legs around his waist. He kissed her deeply once more, his hands palming her ass. Her slick wetness slid over his cock, which was pinned between their bodies. *Take me. Right now.* Her voice touched his mind. *I want you inside me.*

With the speed of a vampire, he whisked over to the wall and pinned her there. Trixie let out a gasp of pleasure mingled with surprise as he slipped his hands from her ass to her thighs. He held her against the cool wood as he stood between her legs, holding them apart, opening her for him in every way. Trixie grabbed fistfuls of his hair and held his silvery stare as he tilted his hips and drove himself deep inside with a powerful thrust.

Trixie shouted his name as he filled her time and again. He moved slowly, pumping his hips and rolling with each pass, hitting her clit in exactly the right spot so that her pleasure would match his own. Her orgasm coiled tightly as he thrust faster and each stroke became more furious and burgeoned with need. The sounds of flesh slapping against flesh and their groans of pleasure mingled in the air.

As Dakota's orgasm crested in unison with Trixie's, he dipped his head and whispered into her mind. *I want all of you and I give you all of me. I love you, Trixie.*

Trixie cried out as his fangs pierced her throat. She came hard and fast as he drank from her, clinging to him as their bodies shook and thundered with their shared climax.

In spite of it all, fear glimmered in the back of her mind. Trixie was terrified of becoming any more addicted to him than she already was. If she had to walk away for whatever reason, she could still do it. But once she drank his blood and tasted his true essence…she might never be free again.

Her own fangs hummed with unfulfilled need as Dakota licked the wound on her neck until it healed. Tears stung her eyes but she willed them away. Even after all he had revealed and the raw truths that he already knew about her, Trixie still couldn't bring herself to complete the bond.

Dakota pressed a sweet kiss to her throat, as Trixie quickly wiped away her tears. She couldn't help but wonder if she'd ever be able to do it. Even now, as a vampire, the fear of addiction ruled her world.

Would she ever be free?

Trixie sat up and rubbed at her eyes, squinting from the bright light and long-forgotten sensation of being out in the sun. She smiled and held up her hand, attempting to block out the almost painful brightness. She rose to her feet and looked around in awe. She was in the dreamscape again, but this time Dakota was nowhere to be seen.

The last thing she remembered was falling asleep naked in his arms after making love for a third time. But she was here and she wasn't naked. She frowned when she saw the dingy white Keds on her feet, cutoff jean shorts, and a pink tank top emblazoned with an ironed-on picture of David Cassidy.

David Cassidy? She grimaced and held the shirt out while shaking her head. *This was an outfit she had worn as a kid. Before she actually got some decent taste in music.* Gross. I must have blocked that out too.

Like the clothes she was wearing, the area was also familiar. It only took her a moment to realize that this was exactly where she had been when she found the coin. She turned and looked over at the unusual rock formation about thirty feet away, the one that looked like a small pyramid. It was an odd collection of round and oval boulders that eons ago, through happenstance, had settled into something that resembled an Egyptian pyramid. The cluster of rocks was surrounded by a group of small trees and brush.

A large dome-shaped mountain, gray and almost shiny, loomed in the background and Trixie laughed out loud. She remembered now. The Langstons had taken her camping at Enchanted Rock State Park. This was it! That odd rock formation was where she'd found the coin. Trixie hooted with victory and pumped her fists in the air, but her joy swiftly cooled when she noticed Dakota's stark absence.

Why wasn't he here? They'd shared the dreamscape once before. It didn't make sense that he wouldn't be dreaming with her now, especially after everything that had happened.

Dakota? *Trixie shouted and looked around her frantically.* Can you hear me? Where are you?

He's not here.

A woman's voice, one Trixie had never heard before, piped up from behind her, scaring the hell out of her. Fangs bared, she spun around to find herself face-to-face with an elderly woman. A tanned face, shriveled by age, was framed by gray hair that hung in twin braids all the way to her waist. She wore a long white nightgown, and a blanket with an Aztec design was draped over her narrow hunched shoulders. Her feet were bare, and her arthritic-looking hands were curled around a crooked wooden walking stick.

Put your fangs away, girlie. *The old woman laughed and pounded her walking stick in the dirt before leaning on it with both hands.* They won't do you no good in the dreamscape. Besides, I'm the one who brought you here. I'm Isadora.

Isadora? *Trixie sheathed her fangs and folded her arms over her breasts, feeling like anything other than a tough girl in her David Cassidy shirt.* Pete's friend?

Well, his daddy's friend. *A cheeky grin cracked the old woman's face and she winked.* Me and Asmodeus used to knock boots back in the day. He ain't the Demon of Lust for nothing! Anyway, that's neither here nor there. From what I hear, you have some witch's blood running through your veins, and Asmodeus's boy thought maybe I could help you sort it out.

She moved slowly but steadily toward Trixie, her frame stooped over and her gaze curious. Without saying a word, the old witch walked a full circle around Trixie, inspecting her like some kind of science experiment. Isadora said nothing but nodded as though she was confirming something before finally stopping and standing right in front of Trixie.

I like your hair. *Isadora placed one hand on the small of her own back and arched a bit, as though stretching out her stiff muscles.* I might have to try something like that the next time I step into my younger self.

Your younger self? *Trixie asked.*

It's a spell I use to make me look like I used to. *Isadora winked.* It's easier to get laid that way. I'd teach it to you but seeing how you're a vampire, you don't need it. Anyway, they're right. You have witch in you.

Okay, *Trixie said slowly.* Great. What's the deal with gargoyles? Why can witches sense them, or whatever?

How can you not? They stink. *Isadora wrinkled her nose.* But not all witches can detect them the way that you can. Only witches who are descended from the Rathbone family line have that particular gift. We thought that line had died out. *Isadora sniffed and pursed her lips while giving Trixie the once-over.* Guess not.

Why? *Trixie narrowed her eyes and let out a growl of frustration.* I mean, why do the Rathbone witches or me or whatever feel pain when the gargoyles come around?

Pilar Rathbone, the last full-blooded witch of your line, got involved with a couple of gargoyles. She loved to mix it up with the menfolk: human, vamp, gargoyle. You name it. She liked a good time. According to the story, she did her gargoyle lover a favor, cast a spell for him, and then he jilted her. Left her high and dry.

Isadora shrugged and adjusted her stance with the cane. All of us witches have different gifts, passed down through the generations. The Rathbone family line was able to detect the presence of gargoyles. But since you aren't a pureblood and you have no training…your gift is diluted.

That's it? *Trixie let out a curt laugh and set her hands on her hips.* I can't learn to control it or anything? The pain keeps getting worse, and the last time I turned into a useless heap.

That's because you let your fear take over. *Isadora thumped her cane on the ground, a ferocious glint flickering in her pale gray eyes.* That is your worst enemy, girl. Fear. We fear what we don't know, what we don't understand. But now you know the truth. That feeling you get when the gargoyles show up is just a warning bell. That's it. It ain't gonna hurt you unless you let it. *She grabbed Trixie's bicep with one gnarled hand and squeezed.* You're a strong little thing. Tough as steel, I bet. You can handle those gargoyles, girlie. They can't take you down—not unless you allow them to. You're a vampire, for goodness' sake. The fear… that is your undoing.

Trixie swallowed any argument she might have had because Isadora was absolutely right. Fear was holding her back—and not just with the gargoyles.

If you want to learn about casting spells and brewing potions, that I can help you with. But not the Rathbone curse. *The old witch walked over to a small round boulder and groaned as she sat down.* Like the gargoyles, we thought that family line was gone. I don't know more than the story I told you.

Curse? *Trixie added quickly.* You didn't say anything about a curse.

Relax, girlie. *Isadora laughed, a dry raspy sound like leaves rustling on pavement.* It's just a saying, an expression.

Then why did you come here? *Trixie asked. Feeling completely defeated she sat down on the rock next to the old woman.* Why even bother?

You ever dream like this since you turned vamp or when you were human? You ever do any lucid dreaming?

No. *Trixie let out a sigh and folded her hands in front of her. An armadillo skittered past before vanishing in some brush.* Just the one shared dream with Dakota. But we're bloodmates, so that's supposed to happen. I'm actually surprised he's not here.

He's not here because I'm keeping him out. I wanted

to work with you in private, which is why we aren't meeting in town like we were supposed to. *She looked sidelong at Trixie.* Besides, I don't make a habit of hanging around vampires in the flesh. My blood is too powerful and I wouldn't want anyone to be tempted to—

We would never—

Save it. *Isadora held up one hand and shook her head firmly.* Don't take it personal. Anyway, like I was saying, as a witch, you also have the ability to manipulate your dreams. You can use them to help you remember things that you may have shut away, or you can come here to solve a riddle that you can't quite figure out. The dreamscape allows us to see the world more completely: a fuller picture than on the earthly plane, where you only see through your eyes. Here, you can see the full picture. *She started to rise to her feet and Trixie gently grabbed her elbow, helping the old witch regain her footing.* My connecting with you here was a way to help you unlock that part of your magic. I uncorked it, so to speak. The rest is up to you.

Thank you but how do I do it? *Trixie looked around and stuck her hands in her pockets.* I mean, how do I get back here?

Your mind and imagination are a witch's most powerful gifts. Like anything else you want to be good at, you have to practice. Set aside your insecurities and don't allow yourself to be intimidated by your own power, Trixie. *Isadora patted her cheek gently.* Anytime you want to come back to the dreamscape, all you have to do is think about it...and here you'll be. Not only that but your mind and imagination can aid you in times of trouble. They are the source of a witch's power.

What about Dakota?

What about him? *Isadora laughed and started walking away.* You want him here and he'll be here. If you don't, then he won't. Remember what I said, girlie. Your worst enemy, and the one thing that will keep you from fulfilling your destiny, is fear. Fear is the killer of dreams.

Wait. *Trixie called after Isadora but her image began to fade.* What if I need your help?

Don't worry, girlie. *She laughed.* I'll be around.

Isadora's words lingered on the warm Texas breeze as she vanished in the distance. The old woman was absolutely right. Fear had kept Trixie from fighting back against the gargoyles. It had stopped her from being involved in Chelsea's life. Fear was what held a human being a prisoner of addiction. And it was the only barrier preventing her from taking the final step with Dakota.

No more. After this craziness was over and they found her granddaughter, Trixie would shove all that fear aside and complete the bloodmate bond with Dakota.

Fear had ruled her life and stolen her past, but she would not let it hijack her future.

Chapter 14

THEY'D MADE LOVE TWICE MORE LAST NIGHT BUT TRIXIE never drank from Dakota. It took every ounce of self-control he had *not* to ask her why—but he didn't. He had promised her that he'd give her time, and that's exactly what he planned on doing.

No matter how crazy it was making him.

He'd seen her blood memories a few times now, but they had gotten fuzzier instead of clearer. He had a hunch it was because of her witch bloodline. Shane had told him that Maya had a similar issue due to her unusual family history. That answer should have satisfied Dakota, but it didn't. He had fully expected to walk in the dream realm with her when they slept.

Yet, they didn't.

Instead of dreamwalking with *him*, she was with Isadora. Dakota frowned and scanned the area below as they flew toward town. He wasn't exactly thrilled that some old witch had invaded Trixie's dreams and kept him out, but at least Trixie had remembered the area where she'd found the gold. A small comfort, but he'd have to settle for that—for now.

Trixie was still hiding from him *and* from herself. He knew she'd been a drug addict when she was human, and she carried a huge amount of guilt for giving up her daughter. But why would *that* keep her from bonding with him?

It was frustrating as hell.

They landed just outside the center of Fredricksville and walked the rest of the way into town. Luckily the sun went down a bit earlier this time of year, which gave them a bit more time to poke around town. He hadn't realized how much he'd missed being back home until he got here, and nothing made him feel more at ease than wearing his own duds instead of a sentry uniform. He'd reclaimed his favorite plaid shirt, his faded Levi's, and the brown-and-yellow snakeskin cowboy boots. Definitely not the usual sentry gear, but he didn't miss the sidelong glance Trixie gave him as she looked him up and down.

"I like it." Trixie walked next to him, matching his stride. "It suits you."

"What does?" Dakota continued scanning the area around them. He'd felt uneasy ever since he woke up.

"The hat, the clothes, the boots." She smirked at him as they rounded the corner onto Main Street. "You are definitely in your element."

"Thank you kindly." He tipped his hat to her and skimmed his gaze over her from head to toe. She was clad in her usual T-shirt and jeans ensemble, topped off by a black leather jacket. Her blond-and-blue-highlighted hair was slicked back, showing off her stellar bone structure. High cheekbones, an upturned nose, and a strong chin came together to form her beautiful face. "We may be on the hunt but I figured my sentry uniform might make us look out of place."

"Don't worry, cowboy." Trixie slapped him on the arm. "I've got the whole looking-out-of-place thing covered."

"If you ask me, you're lookin' beautiful as usual,"

Dakota said with a wink. He pointed up ahead. "The town has grown a bunch over the past couple of years. Gatlin's address is here on Main Street but I don't recall any apartment buildings. It's mostly retail space and restaurants. It's number 640A, and if I'm rememberin' right, then it should be just up here on the left."

"Maybe it's an apartment above a store or—"

"Shit." Dakota came to an abrupt halt, almost bumping into a young couple as they strolled past, hand in hand. "It's a dead end. That's what it is."

Trixie was about to ask him what he was talking about when she saw the business they were standing in front of. "A UPS store?"

"Looks like our boy Gatlin had a post office box. These places give you a regular-lookin' address but really all you get is a box." Dakota adjusted his hat and peered in the window of the small shipping store. "Damn. So much for him havin' a home here."

"Now what?" Trixie cracked her knuckles and her voice wavered barely above a whisper. "Where the hell did he take her?"

"Hey. We'll find him." He settled both hands on her shoulders and turned her toward him. "We knew this was a long shot. Even if he had an actual home here, we knew it was unlikely that he'd still be here."

"Yeah, but we thought at least we'd find another clue or something."

"We still can." He pointed to the sign in the door and kept his voice low, not wanting any passing humans to hear him. "There are too many folks in there now, but they close in about an hour. We'll come by and have a little chat with that young lady behind the counter. We'll glamour her and get a peek at whatever might be in his mailbox. Or maybe she knows him or where to find him. Just because he doesn't have a place here in town doesn't mean he isn't around. He could live on the outskirts or in another town nearby."

"Great." Trixie slipped her fingers around the chain and curled her hand around the coin. "What are we supposed to do for the next hour?"

"You said you remembered a landmark last night when you were with Isadora, right?"

"Yes." Trixie nodded. "Sorry about that, by the way. I mean, about you not being there."

He wanted to grab her and tell her she damn well should be sorry, but they had more pressing matters at hand than his wounded ego.

"That's not important right now," he said curtly. "Anyway, I have an idea how we might be able to find your landmark. Come on."

Dakota spun on his heels and strode along the sidewalk, not waiting for Trixie to respond. Anger and frustration were starting to take hold, and that only made him more pissed at himself. This wasn't him. He didn't let emotional crap get to him. He'd left emotions and love and all that other stuff behind in his human life.

What the hell was he doing?

"Where are we going?" She caught up right away and fell in step alongside him. "You said it yourself—that park is over a thousand acres. How the hell are we going find the spot in an hour?"

"The Internet." Dakota gestured to the tiny brick building at the end of Main Street. "We'll hit the library and see if an online search comes up with any pictures of the rock pyramid you remembered."

Unlike the center of town, the library was deserted. Besides the one young lady behind the counter, Trixie and Dakota were the only other people in the building. It didn't take long to pull up the information on the park, but none of the images that scrolled across the screen matched the rock formation Trixie described.

"We're closin' in five minutes." The young woman from the front desk kept her voice at librarian-appropriate levels and gave them a shy smile. She flicked a glance at Trixie's hair but looked away quickly, making her way around to check the computer screen. "I'm Mary, by the way. Did you folks find what you were lookin' for?"

"Not really," Trixie said with a sigh. She pulled the necklace out and started fiddling with it again. "And all these rocks are starting to look the same."

"Oh!" The librarian adjusted the stack of books in her arms and settled them onto her hip. "You're here to visit Enchanted Rock State Park! I should've known a couple of city folks like you were here to see that."

"She's the city folk." Dakota winked and jutted his thumb at Trixie, who was sitting next to him and glaring at the screen. "I'm a little more local, Mary."

"Are you familiar with the park at all?" Trixie pressed the chain to her lips and clicked the mouse, looking for more pictures. "I went camping here when I was little, and there was this one spot that was really cool. It was a cluster of boulders that looked kinda like a pyramid. Maybe ten feet high?"

"Oh sure, that's on the west side of the Dome, I think.

You know, that huge gray mountain?" Mary said casually. When Dakota and Trixie snapped their heads up eagerly, the poor girl actually took a step back. "Jeez, you folks sure are excited to find it." Her shoulders sagged and she rolled her eyes. "Please tell me you aren't more of those silly people who are runnin' out there lookin' for gold."

Dakota stilled and caught Trixie's eye before turning his attention back to the librarian.

"Gold?" Trixie asked in an almost inaudible tone as she casually made sure the coin was still hidden beneath her shirt. "Y-you know about the gold?"

"Oh please." Mary giggled and waved her free hand before adjusting the pile of books again. "Everyone around here knows that silly old story."

"Apparently not," Trixie murmured. She arched one eyebrow and glared briefly at Dakota. "What story did you hear?"

"Our town has quite a scandalous history, you know. There was this gang of outlaws who hid their loot somewhere in the area, but when they went to get it, it was gone. Each one accused the other of takin' it." She plopped the books on the table and tugged her brown sweater tighter around her before rushing away. She kept talking as she vanished into the book stacks. "I have a book all about the town that'll tell you the whole story. A local fella, he was kind of our unofficial town historian, he self-published it last year. Poor guy. He passed on about a month after it came out. It was his life's work, that book."

As she moved deeper into the stacks, Dakota and Trixie slowly turned to face each other, and she looked no less surprised than he did.

"This gets weirder by the second. Too bad the guy is dead. We could've talked to him," Trixie murmured. "She knows about the gold but obviously not the gargoyles." Her brow furrowed as she rose from the chair, keeping an eye out for the librarian. "Why didn't *you* know about this story? I thought you said that you grew up around here."

"Beats the hell outta me." Dakota stood next to her with his hat both literally and figuratively in hand. "Hang on, now. I do remember hearin' a story about some bank robbers or somethin' like that."

"And you didn't think the two could be connected?" Trixie asked with waning patience. "Maybe Hector and Addie know something. We *could* glamour them if we had to."

"Hell no. They're family and that would be downright rude. They trust me, Trixie. It wouldn't be fair to do that to them. We can ask them about it if we have to, but like I said before—I don't wanna get them involved in this if I have any other choice." Dakota put his hat on and set his hands on his hips and muttered, "How the hell was I supposed to connect bank robberies and gargoyles?"

"Don't ask me, cowboy." Trixie smothered a smile and lifted one shoulder. "You're the one who's supposed to have the inside scoop."

"Hardee har-har." He tried to be annoyed with her teasing, but all he wanted to do was kiss that little grin off those lips. "Let's just get the book and get back over to that UPS store before the gal closes up."

"Oh nuts," Mary huffed. She hurried over with an apologetic look on her face. "*The History of*

Fredricksville is out on loan. But if you're really eager to read it, you could go online and get it if you have one of those ereaders. It's available as an ebook." Her shoulders sagged. "I'd like to help you more but we really are closin'. I'd stay open later, but I have to get home."

"It's fine." Dakota tipped his hat to her and took Trixie by the hand. "We have to be on our way too. 'Night."

"So," Trixie said as they hurried out of the library, "do Hector and Addie have a computer we could borrow?"

Just before they reached the UPS store, the cell phone in Dakota's pocket started playing "Ring of Fire" by Johnny Cash.

"Ha!" Trixie smirked at Dakota as he answered it. "I should've known."

"Hey, Olivia," he said with a smile. However, as he listened, his expression darkened by the second. "I see."

Trixie had seen that look before. Whatever Olivia had to say, it wasn't good.

"Alright then," he said, clutching the phone so tightly Trixie thought it might shatter. "We have one more lead to follow up and then—"

Silence followed as Olivia responded, and with each passing second, the lines between Dakota's eyes deepened. His emotions were clearly getting the better of him, all his anger bubbling to the surface.

"That's just fine, Olivia," he muttered. "It looks like I'm already in a shit pile of trouble, so what's a few more days? You can tell Zhao to keep his fangs on and that I'll be back *after* I find Trixie's granddaughter and not a minute before. And if he doesn't like it, then he can get his moldy old ass down here to Texas and tell me himself."

Trixie's hands flew to her mouth and she stared at him with wide eyes. "Holy shit," she said, her words muffled by her fingers.

Dakota hit the end button and shoved the phone back in his pocket, fury settling in the lines around his mouth and flashing in his eyes. She had never heard *anyone* talk to Olivia that way *or* about the emperor—*ever*. She probably should have been worried about what was going to happen to Dakota for that kind of insubordination, but she was too busy being proud of him.

"I knew there was a rebel hidden under all that cowboy," she said, trying to lighten the mood. She poked him playfully in the chest, but Dakota didn't flinch, fury still etched into his features. "What is it?" Trixie grabbed his arm when he started to walk away, his body tense and tightly wound, like he was going into battle. "Dakota! Wait a minute. Talk to me."

"It was all a lie," he bit out, striding around the corner and heading for a presumably more private spot. "Everythin'. Jonner lied about it all."

He moved swiftly, so fast that a human wouldn't even see him, and Trixie matched his speed all the way to the edge of town. He finally stopped in the parking lot of an abandoned building. He paced back and forth, hands on his hips, but said nothing. Trixie wasn't sure what to say or do.

"Hey," she said, her voice gentle and hesitant. She stepped in front of him and grabbed his face with both hands, instantly bringing him to a halt. "What happened?"

"Jonner lied." Dakota's mouth set in a grim line and the muscles of his jaw twitched beneath her palm. "There was no top secret gargoyle task force. Emperor

Zhao didn't know anythin' about it. Jonner made it all up. Shit. No wonder the czar in the district wasn't read in on it. That's why he never brought me around any of the others.

"Don't you get it?" he rasped. Trixie's heart ached from the pain and regret that edged his voice. "My maker fuckin' lied to me about all of it. There was no mission, no greater good. It was murder. Genocide, pure and simple."

Dakota shook his head and withdrew from Trixie's touch. She wanted to go after him, to comfort him, but he obviously needed some distance. Could she blame him? She was the queen of needing space and time alone.

"I don't understand. Why would he do something like that?" Her brow furrowed. "Why would Jonner want to kill gargoyles?"

"If the son of a bitch hadn't gotten dusted, I'd be askin' him that very question." Dakota squared his shoulders and finally turned around to face her. "Zhao said we have to put the coin back wherever you found it and haul ass to New York. He told Olivia that finding the baby is not Presidium business, and from what I gather, I have some sins to answer for when we get back to the city."

"We can't just leave," Trixie said as her voice filled with panic. "She may not be Presidium business, but she sure as hell is *my* business. Gatlin might not even want the gold anymore, Dakota. For all we know, he's trying to hide to protect his daughter. We have to at least find a way to let him know that we don't want to hurt her. He probably thinks Chelsea is dead. This is *my family* we're talking about."

"Mine too." Dakota cradled her face in his hand. "I meant what I said to Olivia. We aren't goin' anywhere until we figure out where Gatlin took the baby, and as far as I can tell, that gold is our only connection to him. The Presidium may not care about the gold, but whoever trashed Gatlin's apartment and sent those two gargoyles to the city sure does. Besides, I'm already in a heap of trouble with the emperor, so I might as well do what we need to do. I don't think I can make it any worse."

Trixie jumped up and wrapped her arms around him before burying her face against his throat. She breathed in the soothing scent of sandalwood as Dakota held her tightly. She whispered into his mind, *Thank you*.

The rumbling of a pickup truck cut through the night, the headlights bobbing toward them. As it approached, a now-familiar wave of nausea rippled through Trixie's gut. She stilled in Dakota's arms and held him tighter.

It's happening again. She touched his mind and kept her eyes closed, the sensation growing stronger as the vehicle got closer. *There's a gargoyle... It's getting close.*

Stay calm, baby. Dakota reached down and quickly removed the stone dagger he had hidden in his right boot, keeping Trixie cradled against his chest. Dakota flew them over to the side of the building, still holding her firmly, and hid in the shadows before the truck reached the intersection. *You're safe. Remember what Isadora told you.*

Trixie peeled her eyes open and forced herself to shove aside the self-defeating terror. Cowering in the dark was not going to help her find Rebecca. The headlights of the old Ford pickup bobbed over the parking lot as the driver turned to the right and headed into town. There was one man in the car and he sang along loudly to some country song, his windows open, seemingly unaware he was being watched. Intermingled with the scent of exhaust was the clear and pungent, sickeningly sweet aroma of a gargoyle.

"That wasn't Gatlin, but it sure as hell was one of them." Dakota slipped the dagger in the waist of his jeans and kissed the top of Trixie's head. "What do you say we see where that fella is headed and find out if he knows our friend?"

Chapter 15

TRIXIE HAD NEVER BEEN IN A COUNTRY-WESTERN BAR before, and if they weren't tailing a gargoyle, she might have actually stopped to take the time to *try* to enjoy it. But right now, all she could see was the gargoyle sitting at the bar. None of the humans would have any idea what he was. He looked like most of the other men in the place, casually sipping a beer while checking out the different women on the dance floor. The only thing about him that looked different was his complexion. He was downright pasty white compared to the other men's suntanned skin. That was hardly surprising, since sunlight turned a gargoyle to stone.

She and Dakota settled at one of the tall bar tables by the window. Before they came in, she'd taken off the necklace and secured it safely in the front pocket of her jeans. The last complication they needed was this guy getting a glimpse of the gold.

The waitress came by and took their order, beers that they would pretend to drink while keeping an eye on their mark. Trixie didn't miss the flirty smile the woman gave Dakota, and she tried not to let it annoy her.

"What are we going to do?" Trixie asked, her patience waning. "Sit here all night and stare at him?"

"Where there's one, there's bound to be another. We watch and wait. Tail him when he leaves."

"Can gargoyles sense our kind being around?" Trixie

asked with a hint of nervousness. "I mean, didn't they protect humans once? They must have some way to know if we're in the area."

"The older ones did. They can live a hell of a long time and they hardly age once they reach maturity, kind of like the werewolves." He kept his sights on the bar. "But since this one hasn't split, he must be on the younger side and never learned how. The ones I hunted with Jonner were older and usually picked up on our presence." Dakota smiled at the waitress as she placed the beers on the table, and Trixie didn't miss the way the woman's cheeks pinkened. "Thank you, ma'am."

"You're welcome," she simpered. The woman kept her eyes pinned to Dakota, completely ignoring Trixie. "Can I get you anythin' else? Anythin' at all?"

A sudden surge of jealously bubbled up, taking Trixie by surprise. She couldn't remember the last time she'd felt possessive about a guy. She curled her fingers around her beer with one hand and dragged it closer, while shooting Dakota the stink eye. He was flirting right back.

"No thank you." He winked and tipped his hat at the waitress. "But I surely will give a holler if I get an itch for anythin' else."

"Alright then." The tiny brunette giggled before hustling off with an extra swing in her hips. "The name is Carleen," she shouted over her shoulder. "I'll be around."

Trixie held the smooth, wet pint glass in her hand and shook her head while giving him a disapproving look.

"What?" he asked innocently.

"Shameless." Trixie tried not to smile but she couldn't help it. "Flirting with that poor girl and letting her think she might *actually* have a chance with you."

"I was only bein' friendly." He leaned back in his chair and adjusted his hat. "This isn't the big city, darlin'. People here look each other in the eye and say hello."

"Right." Trixie rolled her eyes before turning her attention back to the gargoyle at the bar. "Whatever."

"Are you jealous?" A twinkle glimmered in his blue eyes as they peered at her from beneath the rim of his hat. "Y'know you've got no reason to be…but I kinda like it."

"Is that so?" The band switched to a sappy slow song, and the dancers either paired up or went back to their tables. "Well, I don't have the patience to sit around all night. How about if I see what being *friendly* will get us?"

Trixie hopped off the chair and fluffed up her hair before peeling off her leather jacket. She'd worn her favorite fitted black tank top with the rhinestone skull and crossbones on the front. Underneath was the best push-up bra ever, putting her boobs front and center. At the moment, they basically defied gravity.

When she tossed the jacket on her chair, she found Dakota glaring at her and slowly shaking his head. "What do you think you're doin'?"

"I'm going to ask our friend to dance and see if I can get some information while I'm at it." Trixie blew him a kiss before heading toward the bar. *You're not jealous, are you?* She touched his mind with a teasing tone and laughed. *Keep your spurs on, cowboy. I'm going to see if we can avoid sitting here all night. This music is going to make me crazy.*

She wove her way through the few people lingering around the bar before slipping in next to her mark. The scent of rotten flowers was almost overpowering and her gut clenched to the point of pain, but she pushed it aside. Trixie kept repeating to herself what Isadora had told her. It was only a warning and nothing to be fearful of.

"Hey there," Trixie said as she sidled in beside the gargoyle. "You wanna dance?"

"Hell yes." His brown eyes widened as he looked her up and down. A big grin covered his face as he ran two fingers over his bushy blond mustache. "I'd love to, cutie."

"Great." Trixie grabbed his hand and tugged him toward the dance floor. "Come on."

"What's your name?" she asked as he clumsily tugged her against him and started moving to the music. This dude was totally not smooth. "I'm Trixie."

"Henry," he said loudly. Trixie winced. Little did he know that he didn't need to shout over the music for her to hear him. "Nice meetin' you. I have to tell you. I never had a woman ask me to dance before." He pulled back and nodded at her. "But then again, you aren't from around here, are you? There's somethin' different about you. I can't put my finger on it."

"You're very perceptive." Trixie gritted her teeth against his unpleasant aroma. "I'm from New York City. I'm here with my brother on vacation."

Your brother? Dakota's voice slid into her mind and was edged with mild annoyance. *You couldn't at least say I was your friend?*

What's the matter? Henry spun her around, and she caught Dakota's eye and quickly stuck her tongue out at him. *Jealous?*

Just do what you're supposed to do and get back over here.

Can gargoyles be glamoured?

I never tried. I didn't try to get to know 'em. I mostly just killed 'em. His voice was gruff and serious. *You be careful. If you try and it doesn't work, he might figure out somethin' is up. Besides, I don't like the way he's pawin' you.*

"Your brother, huh?" Henry asked as he slid his hand from her lower back to her butt. "He protective?"

Oh, hell no. Dakota's voice was more like a growl. *That boy is gonna lose a hand.*

"You might say that." She did her best to ignore his hand on her ass. Hell, she didn't like it any more than Dakota did. "I really wanted to dance, and dancing with my brother seemed too pathetic. You looked like a nice guy and I kind of get the feeling you aren't from around here either."

"Not exactly." Henry let out a curt laugh.

He was on the shorter side and only a few inches taller than she was. Based on the feel of him, he was strong but not too strong. Trixie didn't move the guy's hand but pulled back so she could look him in the eye.

It was now or never.

"Henry?" She kept her voice low as she held his stare and pushed into his mind. Trixie braced herself for a barrier but there was none, and like a knife through butter, she was in. "I have a few questions for you but you keep on dancing. Okay?"

"Okay." He sighed. Henry's jaw went slack and his grip on her loosened as his feet shuffled on the dance floor. "Sure."

"You're a gargoyle, aren't you?" Trixie whispered.

"Uh-huh." He nodded and his glassy gaze held hers. "Sure am. I never shift when I'm up here. Too dangerous."

"I thought so."

"Don't tell nobody I came up here." His voice wavered with the unmistakable tremor of fear. "If they found out I came up again, I'd be in a big trouble."

"Up where?" Trixie's brow furrowed and confusion settled over her. "Here? This bar?"

"No. To the surface," he whispered. "We're not supposed to, but I get so sick of bein' down there. I'm tired of hidin'. But the queen demands it."

I think we need to take this outside. She caught Dakota's eye and nodded toward the door.

Done. He tossed money on the table, grabbed her jacket, and made his way out. *And get his hand off your ass while you're at it.*

"Henry, let's go outside and take a walk in that fresh evening air."

The man nodded wordlessly as Trixie took his hand and led him out of the bar. He came with her willingly, as anyone would while in the glamour state, and didn't say anything as they went along the side of the building. She made sure no one was around before pulling him around the corner. Dakota was out there waiting for them, hidden in the shadows of the narrow alley.

As gently as possible, Trixie held Henry against the wall and pushed deeper into his mind while Dakota stood guard.

"Do you know a man named Gatlin Dorsett?"

"No," he said gruffly. Henry shook his head adamantly. "No. He's no good."

She and Dakota exchanged a concerned look.

"But you know who he is?"

"I'd spit on him if I ever saw him." Henry frowned, the lines between his eyes deepening. "He and Franklin were traitors."

"Traitors?"

"They killed the royal family. Alana was the only one left. The queen will be so mad if she finds out I came up here again." He grew more agitated and whimpered. "They took the gold and ruined it for everyone. We're in hiding. They were hunting us all down. Had no choice."

"Who was hunting you?" Trixie asked quietly. She could feel the tension rippling off Dakota's tall frame because they both knew the likely answer. "It's okay, Henry. You're safe. No one is going to hurt you and I won't tell on you. I promise. Tell me…who was hunting you?"

"The vampires," he whispered.

"Damn it," Dakota said. "He must be talkin' about Jonner and me."

"So now we hide. But they can't get into the Dome." Henry grinned, almost like a naughty child. "Only a gargoyle can get in."

"The Dome?" Trixie murmured. "The gargoyles must be in hiding underground. Under the Dome in Enchanted Rock State Park."

Henry's eyes rolled into the back of his head, and a gurgling noise escaped his parted lips.

"It's too much for him, Trixie," Dakota whispered. "Release him."

"Not yet. Stay with me, dude." Trixie shook her head and tapped Henry's cheek lightly. She was doing her best to hold on to the glamour but she could feel him slipping out of her grasp. "One more question, Henry. Is the queen looking for the gold? Did she send them to find it?"

"Can't find it. The witch cursed it." A slightly hysterical giggle erupted from Henry's throat, and his eyes rolled again before he muttered something incoherent. "She cursed it so they couldn't find it. They tricked her too. Never good to piss off a witch."

Henry started shaking violently as his body and mind started to reject the glamour.

"He's startin' to lose it. Send him home, Trix." Dakota kept his voice low. "We'll follow him and find out where the entrance is."

"What? Why?" Confusion fired through her as she pulled Henry to his feet and held him against the wall. "What good will that do? If Gatlin is some kind of gargoyle outlaw, he's not going to be able to go hide out there. They'd probably kill him."

"I have to make this right, Trix," Dakota said quietly. "We aren't putting the coin where you found it. We're gonna find the rest of that gold and get it back where it belongs. It's the least I can do to try and make up for what I done."

Staring into Dakota's eyes, Trixie saw the unrelenting determination of a sentry mingled with the sadness and regret of a man. She knew he'd wanted revenge on the gargoyle that attacked him that night, but Jonner had used it to turn Dakota into his own personal killing machine. It must have cut Dakota to the core to know the way his maker had manipulated, betrayed, and used him.

It was an unforgivable crime.

Trixie nodded her understanding, pulled Henry close, and whispered into his ear. She sent him on his way back to the Dome and the hidden entrance to the gargoyles' lair.

As she and Dakota flew side by side high above Henry's truck and the massive dome-shaped rock came into view, the nausea began to swirl more violently in her belly.

The truck came to a halt when Henry parked it behind a large clump of trees not easily visible from the road. He hummed tunelessly, seeming to be completely unaware of their encounter. Henry stripped off his clothing and tossed it in the back of the old truck.

Dakota and Trixie landed a safe distance away, keeping their senses alert for any other gargoyles or stray humans camping in the area. So far it was only them. Trixie was about to ask why the guy was getting naked in the middle of the park, but a moment later a bright flash of greenish light blinked, briefly illuminating the night. Trixie clasped Dakota's hand and held on tightly as the man she knew as Henry shifted into a gargoyle. He flapped his leathery wings and leaped into the night sky, taking flight. His legs stretched out behind him, his deadly curved talons glinting in the moonlight as he soared toward the top of the enormous gray dome.

Trixie expected him to land and push some kind of

hidden panel, like the ones they had in the Presidium tunnels. But right after Henry reached the top of the dome, he just hovered for a second before he vanished in another blink of green light.

"What the hell?" Trixie whispered. "Where did he go?"

"Son of a bitch." Dakota took a few steps out from the shadows of the trees. "I guess knockin' on the door is out of the question."

"No wonder I was sick when we were camping out here," Trixie whispered. "The gargoyles were never extinct. They've been hiding underground all this time."

"Mary said she thought that pyramid rock formation was on the west side of the Dome," Dakota murmured. He glanced around warily. "That's on the same side as the ranch. But now that we know it's not too far from their hidden lair, I'm thinkin' it's not a great idea to go wanderin' aimlessly, especially with that coin in your pocket. For all we know, if we hang around here long enough or in the wrong spot, a hundred of those things could come flyin' out. I'd feel better pokin' around if I had more weapons with me."

"I hadn't thought of that." Trixie inched closer to Dakota and kept her gaze pinned to the spot where Henry had vanished. She fished the necklace out of her pocket and quickly put it over her head. It made her feel better to have that coin against her skin. "Thanks for that image. It's going to give me nightmares."

"Let's go back to house. I'll get my gear on, and we'll see if we can find any more information in that book. Then we go huntin'."

Chapter 16

TRIXIE AND DAKOTA SAT AT THE COMPUTER IN HECTOR and Addie's spacious living room and were careful to be quiet, not wanting to wake their hosts. Luckily they already had the book app downloaded on the computer, and it only took a few minutes to find what they were looking for.

"Got it," Trixie said. She clicked the cover image and began to scroll through it. "Damn. This book is longer than I thought it would be."

"That's alright, darlin'." Dakota kissed her head and rose to his feet, then went to the window and stared out over the moonlit property. "We still have a few hours until sunrise."

Trixie surfed for a while until she came to a section specifically about the state park. There were four pages of images, all unusual rock formations, but so far none were of the pyramid-like structure she had seen in her dream. She leaned back in the chair and laced her hands behind her head. Dakota was still staring out the window.

"What are you doing?" Trixie scanned the text on the next screen but none of it was what she was looking for. "Are you worried someone followed us back here?"

"No. I was just thinkin' about how much I've missed this place," he said quietly. His tall, broad-shouldered frame was silhouetted in the moonlight from the window. Gone were the cowboy hat and faded jeans, replaced by his sentry uniform. Now though, with him decked out in that gear, Trixie could see shades of the human man he'd been years before. "It's part of me. No matter where I go or what I do, this will always be my home." He glanced over his shoulder at her. "I'm grateful I had a chance to show it to you. Even if it's not under the best circumstances. I just wish we had more time."

"We can come back." A lump formed in Trixie's throat. "After this all settles down…we could…"

"Come on, darlin'." Dakota turned around slowly and cast a serious but sad look in her direction. "You know that ain't true. I have some sins to answer for with the Presidium. Do you have any idea how many gargoyles I killed in the name of the vampire government? Not to mention what I said on the phone to Olivia."

"But it's not your fault." Trixie jumped to her feet and quickly closed the distance between them. She grabbed his hands and pulled him in. "You didn't know. Your maker lied to you."

"Somethin' tells me that won't matter." A sad smile lingered on his lips as he raised her hands to his mouth, pressing a soft swift kiss to her fingers. "Looks like it's a good thing we never completed the bloodmate bond after all. If Zhao does what I think he's goin' to do…my days are already numbered."

"No!"

"Trixie, he can't let me live." Dakota's voice was calm. "If word about this gets out and Zhao doesn't put me down, do you know how bad that would look to the rest of the supernatural community? He can't let a vigilante sentry walk free. There have to be consequences."

She wanted to smack the crap out of him for acting like this wasn't a big deal.

"No way." Trixie turned on her heel and stormed back to the computer. "I'm turning off this stupid computer, and then we are going to scour the west side of that giant freaking rock until we find that pyramid. I don't care if a thousand gargoyles come after us. If we find the gold, then you can give it back to them and make peace."

"Girl, stop talkin' crazy." Dakota's voice was calm and even and totally infuriating. "Just keep lookin' for some clues in that book."

"Ugh." Trixie sat down at the desk and glared at the stupid screen. "This thing is like five hundred pages long. The dude who wrote this must've really loved this town. We'll be here all freaking night trying to sift through it."

"Too bad you can't use some of your witchy whammy to find it," he said with a small laugh.

Trixie stilled, and as silence hung between them, he turned around and caught her eye.

"Why not?" A smile curved her lips. "It sure as hell couldn't hurt."

"I was kiddin'." He smirked.

"I'm not." She cracked her knuckles. "I'm game for anything and we're running out of time."

Trixie placed both of her hands on the screen and closed her eyes. "Use my imagination," she murmured. "That's what Isadora told me… Use my imagination."

With sharply focused intensity, Trixie pictured the

pages of the book flipping by at a rapid pace. She called up the memories from all those years ago... the rock with the glint of gold...the Dome looming the distance.

As the images in her mind blurred, she murmured over and over again: "Show me what we need... Show me what we need... Show me... Show me..."

A buzzing sound filled her head and warmth whispered in her flesh. As the humming and buzzing grew louder, an odd vibration flickered over her skin just before a sharp electric shock shot up her arms. Trixie let out a yelp and yanked her hands away, rubbing absently at the tingling flesh of her palms.

Dakota had whisked to her side and bent at the knees next to her. He rubbed her back gently and pushed a stray hair off her forehead.

"Woman, I thought you were gonna make the damn computer blow up."

Trixie wanted to answer him, but she was far too focused on the picture that appeared on the screen. It made her blood run cold.

The caption above the picture read:

The Stevens Gang: This notorious crew was suspected of robbing several small towns throughout the west. Known for their lethal brutality and bloodthirsty nature, the quartet of killers eventually turned on one another. According to legend, they vanished after a violent public dispute. Neither they nor their loot was ever found.

It looked like one of those old tintype pictures, showing three men and a woman. The men were grizzled and rough, like actors from the old Western movies that were sometimes on television late at night. The woman with them wore the kind of dress common for that time, and she was snuggled up to one of the men on the end. They were standing outside a saloon, and as was typical for photos from long ago, not one of them was smiling. But all that paled beside the thing that caught the rest of Trixie's attention. The man in the center of the photograph, the one with the haunted eyes rimmed with sadness. He was all too familiar.

Gatlin.

Trixie didn't have to say a word. Dakota gaped at the screen with equal shock.

"Oh my God," he whispered. Dakota and Trixie stared at the image for what felt like hours, even though it was only seconds. "It can't be."

"I know," Trixie said with awe. "It's Gatlin. The robbers, the ones who caused all the trouble back in the day, like some supernatural Billy the Kid gang or something, are the same assholes who stole the gargoyles' gold and killed their royal family."

"Son of a bitch," Dakota seethed. He pressed his finger to the image of the man on the right side of the screen. "That's the gargoyle who attacked Chelsea in the cabin."

"It says here that his name was Franklin Southeby." She leaned closer and read the other two names. "There's Gatlin's name and the other guy is listed as John Stevens."

"That's not the name I knew him by," Dakota bit out. Anger punctuated every syllable. Dakota moved his finger over to the man in the left of the image. He was taller than the other two and had a deadly gleam in his eyes. "*That* is my maker. Jonner."

"Holy shit," Trixie murmured. She quickly read the other name below the image, although her gut already knew who it was. "And the woman next to him is the witch… Pilar Rathbone."

"They were all in on it together." Dakota's jaw clenched and fury rolled off him in almost palpable waves. "And he wasn't huntin' gargoyles… He was lookin' for the gold."

———

Dakota had never been this furious in his entire existence. He stormed out of the house into the night air, Trixie close behind. The sky, a deep inky black, was peppered with thousands of stars. That sight usually calmed him and reminded him how small he and his problems were, but at the moment, not even the sky helped. He launched into the sky, shouting his rage, and streaked through the night like a bullet. His body was rigid, every muscle taut. His whole life since being turned vamp was built on lies, deception, treachery, and death. That didn't change, no matter how much he ran all of the facts over in his mind.

His maker had been a traitor, a murderer, and a thief.

Please wait. Trixie's voice, soft and pleading, drifted into his mind. Her silky smooth fingers curled around his at the same moment. She flew next to him, meeting his eyes when he looked.

Part of him wanted to keep flying until the sun came up, to allow the deadly ultraviolet rays to turn him to dust and put him out of his misery. He was a sentry who had lost his honor. What kind of a man was that? Certainly not one who could be Trixie's bloodmate. She deserved better than what he would be able to offer now. But staring into those beautiful brown eyes, and with the moonlight bathing her heart-shaped face, he could only do what she asked of him.

Hand in hand, they flew down and landed by a massive rock formation that resembled a house. Two huge rectangular boulders stood side by side, capped by an even larger one that looked like a roof. Two sprawling trees with low-lying branches curled around the sides, almost like arms reaching out to embrace the night. Hidden in the midst of it all was a small hot spring. Steam rose from the moon-dappled water, a veritable oasis secreted away from the rest of the world.

Dakota pulled his hand from Trixie's and folded his arms over his chest. He had to distance himself from her because he was a selfish bastard. He wanted to wrap himself up and lose himself in the feel of her, to forget for even a short while what a lie his life had been.

"Jonner must have been involved in the murder of the royal family," Dakota bit out. "He was in cahoots with Franklin, Gatlin, and the Rathbone witch. From what that book said, they weren't limited to brutalizing gargoyles. He only turned me so I would help him hunt down his enemies and further his personal vendetta. Hell, for all I know he sicced one of them gargoyles on me just so he could turn me and use me."

Trixie slipped in behind him, curled her arms around his waist, and pressed a kiss to his shoulder. The gentleness of it almost broke his heart.

"How could you still want to be with me?" His voice was rough and strained, but Trixie tightened her grip. "I am a fool, Trix. Here I thought I was on some mission for the greater good and doin' the Presidium's work but I was a puppet for Jonner. He showed me the picture of the gold because that's all he was ever after. All that time, all those nights we were huntin'…he was lookin' for the gold. Son of a bitch. And I helped him." He gritted his teeth and fought the self-loathing that swelled up like a wave, threatening to swallow him whole. "Why would you want to be with a man like that? I was a fool."

Trixie slipped around so that she was standing in front of him, keeping her hands settled on his waist. The moon cast an ethereal glow over her porcelainlike skin, making her look more beautiful than ever before. More than the moonlight, pure love and acceptance glimmered in her eyes. Or was he imagining that? Was he seeing something he wanted to see instead of what was really there?

"Do you remember what you said to me once?" Trixie asked in a steady voice. "You told me that *we* are not the mistakes that we've made in the past. *You* are *not* Jonner. You did not kill that family or steal their gold. Dakota Shelton, you did what you thought was the right thing to do because your maker, the only vampire you knew in the world, told you it was. How could you believe anything else?"

"That's no excuse."

"Maybe not, but it's reality. And now that you do know the truth about what happened, you are the kind of man who *will not stop* until he's made good."

"It's not enough," he rasped. Dakota cradled her face in his hands, carefully and gently as though she were made of fine china. "I don't know if I can ever make it right or if—"

"I'm not finished." Trixie pressed one finger to his lips, immediately silencing him. He stilled as she ran her thumb over his mouth in one slow stroke. "I promised to tell you why I was afraid to blood bond with you. It's because I was terrified of becoming addicted—to you. I was scared that once I tasted your blood I wouldn't be able to shake you—that my every waking moment and thought would be consumed by the desire to be near you. The fear of addiction has ruled my world for as long as I can remember. But it doesn't anymore. Do you want to know why?"

He shook his head but said nothing. If he had any breath in his lungs, he'd be holding it.

"Because of the man that you are. The man that I know would do anything for his people, who always stands up for what's right. He's kind, loving, loyal, and gentle. Your hands may have been used in battle and delivered more deathblows than you can count, but these are the same hands that carve wooden ponies for two-year-old girls." Her voice broke with emotion and tears glittered in her eyes. "And they are the same hands that have cradled the broken pieces of my heart, even when I pushed you away."

"Trixie…" His hand drifted down and slipped around her waist, pulling her close. He rested his forehead against hers.

"I'm the one who's been a fool, Dakota." She threaded her hands through his hair and pressed a kiss to the corner of his mouth. "I couldn't separate addiction and love. But I know now that even if I never tasted your blood, it wouldn't matter."

He held her there, her mouth painfully close to his, and the whisper of whiskey and mint rolled around him in the dark. Dakota wanted to dive deep and lose himself in the feel of her, but how selfish would that be? He lifted his head and pulled away from her, but she tightened her grip.

"I'm not letting you go," she whispered. "Don't you get it? I love you, Dakota. The only thing I'm afraid of losing…is you."

Those words shredded his last ounce of self-control. He crashed his mouth down into hers in an explosion of need. He tilted her head, taking full control of the kiss, licking and sucking those luscious lips like a man who'd been starving. Hadn't he been? Starved for truth, acceptance, and love. And Trixie was giving him all of it, and then some. He trailed kisses down her neck, nudging the chain of the necklace out of the way. Only then did his protective instincts go on overdrive, pulling his lust-fogged head out of his ass.

"Wait." He tore his mouth from hers and shook his head, his fangs unsheathing in protest and need. Dakota held her face inches from his as she tried to kiss him again. "It's too dangerous to be out here in the open. We don't know where the gargoyles are. It's not safe."

"Dakota? You have an arsenal hidden inside this coat," Trixie murmured. "Besides that, did you forget that your bloodmate has a bona fide gargoyle alarm inside her?" She lifted her lip and ran her tongue along the tip of her fangs. She whispered, "Trust me, baby. We are covered."

The sight of her wet tongue sliding over the curve of her gleaming white fang was deliciously carnal and more than Dakota could bear. He dipped his head low, cursing all the while, and devoured her mouth with his. His fang scraped her lip, sending a few drops of her rich blood over his tongue. Light and color erupted behind his eyes and only made him want more. He wouldn't take it—not until she was ready to do the same.

They broke the kiss just long enough to strip the clothes from each other's bodies in a furious rush of limbs. She went to remove the leather sheath and harnesses around his forearm—the ones that held his sentry dagger and the stone dagger—but Dakota shook his head.

"Sorry, darlin'," he rasped before trailing his tongue along her throat. "Those stay on."

"Alright then." Trixie sighed. She trailed her fingertips lightly over the leather sheaths and rubbed her thumbs along the handles. All he could think about was having her hands on him like that. "As long as you don't keep your boots on. A girl has to draw the line somewhere."

Mourning the loss of the taste of her, he quickly captured her lips again. He tasted peppermint and whiskey, and Dakota realized he'd been wrong about something. He'd said that the ranch was his home but that wasn't entirely true. His heart would be with this woman for the rest of his existence—no matter how short-lived it might be. Her spirit, heart, mind, and body. That was where he would worship, and that was all he would ever need to know that he was home.

They stood naked in each other's arms, and Dakota
groaned as he reveled in the feel of Trixie's soft curves
against his body. The cool gold coin pressed against his
chest as her breasts melded to him. The soft curve of
her hips and belly was in stark contrast to him. Every
inch of him was wound tight with desperate need and
anticipation. Kissing her deeply, Dakota scooped her
up in his arms and carried her into the hot, welcoming
water of the pool.

She tangled her arms around his neck and sighed
into his mouth as he dipped her deeper under the surface, letting the naturally heated water wash over them.
He tore his lips from hers and held her tightly, while
taking in the glorious feel of her. Trixie's naked skin
was slick and glistened in the moonlight. Her mouth,
swollen from his kisses, parted and revealed the enticing tip of her fangs. She wiggled in his arms and whimpered, a pleading sound that cried for more of what
they both wanted.

Kissing her deeply, he brought her to the edge of the
pool and set her down gently. He knelt in the water, settling between her legs. He pressed one hand to her belly
and urged her to lie back, then curled his other hand
under the crook of her knee. Trixie nodded and leaned
back on her elbows, her lower lip caught between her
teeth. She let out a moan, a needy whimper, and opened
her legs wide.

"Oh my God," Trixie whispered. She settled on one
elbow but her other hand curled around her breast.
Dakota almost lost it when she rolled her erect nipple
between her fingers. "I want to watch you put your
mouth on me. Please, baby."

Dakota linked his arms under her legs and tugged her wider still before leaning in and blowing softly over the swollen flesh. She flinched but he held her, anchoring her to him as he pressed delicate kisses along her quivering inner thigh.

Tell me, Trix. He touched her mind and felt her shudder when their thoughts mingled. *I want to know exactly where you want me to put my mouth.* He licked a hot trail all the way up to the soft flesh along her hot center. *And my tongue. What will make you come the hardest?* He peered at her over her sex and licked her clit in one slow pass. Trixie shuddered in his arms and pinched her nipple harder, her head falling back.

That was all the information he needed. She tasted sweet and hot, and she was all his. He took his time licking and suckling her clit and alternately sliding his two fingers deep into her tight channel. Trixie writhed and bucked as he continued his merciless assault, and as she grew closer to her climax, her sweet juice bathed his tongue.

"Not yet," Trixie gasped as she grabbed his hair and pulled him toward her. "Kiss me... I want to taste myself on your lips."

Dakota groaned at the wicked decadence of her words, and when his tongue met hers in a frenzy, he knew what they both needed. He slipped his arm around her waist and pulled her into the water. Trixie wrapped her legs around him and impaled herself on his thick hot shaft in one swift move. Dakota knelt in the shallow pool and clung to her as she rode him. But as the pace increased, so did the call for blood.

Trixie broke the kiss and stared into his eyes as she

slid up and down on his cock. Fangs bared, she touched his mind with hers. *Let me taste you, Dakota. All of you.* And as his climax began to crest, he tilted his head and Trixie dove deep. Dakota's orgasm erupted violently when her fangs pierced his flesh, and he clung to her like his existence depended on it. Perhaps it did.

He tangled his fingers in her short hair and returned the favor in kind. His fangs broke the barrier of her skin, and he felt her spasm around him as her own climax reached its peak.

Clinging to one another, connected in every way possible, they shuddered as the delicious waves of pleasure ebbed. Wrapped in her arms and with the fog of lust fading, he heard a sound he almost didn't recognize. Amid the distinct pulses of the waning orgasm came the clear and strong beat of his heart. It was perfectly mingled with hers. Dakota licked the wound on her neck closed and lifted his head as their gazes locked.

Neither one wanted to move.

They remained that way, joined in body and mind. They quietly reveled in the hypnotic sound of their long-dormant hearts beating together as one.

What happened in his past might not be able to be undone, and he would likely have to pay for his actions. But in that moment, with her body curled around his and their hearts beating together, he knew it was worth it.

Whatever happened down the road, no one and nothing could take this away.

Chapter 17

TRIXIE WAS FURIOUS WITH HERSELF FOR WAITING SO long to bond with Dakota. The moment his blood touched her lips had been exquisitely intimate and not one she would ever forget. She had been cradled in the very essence of Dakota Shelton.

She saw the almost idyllic childhood he'd had with his parents, who he'd loved and been loved by with Rockwellian-like perfection. She witnessed the cockiness of youth as he rounded up horses and worked the land of the ranch. Her heart ached from the pain and agony of the night he'd been attacked, the satisfaction of revenge when he hunted down the one who had done it, and the outright regret that haunted him for believing Jonner's lies.

Yet through it all, the one fact, the sole truth that rose above the tsunami of his memories was the core goodness and loyal heart of the man who was Dakota Shelton. What had she ever done to deserve this kind of gift from the universe? She smiled at the memory of her last conversation with Damien.

A bloodmate is a gift and not one that should be squandered.

Trixie let out a groan of discontent because right now that gift was covering up his beautiful body with clothing. What a shame. She was pretty sure that he should be naked all the time. Dakota's gifts were not limited to his huge heart.

"Your body is too fine to be covered up like that all the time." Trixie pulled her clothes on over her wet body. She snuck a glance up at the brightening sky before blatantly staring at Dakota's bare chest. "I think that from now on, when we're alone, you should stay naked so I can stare at that gorgeous bod all day long."

"Fine by me, darlin'." He whisked over and planted a firm kiss on her lips before smacking her butt. "But turnabout is fair play. If I'm naked, then so are you, and I won't keep it to lookin'. There'll be lots of touchin'. But we are burnin' moonlight. Let's get a move on and see if you can find your rock pyramid before the sun comes up."

Trixie couldn't help but laugh as she pulled on her leather jacket.

"We could test it out at sunrise and see if the bloodmate bond worked and we can daywalk like the others." She jumped up into his arms and wrapped her legs around him. She wiggled her hips playfully when he palmed her ass with both hands. "What do you think?"

"I think it would be safer to try it near some shelter." Dakota kissed her before placing her on her feet. "Let's go."

"It's gonna be pretty cool to be in the sun again. I mean, it's only been thirty or so years for me but…" Her brow furrowed and her mind careened back to the picture they'd found of the men. She stopped short. "Oh my God."

"What?" Dakota's jaw set and that steely look came over his face again as he scanned the area. "Are you sensin' a gargoyle?"

"No." She shook her head furiously. "The picture

of the gang. The one of Gatlin and the others. It was outside a saloon."

"So?"

"So? It was *outside*." She slapped his arm. "It was during the day. They couldn't take pictures at night…in the dark. Not at that point in time."

"But that can't be possible," he murmured. "Gargoyles turn to stone in the sun and vamps get dusted."

"Well, not those guys apparently." Trixie tangled her hand with his as they walked down the embankment of a hill back toward the house. "Isadora said that Pilar cast some kind of spell and then her lover jilted her. What if she gave them all the ability to walk in the sun? I bet that's it! She cast a spell to make them daywalkers. Think about it, Dakota. It makes sense. She's a witch and has no problem living a regular life among humans. Wouldn't she want her lover to be able to live in the daylight with her?"

"Could be," Dakota said slowly. "If they attacked the gargoyles during daylight hours, that could explain how they were able to make a clean getaway. The rest of the gargoyles couldn't follow them out of the Dome because they'd turn to stone."

"The most annoying part is that we don't *know*, and until we find Gatlin, we're just guessing. He's the only one left alive." Trixie let out an exasperated sigh. "The more I hear about him, the less happy I am that he's my granddaughter's father. He probably only used Chelsea to try to get that gold piece from her."

"I hate to say it but that's likely the case." Dakota turned his gaze to the sky. "We had better get a move on if we want to cover some decent ground before sunrise."

Trixie nodded her understanding. As the two of them took flight and headed for the west side of the Dome, a pang of disappointment fired through her. She almost laughed at her foolishness. She'd put off blood bonding with Dakota all this time and now that she'd finally done it, she was impatient to see it all come to fruition. She rolled her eyes. It would serve her right if the universe decided to take its sweet time.

For the next two hours, they flew low and scanned the entire west side of the Dome, and while there were several unusual rock formations, it seemed like they would never find the one in question. But right as Trixie was about to give up hope, she spotted a large cluster of trees with low-lying branches—much like the ones that had hidden the hot spring.

Let's check out what's under there. She caught Dakota's eye and pointed to the area in question. *It could be interesting.*

Sun's gonna be up soon. He stopped flying and hovered above the tree line. *We can always come back tomorrow.*

It may not be anything, but let's have a look before we head out. She threw a sultry smile his way. *You never know what might be hidden under there.*

Alright, darlin'. Dakota winked and his voice, full of that suggestive rumble she'd come to adore, tickled her mind. *If it's anythin' like the last little bit of heaven we found in the trees, then sign me up.*

They landed silently side by side and Trixie immediately spotted the cluster of rocks they'd been searching for.

"Jackpot," she whispered, a wide grin covering her face.

Trixie held out one hand, which Dakota promptly slapped in a victory high five.

"It's been forty years since I was here." Excitement shimmied up her back. "Jeez. I didn't take into account the changes to the landscape. Those trees were more like bushes or brush when I was a kid."

"Nice job, darlin'." Dakota slipped his arm over her shoulders and kissed the top of her head. "Now all we have to do is find the rest of that gold. It's probably buried under there. We'll have to come back tomorrow night with some shovels."

"Hang on." Trixie scooted over to the boulders and got down on her hands and knees, checking the crevices for evidence. "Maybe not. I found this one right in here. I mean, it was hardly even hidden."

As soon as she got close to the spot, the earth began to shake and the coin on her chain levitated away from her body, as though reaching out in search of the rest of the treasure.

"Holy shit," she whispered.

Dakota was beside her in a blink. He crouched next to her with his back to the boulders, gun drawn and his keen gaze scanning the area around them.

"I don't mean to sound like an ingrate," he whispered. "I'm glad we found it. But I'd be much obliged if this thing wasn't so damn loud. This is too close to the Dome for my liking."

Trixie's teeth clattered as the ground vibrated and the coin hovered in midair. She held up both hands as if in surrender, kneeling in front of the boulders.

"Take it off, Trix," Dakota said quietly. "It's tryin' to go somewhere, so I say we let it."

Trixie nodded and licked her lower lip as she carefully pulled the chain over her head. She held the chain and let out a shuddering gasp. The coin floated away and slowly up the side of the structure, and the gold links slipped through her shaking fingers. She and Dakota got to their feet and stood side by side as the gargoyles' gold made its journey.

The vibrating grew stronger when the coin reached the pinnacle of the pyramid and erupted in a blinding flash of green light. It was so bright that Dakota and Trixie briefly shielded their eyes. When they dropped their hands, it was to the gritty sounds of rocks moving and grinding against the earth.

The large pyramid of stones began to open, almost like a rock flower that had started to bloom in the sunlight. Dakota linked his hand around Trixie's arm as they backed up to avoid being crushed by the enormous rocks. The earth shook one last time when the last stone hit the ground. The coin drifted gently down before landing with a high-pitched clink on top of an open black bag full of gold.

"Son of a bitch," Dakota murmured. "That Rathbone woman sure did find one hell of a hidin' place."

"We did it!" Trixie jumped into his arms and hugged him tightly. "Everything is going to be okay," she whispered. "We can give it back to the gargoyles and Zhao will have to pardon you."

Her joy was cut short when the familiar scent of rotten flowers drifted over them with the breeze.

Then, as if they'd been doing it all their lives, Trixie and Dakota shifted their positions so that they were back-to-back and ready for battle. *Do you smell that?* Trixie asked.

Sure do. And I can't help but notice that you aren't feelin' sick. Dakota withdrew the stone dagger from the sheath on his wrist and then handed his gun to Trixie. *It's loaded with thirty silver rounds and the safety is off.*

Got it. While she was grateful to not be incapacitated by nausea and pain, she was also confused. *What the hell is going on, Dakota? It smells like a gargoyle but...not.*

The wind picked up and with it came more of the flowery aroma.

But there was something else mingled with it, another scent that she couldn't put her finger on. Trixie sharpened her focus and raised the gun, clutching it tightly in both hands, wanting to be ready for who or whatever was lurking in the shadows.

Don't move. I know that scent. Dakota's voice, dark and serious, filled her head and she could feel his tense form directly behind her. *I'll be a son of a bitch... It's Jonner.*

Before she could say what-the-hell-do-you-mean-it's-your-dead-maker, Jonner shot down from the sky and slammed into Trixie and Dakota, instantly separating the two. Trixie was knocked to the ground and rolled to the right, but quickly recovered and started to scramble to her feet. Fangs bared and gun at the ready, she crouched and spun on her heel in search of Dakota and Jonner.

The two vampires were nowhere to be seen. And as she scanned the area, the rock pyramid closed up, once again concealing the treasure within.

Run, Trixie. Dakota's voice, gruff and pained, echoed in her head. *Get the hell out of here.*

No way. She rose to her feet, gun in hand and desperate to find him. She spun. The sound of grunting and growling cut through the night. She was looking in the wrong place. *I'm not leaving you here.*

They were above her.

Get him on the ground, Dakota. Trixie pointed her gun at the sky as Dakota wrestled in midair with his maker, who was obviously not dead. They tumbled and battled, with the moon looming behind them. She struggled to separate one from the other as their grunts of fury filled the air. Trixie sharpened her focus and aimed her gun toward them. *I can't get a clear shot.*

Don't shoot him, Trixie, Dakota grunted. *This is my kill.*

Trixie lowered her weapon only for a moment. The cramp in her stomach hit her right before a second gargoyle did. The massive creature slammed into her from the right and sent her tumbling to the ground. The fall knocked her gun from her grip and it went skittering across the dirt. Even though she wanted to retrieve it, her bigger concern was trying to avoid the poison-tipped talons of the gargoyle.

Trixie flipped onto her back and grabbed the gargoyle's grotesque arms. The beast had to outweigh her by at least a hundred pounds. Its greenish-gray leathery body was thick and muscular, and a pair of yellow glowing eyes glared at her with blind—almost hypnotic—fury.

In that moment, she knew the monster had only one thought on its mind—to kill her.

It was no wonder these things were tasked with protecting humans. They were as powerful as vampires, and that made them a formidable enemy. With all of her strength, fangs bared and arms shaking, she held it away from her. She only had a moment. Trixie pulled her knees in and planted her feet on its torso. With one massive rush of effort she shoved the creature away from her body. She scuttled onto the balls of her feet and the gargoyle shrieked with frustration, flapping its massive wings.

It shifted its weight from one clawed foot to the other, as though weighing its options. Trixie could hear the clash still raging in the air above her but she dared not look away even for a second.

"That's all you've got?" Furious but surprisingly invigorated by the attack, she fleetingly wondered if all of her fight training had been preparing her for this moment. Trixie narrowed her gaze and waved the crea- ture toward her with both hands. "How about you bring that ugly ass a little closer." She gave it a big, fang-filled smile. "I didn't get a kiss."

Screeching, the gargoyle lunged toward Trixie with outstretched hands. She spun on her left foot, swung her right leg around, and delivered a round- house kick to its face. The gargoyle stumbled back but recovered quickly and slashed at Trixie with its poison-tipped claws.

She dodged to her left and grunted with the effort. The talons whisked by her cheek with a whistling sound, barely missing her. Trixie tried to lunge over and get the gun, but the beast managed to herd her away from the weapon. And as it did, one hand shot out and swiped those claws through the flesh of her forearm.

A horrid burning sensation sizzled in Trixie's blood

as the talons tore her skin and the poison hit her blood-stream. She screamed in pain and rage and stumbled backward, clutching the wound on her arm. Her vision blurred as the poison seeped through her body, but she continued to fight.

The gargoyle kept coming, despite each punch she landed and every powerful kick. For the first time since that night in the tunnels when Olivia found her, Trixie could see death's door. The only difference was that this time she didn't want to die.

For once in her life, human or vampire, she had several good reasons to live. She had too much to lose to simply give up and tumble into the abyss of oblivion.

Dakota. Chelsea. Rebecca. Family. Love.

Trixie's strength drained from her body by the second. She cursed the fact that she hadn't had a live feed for so long. If she had fed from a live human, maybe the poison wouldn't be affecting her so strongly. And that was when she knew she only had one choice left.

Badly wounded and with no weapon, there was only one other option—feed off the gargoyle. She didn't know what gargoyle blood would do to her but she did know that if she drained the beast, at least it would no longer be a threat to her or Dakota.

Almost completely blinded by the poison, Trixie pushed herself off the ground as the creature lunged toward her. With one final rush of strength, she did a flip in midair before landing on the gargoyle's back with a grunt. She hung on tightly as it bucked and shrieked in a desperate attempt to shake her off, but Trixie had an ironclad grip. Her life and her family depended on it.

Dakota had said he wanted to teach her how to ride,

but this was probably not what he had in mind. She'd seen him ride that gargoyle in the alley in New York City, and even through the pain and confusion, it had reminded her of a bucking bronco.

Her arms were clamped tightly around the gargoyle's neck and her legs clenched down like Dakota's had, pinning the wings so it couldn't fly. She reared her head back and with a bellow of rage, she sank her fangs into the gargoyle's thick leathery flesh. As soon as the potent blood hit her tongue, Trixie's entire body lit up like the Fourth of July. Power surged beneath her skin like an electric current, reenergizing her strength like never before. She drank greedily and the gargoyle dropped to his knees, quickly weakened by the loss of blood, but Trixie didn't relent.

Along with the power surge came the blood memories of her attacker. It was Henry.

He'd snuck out again for a night of freedom among the humans. Whiskey. Music. Dancing. A young woman with raven hair and a sexy smile. A quickie beneath the stars in the bed of his pickup truck. He stumbled into the darkness still high off the sex; he was stopped by an evil grin and the seductive whisper of a vampire's glamour effect.

Jonner's face was the final image that filled Trixie's mind.

Chapter 18

DAKOTA WRESTLED WITH JONNER IN MIDAIR, STILL NOT quite believing the truth.

His maker was alive. The son of a bitch had been alive all along.

Dakota swept around Jonner, who glared at him with a familiar wicked grin. The older vampire easily dodged the silver throwing stars that were flung in his direction. Dakota lunged again, wanting to rip Jonner's heart out of his chest for the lies and betrayal, but when he spotted the gargoyle attacking Trixie on the ground below, he lost his focus.

"No!" Dakota's chest clenched with fear when his bloodmate, the only woman he'd ever dared love, went tumbling to the ground beneath the bulk of an attacking gargoyle. "Trixie!"

That was why he didn't see the next blow coming.

Something sharp swept across his back and tore through his leather coat and shirt. The force of it knocked him out of the sky and sent him tumbling to the ground. Dakota didn't feel the pain at first, too consumed by worry about Trixie. But when he tried to get to his feet, he knew his situation was dire. White-hot agony ripped through his bloodstream and sent him to his knees as Jonner hit him with another blow. This time, the pain was instantaneous and almost blinded him.

Dakota gritted his teeth and struggled to stand, but

he was robbed of most of his strength. Jonner must have shot him or stabbed him with silver. That *had* to be what was rippling though his body and killing him slowly. Writhing against the pain, his body contorting, Dakota willed himself to his knees and found himself staring into the unfeeling face of his maker.

"It's fitting, really." Jonner let out a short laugh and adjusted the long coat he was wearing. The flowery scent of a gargoyle rolled off him, only adding to Dakota's confusion. "You almost died out here over fifty years ago, but I needed another pair of eyes and you were in the right place at the right time."

"Why?"

"You were young, strong, and you knew this area like the back of your hand." Jonner braced his hands on his knees and made a *tsking* noise. "Not so strong anymore."

"Fuck you," Dakota seethed. He bared his fangs and pushed himself to one knee before finally standing on his own two feet. "You used me. There was no top secret task force. You were after the gold the whole damn time. You let that gargoyle almost kill me just so you could turn me and get me to help you hunt them down."

"True." Jonner sighed. A wicked grin slithered over his face as he pulled something from beneath his jacket. Dakota shook his head, trying to clear his vision, and a moment later the severed hand of a gargoyle came into focus. "Well, partially true. There was no gargoyle that night, just this handy little souvenir from our heist in the gargoyles' lair. It turns out that the poison on the claws works with or without a living, breathing gargoyle. Their flesh makes a lovely coat too, don't you think? Cloaks my scent nicely."

"You son of a bitch." Dakota wavered on his feet but kept his sights on Jonner. The coat his maker wore was made from the skin of a gargoyle. "You're a psycho. Wiping out the gargoyles for profit?"

"The gargoyles are too stupid to live," Jonner spat out. "The hideous wretches belong hidden away underground. And the witch? She was a great fuck and cast a hell of a spell, turning us into daywalkers for the big heist, but she was too clingy. I gave the whiny bitch her cut of the gold like we agreed on and then told her to take a hike."

"Didn't work out so well for you, did it?" Dakota slid his fingers beneath the sleeve of his coat and stilled when they brushed the handle of the dagger. "She made your gold disappear."

"Stupid whore," Jonner shouted. He waved the gargoyle claw and his fangs glinted in the moonlight. "It all vanished. All of it. Disappeared right in front of me. Before I drained her dry, she told me that only another Rathbone witch would be able to find the gold. She said that was my punishment for refusing her love," he said with sarcasm. "Can you believe that shit? I gave her enough gold to set her up for life and the dumb broad was babbling about love."

"Why fake your death?" Dakota tried to keep him talking, fighting the panic when he realized Trixie wasn't moving. "Why didn't you keep doing what you were doing?"

"The Presidium kept getting in my way," Jonner scoffed. "I didn't want them running my entire existence. I had another fifty years to serve as a sentry and that was more than I wanted to do. You know how they are. Honor, duty, and all that crap. Death was more appealing." He grinned. "I had enough money squirreled away from some of my other enterprises… so I waited. I knew if I waited long enough, eventually I'd find one of the Rathbone witches. Pilar was smarter than I gave her credit for though. She not only hid the gold but she hid her kids too. She knew I'd go after them to use them to find the gold, so she cloaked them in a spell. But like most spells, it eventually wore off."

Jonner moved slowly to his right and Dakota countered, matching him. When he caught sight of where Jonner was heading, fury fired through him. Trixie.

"You waited for one of her descendants to surface." Dakota blinked to try and clear his vision, but it was getting worse.

"Looks like my waiting paid off."

In a flash, Jonner grabbed Trixie by the neck and pulled her to her feet. She was barely conscious, the gargoyle at her feet close to dead. Dakota started toward him but Jonner held the gargoyle claw to Trixie's throat, stopping him in his tracks. Jonner held her limp form against his chest and leaned in before running his tongue along her throat. "Mmm…I bet she tastes sweet. Tell me, Shelton. Is she as good a fuck as her great-granny?"

Rage-fueled bile rose in Dakota's throat. "Put her down." He steadied himself and slowly moved his hand toward his other wrist. The sterling-silver sentry dagger—the one he'd cherished for so many years, the one he'd thought was an honorable weapon left over from his dead maker—was mere inches from his grasp.

"You got what you wanted. The gold is under there. Take it and get the fuck away from us."

"I need your little vampire-witch slut to open it up for me." He shook Trixie violently and shouted, "Anyone home? Wake up, witch. You have a job to do."

Trixie's eyes snapped open at the same moment Dakota's fingers curled around the leather-bound handle of the sentry dagger. Movement to the right caught Jonner's attention momentarily, and at the same instant, the pungent scent of a gargoyle filled the night. The older vampire hissed and snapped his head toward the disturbance in the air.

"I have something of yours, Jonner," Dakota murmured. "It's about time you get it back."

Now, Dakota. Trixie's voice shouted into his mind. *Throw it.*

At the same instant Dakota threw the dagger, Trixie grabbed the vampire's arm and hurled her legs up, flipping herself over Jonner's head and out of his grasp. She landed in a crouch behind Jonner as the dagger slammed into his chest. The only sight more satisfying than the look of shock on his face was the moment when the traitorous bastard burst into flames and dissolved into a pile of dust.

Exhausted and barely able to stay conscious, Dakota fell to the ground in a heap. Trixie was safe. The gargoyles would get their gold back. As the world around him faded, a smile curved his lips because he had done what he wanted.

He made things right.

Dakota Shelton could die a happy man.

"Dakota!" Trixie screamed his name and flew to him. She knelt by his side and pulled his head into her lap, but he was completely unconscious. "Baby, please wake up."

Blood seeped from the wounds on his back, soaking her jeans, a sickening sign of the severity of his injuries. That poison was ravaging him from the inside out. Without gargoyle blood, Dakota was going to die.

A sob of desperation escaped her lips. She looked around frantically but Henry was gone. He must have come to and run off. Not that she could blame him; he was as much a victim as anyone else. Yet another person manipulated and used by Jonner.

Trixie pierced the skin of her wrist with her fangs before holding it over Dakota's mouth and allowing the blood to do its job. She knew the odds of her blood helping him were slim, but it was her last hope.

Tears spilled down her cheeks as the sun began to make its arrival but still he did not stir. She clung to him and whispered into his mind. *Dakota...please don't leave me. I love you.*

She was met with deafening and heartbreaking silence.

Trixie let out a shuddering sob as a pale glow burned brighter on the horizon.

If the bloodmate bond hadn't worked, they'd both be dead in a few minutes anyway. Trixie pushed a lock of hair aside and pressed a kiss to Dakota's forehead, allowing his distinct scent of sandalwood and leather to surround her.

If they were going to die, then at least they would be together.

Movement in the trees caught her attention. Trixie bared her fangs and hissed a warning. The raspy voice of a man whispered through the trees and with it came a gargoyle's scent. "Let me help."

At first she thought that Henry had returned. Trixie glanced to her left and a man emerged from behind a tree trunk. To her surprise, she found herself staring into a familiar face—it was Chelsea's boyfriend, Gatlin.

"Gatlin?" Trixie sniffled and held on to Dakota protectively, but when she realized Gatlin was alone, it only increased her panic. "What are you doing here? Where's my granddaughter?"

"Rebecca is safe." He held up both hands and dipped his head. "I promise. I'm sorry I ran, but I knew Jonner was back and I had to keep her away from him." He extended his arm to Trixie. "Here. Use my blood to heal him."

"Are you serious?" She flicked her gaze to his bare forearm. "After everything you've done, why should I trust you?"

"Because I love your daughter." Gatlin dropped to his knees, his arm extended. "If you let me help Dakota, he'll be able to tell you everything when he wakes up."

Trixie paused and bit her lower lip before casting a glance to the ever-brightening sky. A sliver of the sun had crested, and though the shade of the trees would buy them some time, it definitely would not be a lot.

"You should hurry," he whispered. "The poison moves fast and gargoyle blood is the only cure."

Trixie hesitated. Could it be a trick?

"Time's running out." He jerked his head to the horizon. "In a few minutes, I won't have anything to offer.

After all, you can't get blood from a stone." A sheepish grin curved his lips. "And make sure he takes it all. Jonner dosed him heavily."

"All of it? But if he takes too much—"

"Just do it," he snapped. His expression softened and his mouth set in a grim line. "I can't change what I did all those years ago, but I can do this. I can make Chelsea and Rebecca proud of me. I want to leave my daughter more than a legacy of betrayal."

"Fine." Trixie snapped her mouth open and bared her fangs. "But if you make one wrong move, make no mistake about it, I *will* eviscerate you."

"Right." Gatlin's eyes widened and he swallowed hard but he kept his arm out. "I-I understand."

With no other options, Trixie took his wrist in her hand and bit down, keeping her eyes locked with his. He winced and when the wound began to bleed, Gatlin brought it to Dakota's mouth. To Trixie's utter relief, within seconds Dakota's lips clamped over the gargoyle's wrist and he drank greedily.

A few minutes passed, and with each second, Dakota grew stronger. At the same time, Gatlin was starting to fade. He slumped to a sitting position and his eyes fluttered closed, all the color draining from his face. Trixie helped Dakota sit up as he released Gatlin's arm and licked the wound closed. She barely noticed when Gatlin crawled over to the base of one of the trees, seeking out the protective shade.

Without waiting for Dakota to say a word, she wrapped her arms around his neck and hugged him tightly, her mind instantly seeking out his. *I almost lost you.* She pressed her face into the crook of his neck and squeezed her eyes shut, reveling in the feel of his strong body and the beautiful, comforting scent of sandalwood.

Dakota pulled back and cradled her face in his hands. He pressed a firm kiss to her lips, and when his mind slipped into hers, she almost wept with relief. *Baby, you ain't never gettin' rid of me.*

Trixie giggled and rested her forehead against his. She was so caught up in the feel of him that it took her a moment to realize that the sun had risen. A delicious blanket of warmth, one she vaguely could recall from her human life, spread slowly over them. Trixie linked her fingers with his. Golden rays of sunlight danced over their intertwined hands, and for the first time in decades, neither of them was burned by it.

"Oh my God," Trixie said with pure wonder. "It worked. The bloodmate bond worked."

"See that, woman." Dakota pushed himself to his feet with a grunt and pulled her up with him. "Now you're never gettin' away. Daytime. Nighttime. Darlin', I'm not gonna give you a moment's peace."

"You better not." Trixie punched him playfully in the gut, but her smile faded quickly when she spotted Gatlin. "We might be daywalkers, but Gatlin isn't."

Dakota and Trixie went to him and as the sun began to peek through the leaves, it was clear that Gatlin was no longer immune to the sunlight. Whatever spell Pilar had cast all those years ago was long gone.

"What can I do?" Dakota asked. His eyes were rimmed with empathy as he laid a hand on Gatlin's shoulder. "After what you did for me. How can I repay you?"

"Let's call it even," Gatlin bit out. "No one owes me anything."

A look of understanding passed between the two men and Trixie knew that there had to be more to Gatlin's story. Now that Dakota had read his blood memories, he seemed to have sympathy for him.

"Help me up." Gatlin gritted his teeth. Trixie and Dakota each took a hand and helped him to his feet. "I will not die sitting on my ass."

"Die?" Trixie looked from Gatlin to Dakota, whose expression was grim. "What are you talking about? What about Chelsea and Rebecca?"

"They'll have both of you." Gatlin limped away and put his hand up when they tried to stop him. He shuffled closer to the encroaching sunlight and a green glow began to emanate from his body. "I've caused enough misery for one lifetime. He knows how to get into the Dome now." He stood taller and flicked his serious dark eyes to Dakota. "You tell them what happened. Will you? Tell Queen Alana that I tried to make it right. Promise me that you'll return the gold to them and tell my story. I never meant for anyone to get hurt."

"I will." Dakota tilted his head in deference and linked his arm around Trixie's waist. "You have my word."

"Hang on," Trixie shouted. "What about Chelsea? What do I tell her?"

"You tell her that I love her." He clutched his side and grimaced but continued toward the sunlight. "When we met that first time at the coffee shop to talk about the coin…she flashed that beautiful smile and I was a goner." He sighed. "It was like she flipped a switch inside me. Woke me up. I think I fell in love with her that afternoon."

"You should be the one to tell her all of this," Trixie pleaded.

"No more time." His boots touched the edge of the shade line and he cast one last glance at Trixie over his shoulder. A sad smile curved his lips. "I do love them, you know. Please make sure Chelsea and Rebecca know that."

Trixie moved to stop him, but Gatlin stepped into the sun, and an emerald-green light erupted from him. He shifted into his gargoyle form and spread his massive wings wide. A crackling sound split the early morning air. The sunlight shining over his weakened form grew stronger, and a split second later, two massive fissures rippled up Gatlin's stone body.

As the sun moved higher in the sky, Gatlin's body exploded, then crumbled into a pile of dust.

A combination of sadness and relief settled in Trixie's chest as she snuggled deeper into Dakota's strong embrace. Gatlin gave his life to save Dakota. It was a clear example that mistakes and poor choices from the past didn't have to define the future. Gatlin may not have lived most of his life like an honorable man, but he chose to die like one. Would that be enough to soothe Chelsea's broken heart? And what about the baby? Rebecca would never know her father.

"Please tell me that you know where the baby is," Trixie said, grimacing. She pulled back to look him in the face, and when his eyes crinkled at the corners, relief flooded her. But that was quickly replaced by excitement. "Well, don't keep me in suspense. Where is my granddaughter?"

"She's with Hector and Addie. The boy went

old-school and put her in a basket on their front porch with a note sayin' she belonged with you and me." Dakota squinted in the sunlight. "Gatlin knew what the endgame would be, what it had to be."

"The endgame for him, sure." Trixie hugged him tightly and peered at the Dome, a shudder rippling through her. "But what about for us? What if the gargoyles and the emperor aren't as forgiving as we hope they are?"

"How about we get on over to the ranch and see that baby girl?" He kissed the top of her head before tangling her hand with his. "Once we get the ball rolling to bring the gold back to the gargoyles, I'm going to have my hands full with Presidium politics. I say we take one more day...and one more night...just for us."

Trixie nodded but said nothing. If she tried to speak, she'd start blubbering again like a lovesick teenage girl. He squeezed her hand and sadness flickered behind those pale blue eyes before he led her into the sunlight and toward an uncertain future.

Chapter 19

LUCKILY, HECTOR AND ADDIE HAD HEARD THE BABY crying within a few minutes of Gatlin leaving her on the porch. They'd brought her in and Addie immediately went about fixing her up a bottle with some of the formula that was in the bag. When Dakota and Trixie got back to the house, it was as if the baby had always been there. Addie and Hector were doting on little Rebecca like she was their own. Dakota even caught cranky old Hector making silly faces at her.

Dakota leaned against the wall with his arms folded over his chest, taking in the oddly normal scene, but he couldn't stop stealing looks at Trixie. She was curled up on the couch with the baby in her arms. That's where she'd been since they got back to the house hours ago. The expression on her face was one of pure peace and love. It was the first time he'd seen Trixie look totally and completely at ease, and he was pretty sure he could watch her hold that baby every minute of every hour of every day for the rest of his existence.

To say she was in her glory would have been an understatement. But the truth was, so was he. He never thought he'd have a family like this once he'd been turned vamp. The joy was only tempered by the fact that his undead life was probably on borrowed time.

Dakota had already spoken with Olivia, and it wasn't looking good for him. He'd told her what had happened and what he and Trixie planned on doing with the gold, but she didn't seem overly optimistic about his future. All he knew was that Emperor Zhao was on route to the States and wanted to speak with Dakota face-to-face.

Great. The most powerful vampire in the world was pissed at him. This was exactly his kind of luck. Here he finally had the family he never dared dream possible, and a three-thousand-year-old vampire was coming to New York to execute him.

He was screwed.

"Now, Dakota," Addie said sweetly. She was wiping down the big table, cleaning up after dinner, when she flicked her big eyes to his. "Gettin' a sweet baby girl dropped on my porch before sunup was more than enough surprise for one day, but when you and Trixie came strollin' up to the house in the light of day?" She waved a hand like she was having heatstroke. "Well, that almost had me thinkin' I was hallucinatin'!"

"Sorry, Addie." Dakota took off his long coat and draped it over the back of the large sectional. He smiled at Trixie and reminded himself that Hector and Addie didn't know about the gargoyles or little Rebecca's true parentage. "It looks like our visit has caused you two more stress than I intended."

"No worries," Addie said with a nervous laugh. She wrung the dish towel between her pudgy hands and hurried back into the kitchen. "Does that mean y'all are cured?"

"No, ma'am." Dakota settled his hands on his hips and chose his words carefully. "Let's just say that me and Trixie got an extra bonus. Sunlight isn't a problem for us anymore, and I want to assure you that we'll be out of your hair tomorrow. We have one more item to take care of before we head back to the city with little Rebecca."

"She's your *granddaughter*, Trixie?" Addie's confused expression was almost comical. "Is that right?"

"Yes, ma'am." Trixie shifted her position and put the baby on her shoulder, gently patting her back. She peered across the room at Dakota and smirked. "But she's just a regular human baby. She's one of my descendants and I'm going to take her back to New York City to her mama. Her daddy couldn't take care of her anymore."

Silence filled the house for a few moments, but Dakota didn't miss the look that Hector and Addie exchanged. Hector was finishing his dinner, and as usual, he hadn't said much all day.

"I see y'all got that book about the town's history and downloaded it on the computer." Hector pushed himself away from the table and hitched up his pants. "Anythin' interestin' in there? I've been meanin' to read it myself."

"Thank you for that, but no...nothin' of any interest really." Dakota shook his head slowly, but a tickle of warning flickered up his back. "I just thought it would be fun for Trixie to learn more about where I grew up. After all, the Shelton family has been here for generations."

"It surely has," Hector said quietly as he grabbed his hat by the front door before pulling on his coat. "There's been a Shelton here since the town rose up out of the dirt." He tugged the door open and a brisk wind blew in, prompting Trixie to cuddle the baby back into her arms. She cooed and tightened the pink blanket around the sleeping infant. "I best be gettin' back out to the horses. Miguel already headed home for the day. Thanks for dinner, Addie."

The sun was beginning to set, and even though Dakota would like nothing more than to let Trixie hold Rebecca through the night, there was one more job to do. They had to get that gold and return it to the gargoyles beneath the Dome.

He rose to his feet and touched her mind with his. *Time to go, darlin'.*

"Already?" Trixie's shoulders sagged but she nodded her agreement. She carried Rebecca into the kitchen and passed the adorable little bundle to Addie. "She finished that whole bottle and burped a bunch. She should sleep for a while. I can come back and get her later," she added quickly.

"Don't be silly," Addie cooed. She kissed the baby's forehead and kept her voice to a whisper. "You two go do what you need to do. She'll be just fine. Babies need a schedule and some normalcy. No point in shufflin' her around tonight. I'll put her bassinet in the guest room and sleep in there with her."

"Will Hector be okay with that?" Trixie asked.

"Oh please." Addie rolled her eyes. "He probably won't even notice I'm not there. The man sleeps like a log and snores like a freight train. Besides, the Lord never blessed us with a baby of our own. It'll be fun for me."

With Trixie's hand planted firmly in his, Dakota practically dragged the woman out of the house and down the steps. That didn't stop her from repeatedly looking over her shoulder and nibbling on her lower lip, the sweet gesture that belied her nervousness.

"She'll be fine, darlin'." He brought her hand to his lips and pressed a kiss there. "And you need to focus."

"I know." Trixie sighed. "But after everything that's happened, I hate to let her out of my sight."

"Then let's do what we need to do so we can get on with our future."

Once they were past the barn and had hiked over the ridge, putting the ranch house and the barns out of sight, Trixie and Dakota leaped into the early evening air. The sun had finally dipped below the horizon and the stars were beginning to glimmer in the deep purple sky. Being able to walk in the sun again had been wonderful, especially with Trixie by his side, but Dakota would never tire of the night. Evening was peaceful and comforting, and he hoped like hell that the emperor would have mercy on him so he could enjoy many more nights like this one with Trixie.

They landed quietly by the pyramid of rocks, and as far as Dakota could tell, it looked exactly like they had left it hours ago. Trixie rubbed her palms on her jean-covered thighs and cautiously approached. He scanned the area, assuring there was no imminent threat, and provided cover for her while she knelt next to the rock formation.

Unlike before, this time nothing happened.

"Now what?" Trixie sat on her heels and glowered at the pyramid. "Maybe I needed the gold to open this thing up."

"Damned if I know, darlin'." He holstered his

weapon and rubbed his hands together before waving her away. "Maybe what we need is some good old-fashioned brute strength."

"Right," Trixie snorted with laughter. "This pile of gold is hidden with a witch whammy, and you think you're just gonna knock these over like bowling pins?"

"Can't hurt to try."

Dakota spit on both hands and rubbed them together before using all of his strength to try to push one of the rocks aside. He grunted and strained but the damn thing didn't move an inch.

"Well, shit." He dropped his arms to his sides and stepped back, feeling more than a bit embarrassed. Avoiding Trixie's gaze, he rolled his shoulder, which was actually feeling strained from the effort. "It's the spell… Has to be."

"Uh-huh." Trixie smirked and patted him on the arm. "It's okay, babe. I know you're strong. Let me try something." Trixie stepped between Dakota and the pyramid, raising her hands so they were just inches from the boulders. She closed her eyes. "Maybe if I imagine the rocks opening up, just like they did before…" Her barely audible voice trailed off and her focus was intense.

Within seconds, Dakota detected a subtle pulse in the air that rippled and throbbed off Trixie's body, much like it had with the computer. He took a few steps back, wanting to give her space. As the waves of energy increased, the earth began to shake.

"You're doin' it, Trix," Dakota whispered. "It's working." His chest puffed up with pride as the rocks opened up and revealed the treasure hidden within.

When the massive boulders slammed onto the ground,

Trixie's arms dropped to her sides and she wavered on her feet. Dakota caught her before she fainted.

"Trixie?" He knelt down and cradled her in his lap, while trying to shove aside the cold finger of dread. "You did it...baby?" His gut clenched with fear when she didn't respond right away, but a few seconds later, those gorgeous brown eyes fluttered open.

"Oh, hey," she murmured, a small smile curving her lips "Did it work?"

"It sure did. But if you're gonna pass out when you use your witchy wiles, I'd just as soon you didn't pursue that particular hobby." He helped her to a sitting position and tapped the tip of her nose. "I like my women to be conscious, thank you very much. Even if you do enjoy fightin' with me half the time."

"Oh, please. You love it." She rolled her eyes and pushed her blond-and-blue-streaked hair off her face before pushing herself to her feet. "Is all the gold still—" She stopped mid-sentence and her body went completely still. Trixie's hand curled around his and she inched closer as the distinct scent of gargoyle rushed over them. *We've got company.*

Gargoyles. Definitely more than one. I'm bettin' on several by the smell of it. Dakota slowly removed the gun from his holster and lowered it to his side as he scanned the area. But even with his night vision, he saw nothing. *No pain this time?*

No. Now it's more like a tingling in my belly, but it's not painful. Trixie shook her head, but he could feel the tension in her body as she inched closer to him. *This is so weird. I don't know what's going on. Maybe we should just go and let them take the gold.*

No way. Dakota caught sight of movement above them and the unmistakable sound of wings filled the air. *We don't know who they are, and there's no guarantee they'll take it back to the gargoyles in the Dome.*

Before she could answer him, two massive gargoyles swept down and landed in front of them, their wings spread wide. They were bigger than the others he'd seen recently. Each of them stood over six feet tall and had a ten-foot wingspan. Seconds later two more hulking beasts landed behind Dakota and Trixie, along with one on either side.

We're in trouble, darlin'. Dakota's gruff voice sounded in her head as pulled her into his embrace and held her tightly against him. *We're surrounded. I count at least six.*

Something is definitely different. Their eyes aren't glowing. The two at the club, their eyes glowed yellow and so did Henry's last night. Trixie looked around at the six massive creatures. Moving slowly, obviously not wanting to incite the creatures, she slipped from Dakota's arms and turned so that they stood back to back. *Why aren't they attacking us?*

A rustling in the air above captured his attention, and when he looked to the sky, he spotted at least eight gargoyles flying in formation. He and Trixie were corralled like horses and there was nowhere to go. He wished he was better at politics and diplomacy, because fighting their way out wasn't a viable option.

Stick close. Dakota's voice touched her mind as his hand linked with hers. The tension in his voice was matched by the tension in his body. *If this goes bad, you fly your ass out of here and don't look back.*

Yeah, right. Trixie retorted. *Do you know me at all? I don't cut and run, baby, and I'm not starting now.*

Woman…

Save the bossy bloodmate crap. Trixie gave his hand a reassuring squeeze. *Or I might have to kick your butt in front of all these gargoyles.*

Promises, promises. Besides, I have a plan.

"You have something that belongs to us." A woman's voice, almost angelic in nature, rippled around them like music.

At first, Dakota couldn't tell where it was coming from. His answer arrived when two gargoyles in front of him lowered their wings and revealed a gorgeous young woman. Her petite form was covered by green gown with a billowy skirt, her long flowing sleeves glittering like emeralds in the moonlight. She had waist-length platinum blond hair and the biggest, greenest eyes Dakota had ever seen on any creature—human or supernatural. Given the jeweled crown on her pretty little head, he could only assume this was Queen Alana of the gargoyles, the sole remaining member of the royal family.

She moved slowly toward them, and the two gargoyles on either side of her bowed low as she made her approach. The minute she passed them, they stood tall and spread their wings wide, once again creating a complete circle around him, Trixie, and the gold.

"I never thought I would meet one of the executioners in person," the queen said with little humor.

"I assume you're talkin' about me." Dakota kept his gun at his side and his gaze on the queen.

"You assume correctly. You can put your gun away,

sentry," she said calmly. Her hands were clasped in front of her and she exuded serenity. "If I wanted to kill you, then you would already be dead. As you can see, you are quite outnumbered."

"That's comforting," he murmured with a smirk. He holstered his weapon and bowed his head. "You must be Queen Alana."

"Yes." She flicked her enormous green eyes to Trixie. "And this is a Rathbone witch who is also a vampire? Interesting."

"Mostly vampire, by the way. And for the record, we don't want your gold," Trixie chimed in. She jutted her thumb over her shoulder to the open pyramid behind them. "In fact, we were coming to get it so that we could give it back to you. I know you probably won't believe—"

Alana held up one hand and her lips curved in a smile, but there was strength and determination in her eyes. "I know why you are here." She waved her hand and the gargoyles behind her dropped their wings. "And what has recently transpired."

A moment later, Henry shuffled out of the darkness with his head down and a sheepish expression on his face. He hurried in and stood beside the queen with his cowboy hat in his hands, all while avoiding Dakota's gaze.

"Henry?" Trixie said with obvious relief. "Oh man, I am so glad you're okay. But, dude, you totally tried to kill me."

"I'm sorry, I—"

"Silence." The queen's voice was quiet but commanding, and Henry immediately shut up. "You'll have to pardon my son. He sometimes forgets his place."

"Your son?" Dakota and Trixie asked in unison.

You weren't kidding about the slow aging thing. Trixie touched his mind and even though she was trying to be playful, he could tell how nervous she was.

"Yes. It seems he's been getting himself into trouble and coming up to the surface, even though it has been forbidden. I caught him sneaking back into the Dome, and after some coaxing, he told me what happened."

"Right, about that..." Trixie cracked her knuckles and let out a nervous laugh. "Sorry about the whole drinking-your-blood thing, Henry, but—"

"Normally, I would not approve of a vampire feeding on any of my people, let alone my own child. However, if you had not done that, Jonner's glamour effect might not have been broken and my son might well have been lost to me. And I have already lost enough."

"That's why Henry's eyes were glowing all weird!" Trixie elbowed Dakota. "Just like the two that attacked us in the city. Jonner must have glamoured them to attack us."

"It would seem so," the queen said quietly. "Two of my guards went missing recently while patrolling on the outskirts of the Dome. We detected some unusual activity in the area, and though I was reluctant to do so, I sent them to the surface. They never returned. I can only assume they are the two you speak of."

"So"—Trixie arched one eyebrow—"you're not pissed?"

"Henry told me what you did." She flicked her gaze to Dakota. "You destroyed Jonner and recovered our gold."

"Yes, ma'am." Dakota squared his shoulders and

bit back the regret that bubbled up from the sins of his past. "But that doesn't erase the damage I did as an...executioner."

"From what I am told, you were manipulated and lied to by him, much like we were. He was allowed into the Dome under the guise of creating a peace treaty between our people and the vampires. But he betrayed my father's trust, slaughtered my family, and stole our gold."

"You have to know that Emperor Zhao and the Presidium had nothin' to do with that." Dakota stood tall and braced himself for whatever this woman was going to throw at him. "Gatlin didn't know what Jonner was plannin' either, but I can tell you that he gave his life to save mine. I know 'sorry' ain't gonna cut it, but that's about all I've got. If I could go back and fix it, I would. All I can offer you is my regret."

"Do you think an apology is going to atone for the lives you took?" Her voice remained as calm as her demeanor. "Erase what has happened?"

"No," he said firmly. "But you can take my life if it will make you feel better. All I ask is that you let Trixie go."

"No way," Trixie shouted. She punched him in the arm. Hard. "You're a big jerk. That's your plan? Say that you're sorry and throw yourself on their mercy? That's a shitty-ass plan."

"If it will keep you safe, that's all that matters," he responded. "Damn, woman. Stop arguin' with me. Now is not the time."

"I do not wish to kill you, sentry." Alana strode closer and the gargoyles behind her growled as they followed. "Do you know what it is that I do wish for?"

"No, ma'am," he said with a hint of apprehension.

"Peace," she said quietly. "Peace and the ability to have my people live on the surface without fear of extermination. I was a baby when my family was killed. Since the gold was stolen, we've lived a meager existence within the Dome. I want more than that for my people and their future."

"Not to be rude," Trixie interjected, "but didn't you have any other money?"

Queen Alana's brow furrowed and confusion flickered in her eyes before a look of understanding passed over her face.

"Of course...how could you know the truth?" Her melodious voice drifted around them in the wind. "So much about our people has been misunderstood, so why would the gold be any different? The gold is not only of monetary value to our people. It represents far more than you could understand, and returning it will mean returning dignity and purpose to those within the Dome."

"It's all yours," Trixie said, holding up both hands. "Seriously, Your Highness, take it."

Though Dakota didn't hear the queen utter a word, one of the gargoyles swept down from the sky and grabbed the bag of gold with his massive claws. Moving on instinct, Dakota grabbed Trixie by the arm and pulled her away from the pulsing wings of the beast. The gargoyle ascended, the rocks rumbled and scraped against each other, and the pyramid closed back up. All of it happened in a matter of seconds, and then the gargoyle was once again flying in formation with the others. Except now, he had the huge sack of gold coins hanging from his clawed feet.

"I have one request," Alana murmured. She extended her hand and held out a gold envelope. "Give this to Emperor Zhao. I would like to take my rightful place on the committee and attend the annual summit with the rest of the supernatural leaders. It's time that we come out of the shadows and put the past behind us."

"That's it?" Dakota eyed the envelope warily as he took it from the queen. "You don't want to see me hung up by my fangs or staked out with silver?"

"No." She took a step back and kept her gaze pinned to his. "You will be more use to us alive." She smirked. "Well, as alive as a vampire can be."

"That's it?" Dakota asked incredulously. "Why would you let me live?"

"Dude"—Trixie elbowed him—"shut up."

"She showed me what you are going to do and how important you are to her." Alana let her brilliant green gaze drift over him and then to Trixie. "Both of you."

"*She?*" Trixie held up both hands and shook her head. "Wait a minute. Who is she?"

"The child," Alana murmured. A twinkle glimmered in her eyes when they crinkled at the corners. She was obviously amused by Trixie and Dakota's confusion. "As a child born of gargoyle and witch bloodlines, Rebecca has some exceptionally unique gifts."

"But she's only a baby," Trixie scoffed. "How can she tell you anything? All she does right now is eat, sleep, and poop. Although she does look adorable while doing it."

"And until a few days ago, you were only a vampire and my people were extinct." Queen Alana strode backward with a peaceful smile on her face. "You should know by now, Trixie, that nothing in this world is ever as simple as it seems." She bowed her head and turned her attention back to Dakota. "I'll await Emperor Zhao's response."

In a flash of blinding green light, Alana shifted into her gargoyle form and launched into the night with a shriek. The others followed their queen immediately, leaving Trixie and Dakota alone again in the quiet Texas evening.

"Holy crap," Trixie muttered. "She let us go."

As the gargoyles faded in the distance, Dakota couldn't help but wonder if the emperor would be as forgiving.

Chapter 20

CHELSEA HAD STEPPED INTO HER NEW LIFE AS THOUGH she were born to be a vampire. Their reunion had been everything Trixie had hoped for and then some.

"I can't believe you knew," Trixie whispered. She hugged Chelsea tightly and forced herself not to cry. Again. "All this time…you knew."

"Well, sort off." Chelsea giggled and kissed her mother's cheek. "I didn't know you were a vampire but I really did think you were my guardian angel. I always knew I was different. I was really good at reading people, kind of seeing through their lies and pretenses. My adoptive family was awesome, but they did *not* understand my obsession with tarot cards and crystals. I mean, I didn't know I was a witch…but I knew I was strange."

The two women sat next to each other on the bed in the guest room of Trixie's apartment. Rebecca made a cooing sound from her bassinet, and Chelsea made quick work of scooping her up in her arms. She settled onto the bed again next to her mother and adjusted the blanket around the baby's face.

"Well, the glamour obviously didn't work." Trixie sat cross-legged on the bed. "I wonder if it's because of the witch genetics."

"Maybe." Chelsea shrugged and laughed softly. "I don't know. But whatever the reason, I'm grateful for it.

I knew you were watching out for me and you sparked my interest in coin collecting. The one you gave me was unique, so I started looking for others." Rebecca smiled at the baby and then looked at Trixie, tears glimmering in her eyes. "If you hadn't given me that coin, then I never would have met Gatlin. I loved his smell... It was like roses."

Trixie arched one eyebrow. They say love is blind, but obviously it has a weird sense of smell too.

"And you wouldn't have that gorgeous baby girl," Trixie said wistfully. She bit her lower lip nervously. "Can I hold her?"

"Of course," Chelsea said quickly. She leaned over, the bed creaking with the movement, and gently placed Rebecca in Trixie's arms. "She's your granddaughter."

Trixie cuddled the baby close and her chest clenched as she stared at Rebecca's serene expression.

"I can't believe I finally have my family with me," Trixie said with pure awe. "I never really believed it would happen."

"From what I can tell, you already had a great family." Chelsea stretched her arms over her head before fluffing up the pillows behind her. "Olivia and Doug are so cool, and little Emily is freaking adorable. Maya has already offered to babysit, and Damien is a sweetie pie. When I woke up, they were all standing around me with big smiles."

"They are one weird bunch, aren't they?"

"Honestly?" Chelsea laughed and shook her head. "Nothing has seemed weird to me for a long, long time. And this vampire family, weird or not, loves *you* a whole lot."

"They do, don't they?" Trixie was quiet for a moment and her thoughts went to Gatlin. "He loved you, you know."

She turned her eyes to Chelsea's and finally brought up the one subject they hadn't touched on.

"Gatlin really did love you. He told us that the day he first met you in the coffee shop, he fell in love the minute you smiled at him."

"He was so corny." Chelsea laughed through her tears. She swiped at them with the back of her hand. "And he was so excited to be a daddy, but right before Rebecca was born he started acting weird. He was nervous all the time and always running off to secretive meetings. At first, I thought he was stepping out on me but he came clean. Told me about his past and about the coin. A couple nights later, Franklin showed up at the cottage while Gatlin was in town picking up some things at the store. He got back after Franklin went after me… then he left with Rebecca…"

"He must have sensed us coming," Trixie whispered. "He wanted to protect her."

"And he did."

———

Even though she wanted nothing more than to sit in her apartment to play catch up with Chelsea and fawn over Rebecca, Trixie and Dakota had been summoned to the Presidium's offices.

Emperor Zhao had arrived, and whatever was in that letter had captured his attention.

Trixie clutched Dakota's hand tightly as they strode side by side down the stone hallway that led to the main office. With their footsteps echoing along the stark corridor, Trixie couldn't help but notice how barren and empty it was. Everything was gray and cold, and she found herself longing for the sun. All of this, the whole place, represented her life before *him*...before them.

Before she was free of fear and addiction. Before she stopped hiding.

They rounded the corner, and the instant the door to the Presidium's main office came into view, it swung wide open. Suzie stood in the doorway, looking like her typically nervous self.

"It's wonderful to see you both," she said with a shy smile. Suzie closed the door behind them and gestured to the brown leather sofas. "Have a seat. I'll let them know that you've arrived."

"Thanks, Suzie."

But before they even had a chance to sit down, the door to the conference room swung open and they were met with Olivia's serious green stare.

"Time to face the music," Dakota murmured.

Hand in hand they went into a meeting room that was so quiet it was almost painful. Emperor Zhao sat at the head of the long table and Doug was seated to his left, but when Trixie saw who was sitting on the emperor's right, she was unable to hide her surprise.

"Holy crap," she said none too delicately. "Queen Alana? What the hell are you doing here?"

"Girl, really?" Olivia plastered on a tight smile and shot them a look before gesturing to the two empty seats at the end of the table. "Sit down, you two. Trixie, try to control yourself."

"Sorry." Trixie shrugged sheepishly. "But I wasn't exactly expecting to see her here."

"Lovely to see you too, Trixie," the queen said with her hands folded on the table. "How is Rebecca?"

"Um…she's good." Trixie shrugged. "You know. She's doing her baby thing. Eating, crying, pooping, and sleeping."

"Yes, of course." The queen sat up straighter in her seat and flicked a glance to Emperor Zhao, who was glaring at Dakota with his trademark emotionless black-eyed stare. "Emperor Zhao, may I?"

Zhao said nothing but tilted his head in agreement. The formidable vampire exuded more power than any other Trixie had encountered. His hulking, broad-shouldered form was clad in one of his fancy expensive suits, and he kept his gaze fixed on Dakota, which made Trixie incredibly uncomfortable. *Dude, if looks could kill, you'd be dusted.*

Yeah, I'm gettin' that. To his credit, Dakota sat tall in his seat and met the emperor's icy stare with one of his own. *Looks like moldy old Emperor Zhao is ready to hand me my hat. What do you think he'd do if I flew across the table and gave him a big smooch?*

Trixie stifled a giggle and settled her hand over Dakota's. Even in this bizarre situation, with him staring death in the face, he was trying to make her smile. That was love, wasn't it? He was looking at possible execution but he was doing his best to put *her* at ease.

"Emperor Zhao and I have agreed to a new treaty." The queen smiled at the emperor. "It is one that will allow my people to integrate back into the supernatural world."

"Awesome." Trixie gave them a thumbs-up and pressed her lips in a tight line. "I'm not sure what that has to do with me and Dakota."

"Dakota will no longer be a sentry here in New York," Emperor Zhao said. His voice was deep and barely audible, but it carried a wallop. "He is relieved of his duties."

"As you wish," Dakota said quietly.

Trixie's heart clenched in her chest, and even though Dakota didn't flinch, she knew how much this hurt him. He loved being a sentry, and part of her wondered if Dakota would see this as a fate even worse than death.

"You will need to relinquish your sentry dagger." Zhao flicked his gaze to Dakota's left arm. "Immediately."

Without a word, Dakota removed his hand from Trixie's grasp and undid the leather straps of the sheath around his forearm. Holding the emperor's stare, he removed the dagger and sheath before tossing them across the table to Zhao. They landed with a loud thud directly in front of the emperor, who didn't even glance at them.

"Was never really mine, anyway," Dakota murmured. "It was Jonner's. And in case you were wonderin', I killed him with it."

"Very well." Zhao made no move to take the dagger. "You'll have no need for it where you're going."

Panic fired through Trixie's chest and she hopped to her feet, slamming both hands on the table.

"You're an asshole!" she shouted at Zhao.

"Trixie, stop." Dakota rose to his feet next to her. "This isn't gonna do you or me any good."

"No. I will not stop." Anger had taken over and it took all her restraint not to flash her fangs at the emperor. "Dakota was tricked and lied to by Jonner, the same as the gargoyles were. Shit, man. Dakota's the one who fixed this whole stupid mess. If it weren't for him, the gargoyles wouldn't have their gold back and Jonner would still be out there. Not to mention what could have happened to Chelsea and Rebecca. He saved them and he saved me and I'll be *damned* if I'm going to let you harm one hair on his gorgeous head. He is my blood-mate, and if you kill him, then you kill me. I'll kick your moldy old ass before I let you hurt him."

The emperor said nothing, merely raising his eyebrows at her outburst, which only pissed her off more. She wanted to bite that smug look off his stupid old face.

"Who said anything about killing him?" Zhao said in a calm, matter-of-fact tone. "All I said was that he would no longer be a sentry here in New York."

"Wait...what?" Trixie stilled and looked around the room at the various faces. "You're not going to execute Dakota?"

"No, but might I say that you have lived up to your feisty reputation," Zhao said. "Your youth, exuberance, and love for your mate are...enviable. Nonetheless, you are still incorrect."

"Oh..." Trixie let out an awkward giggle and sat down. "Sorry."

"Like Queen Alana, I am tired of war and vengeance. I am three thousand years old, Ms. La Roux, and I have seen more death than you could possibly imagine. We have made peace with the werewolves and the Amoveo. There is no reason we can't include the gargoyles in our dealings. It is the least I can do after the pain that was inflicted upon them by Jonner."

"Jumping the gun, as usual." Olivia rolled her eyes and shot Trixie an annoyed look.

"What was I supposed to think, Liv?"

"As I was *trying* to say," Zhao continued, "Dakota will not be staying here as a sentry. I am sending him to Texas to serve as a senator and work with the gargoyles. Unlike most senators for the Presidium, he will not report to the local czar but directly to me. There have been several misunderstandings and an abundance of misinformation about their people and ours.

"Dakota will be a liaison to help us dispel some of the…confusion. Rebecca and Chelsea will be going as well. The child is of some importance to the gargoyle community, and it's my understanding that she will need to complete training as she grows up. Training that she can *only* receive from Queen Alana."

"Chelsea already knows what we are asking and she has agreed to come. Gatlin still has family there, and this will allow Rebecca to learn about both sides of her heritage," Alana added. "Chelsea and Rebecca will live within the Dome by day and can learn to navigate the human world by night." She smiled. "With your help, of course."

"Do you accept?" Zhao directed his attention to Dakota. "Will you serve as a senator on behalf of the Presidium?"

Trixie's throat tightened. They'd mentioned everyone but her. Could she do it? Could she let them all go?

"I don't know which is worse," Dakota drawled. "Dyin' or bein' a politician."

Trixie gritted her teeth when no one said anything and

all eyes went to the emperor, but to everyone's surprise, Emperor Zhao burst out laughing. His shoulders shook, a deep baritone chuckle rumbling through the room. Finally after a few awkward glances between them, the rest of them joined in.

"Then it's a yes?" Alana asked hopefully through a wide smile.

"Yes for me." Dakota turned to Trixie and gathered her hand in his once again. "But on one condition."

"What's that?" Zhao arched one dark eyebrow.

"Trixie comes with me."

"Of course." A flicker of confusion washed over the emperor's face. "She is your bloodmate. We assumed she would be going with you. I would never deign to come between a bond as special as that."

"Cool. Thanks." Trixie let out a sigh of relief. "Sorry about the asshole thing and the 'moldy old ass' comment."

"I've been called worse," Zhao said with a small smile. "But I trust you will work on your diplomatic skills."

"Me?" She jutted her thumb at her chest. "A diplomat?"

"I'd like you to train with Isadora. Asmodeus gave her a glowing recommendation. She can help you to learn as much as you can about the witches." He leaned back in his chair, exuding pure confidence and power. "I've already been in communication with her and she is…agreeable."

"Okay." Trixie looked from Olivia and Doug to Dakota. "Will we be able to come back and visit?"

"I don't see why not," Zhao said casually. "This is not a prison sentence. You are free to refuse, but I'm afraid that either way, Dakota will not remain as a sentry."

Emperor Zhao's expression grew serious. "I'm sure you can understand why."

"Yes, sir," Dakota murmured. "I do."

"Well, if our agreements have been met"—Alana rose from her seat with graceful elegance—"I will be on my way. I have much to attend to in my own community."

"Of course." Emperor Zhao stood up and took her hand in his before kissing it regally. "I look forward to building the bridge between our races, and I will see you at the summit next month in Geneva."

"I shall see you in Switzerland." Queen Alana pressed her hands together as if in prayer. As a green light began to emanate from them she whispered, "Until then."

The light flashed, filling the room. A split second later, Queen Alana had vanished along with the light.

"The woman knows how to make an exit," Doug said. "I'll give her that."

"Now that the gold has been returned to them, so have many of their powers." Emperor Zhao leaned forward and pressed his fingertips to the table, directing his attention to Dakota and Trixie. "You have two weeks to complete your relocation to Texas. It's my understanding that you already have a residence there?"

"Yes, sir." Dakota nodded and pulled Trixie into the shelter of his body. "I surely do."

"Fine, then. On your way. I'll expect weekly reports from both of you. Suzie will provide you with the proper procedure." Emperor Zhao sat down and gestured to the door before giving them a sly smile. "We have other business to attend to, and I'm sure you do as well."

Dakota lay naked on the bed in their cottage, only a thin black sheet covering him to his waist. He stared at the closed bathroom door. What the hell was she was doin' in there that was takin' so long? He'd heard the shower and then the hair dryer, but so far Trixie hadn't emerged. It had been a month since they moved down to Texas and so far so good. Trixie's training sessions with Isadora were going off without a hitch, and by all accounts, Chelsea and Rebecca were like a couple of rock stars in the gargoyle community.

After a few tense meetings, he'd even begun to develop friendships with the gargoyle guards. They were a bunch of tough sons of bitches and it was a refreshing change to be fighting with them instead of against them.

He'd even gotten Trixie to start riding horses. A smile played at his lips and he pulled the small gift from beneath his pillow. He'd been working on it ever since they got back and he couldn't wait to give it to her. When he heard the door click open, he quickly hid the present under the sheet.

"No laughing," Trixie said from behind the closed door. "I mean it, and if you tell me it's *swell*, I'm going to deck you."

"No promises." He clapped his hands. "Get your fine-lookin' fanny out here so I can see what you're talkin' about, woman."

When she finally opened the door and stepped into the room, Dakota was rendered speechless. Her hair, which was usually one crazy color or another, was now a deep chocolate brown with a few streaks of purple. Instead of sticking up in a hundred directions, it was smooth and sleek; and her lovely face was free of makeup. Hands at her sides, she strode toward the bed. Dressed in a tiny black slip, which only served to highlight her creamy white skin, the woman was a thing of beauty.

When he didn't say anything, her hands flew to her head and she grimaced.

"You hate it, don't you?"

"No, baby." He scrambled off the bed and immediately swept her into his arms, not caring that he was stark-ass naked. "You're beautiful." He cradled her face in his hands and urged her to look at him. "I love it no matter how you wear it."

"I don't want to hide anymore," she whispered. "I-I'm ready for people to see me... I mean really *see me*. I thought maybe if I toned it down a little..."

"I see you," he whispered. Dakota rasped his thumb over her cheek. "I've always seen you. I don't care what color your hair is or how much makeup you wear. I love you, Trix, and I'll take you any way I can get you."

Trixie popped up on her toes and pressed her lips to his. His desire grew swiftly as she pushed her tongue into his mouth, seeking, touching, and tasting. Dakota groaned and slid his hands to her shoulders, hooking his fingers in the straps of her nightie and pushing it off. The flimsy fabric fluttered soundlessly to the ground, and she pressed her soft, curvy body tightly against his.

He kissed her deeply as their hands eagerly explored each other. Dakota was always amazed how quickly they were ready for each other, how easily and naturally their bodies reacted. With lightning-fast reflexes and the need to be inside her, to touch her in every way possible, Dakota whisked her to the bed.

He linked his arm around her waist and spun her so that her ass was nuzzled against his hardening cock. He trailed hot kisses along her throat and she tilted her head, giving him access to the sensitive flesh, but he wanted more.

She bent over and braced her hands on the bed. Fangs bared, she glanced at him over her shoulder and wiggled her ass before spreading her legs wide. Seeing her open and exposed to him like that was more than he could take. He grabbed her hips and thrust his shaft into her to the hilt. He pumped into her with swift sure strokes, and his climax coiled deep in his gut.

Trixie knew what he needed without him having to ask.

With preternatural speed, she flipped over onto her back and pulled him down to the bed with her. Dakota slipped inside her without missing a beat, and as Trixie wrapped her legs around his waist, he unsheathed his fangs. Her hips rose to meet his as he pumped into her wildly. She threaded her hands through his hair, pulling him to her.

He nuzzled her neck and shouted her name into her mind as his climax began to crest. As thoughts and bodies mingled, their fangs pierced each other's flesh at the same moment, sending them both over the edge and into the abyss.

As the powerful blood flowed, and Dakota remained locked inside the warmth of Trixie's body, he reveled in the sound of their jointly beating hearts.

Once. Twice. Home.

They lay naked and wrapped up in a tangle of limbs and bedsheets as the exquisite haze of lust faded. Trixie was curled up on his chest with her arm and leg comfortably thrown over his.

"I could stay right here forever," Dakota murmured.

"Me too." Trixie sighed. She wiggled and adjusted her position. "But something is poking me in the shoulder. What is that?"

She pushed herself up and started searching the sheets. A moment later she pulled out the gift that Dakota had made for her. The genuine expression of surprise on her face was all the thanks he needed.

Trixie held the small wooden horse in her quivering fingers. The rearing mare was smooth and polished. Her head was held high and her tail perked up as she kicked her front hooves in the air and whinnied at the world.

"Did you make this?" she asked in a shaky whisper. "For me?"

"I surely did." He settled his hand on her lower back and trailed his fingers along the soft velvety skin. "Ever since I first set eyes on you, the one image that came to mind was a wild horse. Unbroken. Spirited. Feisty. Free. I dunno… When I saw the way you reacted to little Emily's horse…I figured I should make you one of your own."

"Thank you." Her eyes filled and she blinked, sending one big fat tear down her cheek. "No one ever made me a present before… I love it."

"Girl, you and I are gonna have plenty *firsts* and *never befores*." He dragged her back into his arms and pulled her next to him. He pressed a kiss to her cheek as she fiddled with the horse. "I know you miss the girls back in the city. If you want I could whittle you a little coven, maybe a wooden Olivia and Doug? Shane is pretty stiff, so he'd be real easy to carve."

"Boy, you are too much." Trixie shook her head and laughed as she reached over and placed the horse on the nightstand. She rolled onto her side so that they were face-to-face, her arms curled between them and her leg hooked over his. "But what else should I expect from a vampire who eats human candy. Speaking of which, where are your lollipops? Aren't you going through some kind of withdrawal? You usually have one dangling from that gorgeous mouth of yours. You said that they made you feel human or something, right? I haven't seen you with one in a while."

"That's true." His brow knit together and he let out a short laugh as his gaze skittered over her face. "I hadn't really had the urge for one lately," he said quietly.

"Why?"

Dakota cradled her cheek and rested his forehead against hers. His gruff voice settled in her mind. *Because I have you.*

In case you missed it, read on for an excerpt
from *Tall, Dark, and Vampire*, the first book in
the Dead in the City series

———⟪∿∿⟫———

THE TANTALIZING SCENT FILLED HER HEAD THE MOMENT
she slipped the key into the front door of her club.

Blood.

The sweet, cinnamon flavor titillated her heightened
senses. Olivia's head snapped up sharply as fangs burst
in her mouth. She closed her emerald green eyes and
stilled as she breathed deeply and listened to the comforting noises of the night that blanketed her. The chatter
of humans passing her on the city streets, cars idling,
and horns honking filled her head.

Olivia sharpened her focus on the sounds within her
club—her home. What the hell was going on in there?
She remained motionless as the sound of light, feminine
giggling came from deep within the building.

Her fangs retracted, and she swore with frustration.
"Maya, you incredible asshole," she hissed.

Olivia threw the lock and pushed open the enormous
mahogany doors, slamming them shut behind her with
ease as she threw the main house lights on. She stood in
the cavernous foyer of the old church with her hands on
her hips, while she delivered a withering stare to the young
vampire. Instead of looking contrite for being caught,
Maya looked rather pleased with herself. As a human,
Maya had been a giggling fool who delighted in toying
with men, and now, as a vampire, she was in her glory.

She sat demurely on top of a human male, who was currently on all fours, acting as her makeshift throne. Maya's long blond hair washed over creamy, bare shoulders as her hands remained folded in her lap and her legs crossed sweetly at the ankles. The innocent pose was a stark contrast to the black leather bustier and miniskirt she wore.

She blinked her large blue eyes and laughed again, while the human grunted helplessly beneath her. Based on the look of him, if he weren't under her spell, he would never submit like this for a woman—ever. He was an enormous muscle-head who likely spent most of his waking hours at a gym in a desperate attempt to be the next Arnold Schwarzenegger.

At the moment, he was doing a great impersonation of a bench.

"How many times have I told you? Never play with your food in the club." She let out a sigh and softened her tone, reminding herself that Maya was still young. "It's not safe to do things like this, Maya. We don't want to draw unnecessary attention to ourselves, remember?"

Olivia pushed her thick, curly red hair out of her face and shrugged her long black coat off her slim shoulders. She knew that reprimanding Maya was useless, but felt the need to remind her of the rules. She'd only been turned a few years ago and was still in the defiant adolescent phase. Since Olivia was her sire, Maya was her responsibility for the first century of her immortality, but at the rate she was going—it was going to be longer than that.

"Maya?" Olivia folded her arms as her green eyes flashed with impatience at her uncooperative offspring. "Please get him out, and don't leave any loose ends."

"Oh, you're such a poop." Maya waved dismissively and looked at the pathetic fool beneath her. "We were just having a little fun," she said, stroking his head the way one would pet a dog. "Weren't we, baby?"

Maya smacked him on the ass, and he whimpered, a sound that hung somewhere between pleasure and pain. She straddled him like a horse and leaned in, slowly licking the blood that still dripped from the wound she'd made in his neck. Maya looked like a cat playing with a mouse. The poor bastard had probably been toyed with like this all day long, which meant Maya had not slept.

Great.

The smell of blood grew stronger, and Olivia watched Maya lick a trickle of red from his neck as she writhed seductively on his back. He closed his eyes, grunted, and shuddered as the orgasm ripped through him.

Olivia's fangs erupted, but she quickly willed them away, disgusted by her lack of self-control. It was no wonder this mess aroused her. Between the blood, the sexual energy, and her abstinence, it was bound to happen. Her maker, Vincent, never understood her self-imposed celibacy, although that wasn't terribly surprising—he'd never been in love. If he had watched the love of his life die in his arms, then he might have a better grasp of why Olivia was unwilling to open her heart again. Most vampires could separate sex and love, but that was one little piece of the vampire world she never adjusted to.

Olivia. She jumped as Vincent's sharp voice cut into her mind. *Just because you haven't had sex in centuries, that is no reason to start salivating over this childish nonsense.*

Speak of the devil. Olivia had not seen hide nor hair

of her maker in over fifty years, but given his emotional eavesdropping, he must be back in the city. If he had been more than fifty miles away, he would not have been able to sense her feelings so easily. *What can I do for you, Vincent?*

Do for me? Nothing, my dear. Can't a maker check in on his favorite offspring? Olivia tore her gaze away from Maya and swiftly walked behind the bar, creating busywork for herself in an effort to quell the bloodlust and the plain old lust. *I'm fine, Vincent.* She looked at Maya again briefly, before tending to the stock again. *I take it that you're back in the States? Does this mean that we can expect a visit from you this evening?*

Still celibate, Olivia? It's obviously not doing you any favors. I can smell your sexual frustration from miles away, and it's really quite unattractive.

Are you coming by the club or not? Olivia shielded the telepathic conversation between them because the last thing she needed was Maya, a youngling vampire, butting into it. Vampires could telepath with their sire, progeny, or siblings, and though Maya was her progeny, this conversation was definitely not for her.

Perhaps. His voice faded as the connection was broken.

Great. She shoved a stray curl from her face and swore under her breath. Maya decided to act up just when her own maker comes to town. What shitty timing.

"Maya," she said more firmly. "Your boy toy has to get going, and you've got to get to work."

This was her place of business, and she refused to encourage behavior that could jeopardize it, especially by a member of her own coven. She hated to admit it, but Vincent was right. The fact that she had been celibate for almost three centuries was really starting to grate on her.

At least she had sex dreams.

Her lips curved at the memories. She might've gone bonkers if it weren't for her dream lover and his talented hands. Three hundred years ago, he'd been her human lover and the only man she'd ever loved, but he was long dead and now only existed in her dreams. The dreamscape was the one place she could find pleasure after all these years.

There was just one problem. Vampires did not dream.

Aside from the lack of sunlight, the absence of dreams was one of the hardest losses for new vamps to adjust to. After over two centuries of enduring the leaden dreamless sleep of a vampire, Olivia had practically forgotten what it was like to dream, to fall through the mystical dreamscape and revel in fantasy.

Then, almost twenty years ago, out of nowhere, she began to dream again.

The first one freaked her out. It was a sudden burst of color and light after years of slumbering in utter darkness. Her dream lover looked just as he had when she first met him, a young boy entering manhood. Over the years, he aged in her dreams, just as he had when she knew him as a human.

As fascinated as she was by the dreams, as curious as she was to decipher their meaning, she did not dare mention them to anyone.

Olivia had heard of only one instance when vampires could dream—the bloodmate legend. Vincent told her the story soon after he turned her, and it gave her hope that her life would not be forever shrouded in the night.

However, when she tried to get him to tell her more, he dismissed her harshly and said he knew nothing. He scolded her for being a foolish child and told her the entire story was made up to placate new vampires while they got used to their new lives.

No one else had ever spoken of it, and the whole legend remained shrouded in secrecy and possessed an air of danger.

When the ghostly visits first began, she did some research online but found little information, and any references to the bloodmate legend were few and far between. According to the tale, when a vampire found a bloodmate and performed a blood exchange, then both became daywalkers.

She rubbed at the tattoo on the back of her neck absently. When Douglas's ghost began visiting her, she had the symbol of eternity inked on her neck, a private reminder of her lost love and her promise to love him, *and only him*, for eternity.

Olivia shook her head at her foolishness. Even if there were truth to the whole legend, it was a moot point, since Douglas was long dead. However, dead or not, she kept her pledge of devotion. Maybe the young, innocent girl she used to be lingered inside, because as far as Olivia was concerned, being devoted to someone meant that you did not diddle with anyone else.

Celibacy was a ridiculous notion for many humans, and positively insane for most vampires, at least the ones she encountered.

She sighed as she wiped the bar down and glanced at Maya with her flesh-and-blood plaything. Sympathy for the man tugged at what was left of her heart. Olivia didn't hate humans, quite the opposite in fact, but she did hate the idea of them being feasted on inside her club.

"Come on, Maya." She kept her voice even and her eyes trained on the bar stock, noting what needed to be refilled. "You've had enough fun for one day. Now, get him out, and don't forget to glamour him again before you leave him. Why don't you give him a pleasant memory? He was kind enough to provide you with life-giving blood, so the least you can do is give him a memory that will make him smile."

"Oh fine," she pouted. "He'll think we fucked like rabbits all day long and that he rocked my world."

Maya leaned in and licked his wound closed, leaving no evidence behind. She whispered to her prey, erasing all memory of their day together and replacing it with something palatable. He stood slowly and adjusted his crotch, while looking around the empty club somewhat bewildered.

"You better be back here in an hour ready to work," Olivia shouted. "I don't want to hear any complaining. You *chose* not to sleep, so don't make that *choice* a problem for the rest of us."

"My goodness, Olivia," Maya sang. "Getting cranky in our old age?"

Her singsong tone made Olivia want to smack her, but she could not prevent the smile that played at her lips. Maya was right. She was a little cranky, but three centuries of no sex or intimacy would do that to anyone.

"Cut the chatter, and get him out of here," she said more sharply than intended. She did not want Maya to know that she had been rattled by the situation, because she would never live it down. Olivia glanced at the human who stood there looking confused and found herself feeling sorry for him. "Seriously, let the poor guy off the hook."

"Hey… I gotta get going. I'm really tired. I think I should go." The big oaf babbled absently. "Man, my knees are killing me," he mumbled.

"Poor baby," Maya purred in a velvety soft voice as she glamoured the boy, giving him false memories in place of the real ones. "We should probably get going. Come on, kitten. I'll walk you out, but didn't we have fun at the park today? You're such a sweetheart for walking me to work this evening and for giving me multiple orgasms last night. You big stud."

Maya winked a long-lashed eye over her shoulder at Olivia, as they disappeared into the crisp winter night. Olivia shook her head and smiled in spite of how irritated she was. Maya absolutely loved being a vamp—she genuinely loved it, and there was something refreshing in her enthusiasm. Olivia never found that kind of passion for what she had become, and part of her was a tad jealous of Maya's love for her vampire life.

At first, Olivia had been disgusted and frightened, but Vincent had been a patient teacher, and eventually she accepted it.

But she never loved it.

Even when she served as a sentry for the Presidium, the vampire government, she did it out of duty, loyalty, and respect. She served her one hundred years as a soldier but retired as soon as her term was up and never looked back. Olivia enjoyed the quiet life of a private citizen, even though she never expected that to include a coven of her own.

As she readied the club for that evening's patrons, her

mind wandered to the night she sired Maya, and her smile quickly faded. She found her in the alley behind the club just before dawn, raped and beaten to within an inch of her life. The dirtbag who had done it dumped her there like garbage, and raw anger still flared at the memory.

Olivia sensed it the moment he dropped her broken body next to the dumpster. Maya would have died if she hadn't been turned; there was no time for ambulances or hospitals, and even though it had been almost five years since that night, she remembered it like it was yesterday. It was the last time she killed a human.

The memory both sickened and frightened her because when she drained that piece of shit dry—she loved every fucking minute. Olivia relished watching the fear in his eyes as she pinned him against the wall of his bedroom and savored his whimpering pleas for his life as he struggled uselessly. She took pure pleasure in feeling his heart slow, beat by beat, as the life faded from his eyes.

The red haze of rage consumed her, took her over, and blinded her.

Olivia swallowed the bile that rose in her throat, disgusted with her basest instincts and the primal pleasure she took from eviscerating him. She was a monster. A killer. No different from the vicious, pathetic excuse for a man she killed.

But there was a price to pay for her vengeance— there's always a price.

His blood memories would remain with her for eternity, and that was her penance. The horror and fear of all the women he raped lingered in her memories now, including Maya's last conscious, horrifying hours as a human.

Monsters don't go unpunished, and Olivia knew she was no different.

———

The music pounded loudly through the club as it reverberated through Olivia's body. She walked the dance floor, taking note of the various humans writhing with one another amid the pulsating lights. She stuck out like a sore thumb, since she was the only one wearing a black Armani suit, not the leather or spikes of her faithful patrons.

Olivia waved at the regular customers peppered throughout the club and allowed herself a moment of pride. The Coven had become one of the most popular dance clubs for the Goth set in NYC, and she had worked her ass off to make it happen.

She paced the floor more than usual tonight because she had been on edge ever since walking in on Maya. She could not afford any mistakes that would draw human attention or piss off the Presidium. Humans were easy enough to deal with, but she was less than pleased at the idea of vampire officials butting their noses into her life.

She liked it here and had no desire to leave, but the drawback of immortality was that moving on eventually was an annoying necessity—can't stay somewhere for thirty years if you don't age. Although, the prevalent use of Botox among humans certainly helped explain her lack of facial wrinkles.

Olivia scoped out the club and marveled at how far society had come—and yet not.

Humans who loved to dress like vampires, or what they thought vampires looked like, flocked to this place every night as the sun went down. Except Sunday—she closed the joint on Sunday, since the place used to be a church. She figured it was the least she could do. Olivia grinned and shook her head as she watched the humans wooing one another in their *vampire* garb.

Ironically, most vampires did not dress like horror-movie rejects; many adopted the fashion of the era they lived in, but not all did. Vincent, for example, liked the Victorian era so much that sometimes he still adorned himself in a top hat and ascot, although she thought it looked ridiculous. Vampires retained their individuality at least.

Imagine if they knew this club was owned and operated by an actual vampire who preferred silk and cashmere to leather and spikes. Olivia had to wear the leather sentry uniform every day for a century and loathed the idea of wrapping herself in it again.

I'd be a sad disappointment to them.

She glanced to the bar as she made her way to the DJ platform. Maya was playing up her charms with various drooling idiots who were only too happy to give her enormous tips in exchange for the smallest bit of her attention.

Trixie, her other bartender, was Maya's opposite but worked her charms with equal fervor. Her short pink-spiked hair and black eyeliner were a stark contrast to Maya's blond, innocent look. Both vamps were great at bringing in the crowd and keeping them happy. They gave a quick wave to Olivia as she passed, and Maya stuck her tongue out in her usual flippant, childish manner.

Olivia climbed onto the DJ's platform and gave Sadie a pat on the back. Sadie was one of the best spinners out there, living or undead, and Olivia's oldest, most trusted friend. She was dressed much like the patrons of the club, except Sadie actually *was* a vamp, and the girl had a serious passion for leather and lace.

"Hey, boss. Feels like a lively crowd tonight." Sadie winked and smiled. "No pun intended."

"Did you hear what Maya did?" Olivia kept her eyes focused on the crowd, her senses alert for anything out of the ordinary. A sense of impending doom flickered up her spine. Trouble was coming. "She's a pain in my ass."

"Sure did, and she sure is." Sadie put her headphones around her neck. "Think that girl will ever listen?" she asked with a nod toward the bar, as she laughed and pushed her long brown hair out of her eyes. "'Cause I don't."

"Maya's still young." Olivia gave Sadie a friendly nudge with her elbow. "It took you a little while to get the hang of it, if I'm not mistaken?"

Sadie was the first vamp she had ever turned. Olivia and Vincent were traveling through a largely unsettled part of Arizona and picked up the distinctly potent scent of blood. The Apache Indians had been attacking settlers at that time, not that Olivia could blame them, and Sadie's family had been among their victims.

Sadie was barely alive when she found her. The faint beat of her heart called to Olivia, and before she even knew what she was doing, she turned her. It was an instinctive need to save her, to help this poor girl who had lost everything, left seemingly alone in the world.

Vincent, of course, was less than pleased, and that was the beginning of the end for them.

Olivia looked fondly at her friend and smiled. "You

have been around a couple hundred years longer than she has."

"Truth." Sadie winked and adjusted the headphones around her neck. "You're just a sucker for hard-luck cases. Face it. You would rescue the world if you could."

"Not the *whole* world," Olivia said dramatically. "Just the ones who really need it."

"I sure needed it," Sadie said with a warm smile.

Olivia swallowed the surprising lump in her throat before looking back at the crowd. Sadie had tried to thank her on several occasions, but Olivia never let her get the words out. Deep down inside she felt as though she hadn't saved Sadie or the others. Perhaps the vampire hunters of the world were right. What if vamps really were damned to burn in hell for eternity? Would anyone thank her then?

"I should get back down there before Maya finds another boy toy."

Sadie grabbed the microphone and Olivia's arm before she could escape.

"Everyone having fun?" Sadie bellowed into the silver microphone. The crowd responded with insanely loud screaming and whistling. "Then I think we should all give it up for Olivia Hollingsworth, the owner and proprietor of The Coven."

Olivia waved to the screaming crowd and shot her friend a narrow-eyed look as she made her way down from the altar. She hated being the center of attention, and Sadie knew it but delighted in razzing her on occasion.

Another loud, bass-driven song tumbled over the crowd as Sadie's voice floated into her head. *Hey, boss.*

I see our VIP table is full again tonight with your boy-friend and his crew.

Olivia threw an irritated glance over her shoulder at Sadie and shot back. *He's not my boyfriend. He just wishes he was. What a termite.* She could hear Sadie stifle a giggle as she navigated the crowd and made her way to Michael's table.

How long has it been since you got laid? I forget. Olivia did her best to ignore that last jab from her friend. Other than Vincent, Sadie was the only one who knew that Olivia had been celibate since becoming a vampire. *Don't you think you've tortured yourself long enough? I never knew this Douglas guy, but if he really loved you the way you say he did, would he want you to spend eternity alone?*

I'm not alone. Olivia threw a wink over her shoulder. *I've got all of you, and sex is overrated anyway.*

Damn. Sadie's laugh jingled through Olivia's mind. *Now you're just talking crazy.*

Olivia shook her head and smiled. Her heart had been stolen long before Vincent made it stop beating, and besides, even if she did have her heart to give, Moriarty certainly would not be a candidate.

Michael was a greasy little worm who used his family's reputation to get what he wanted. He came to The Coven every Saturday night with his gaggle of dirtbags, and Olivia could smell his fear and feelings of inadequacy a mile away. He'd been trying to get into her pants for months now, and apparently was still trying, even after a multitude of rejections.

She felt his eyes on her all night and had managed to ignore him, but now it was time to play the game.

She had to placate the little weasel. Jerk or not, he was a customer—a customer who spent a lot of money in her club.

Olivia flashed the most charming grin she could muster as she approached Michael and his motley crew.

"Hey there, hot stuff." He leered at her and his lips curved into a lascivious grin. "I was wondering how long it was gonna take you to get your sweet ass over here."

She wanted to bite his face off. What an asshole.

"Hello, Mr. Moriarty," she said through a strained smile. "Are you gentlemen finding everything satisfactory this evening?"

"We're just fine, aren't we, boys?"

He took a long sip of his martini as he ran his hand up the leg of some young girl who was draped all over him, probably believing he'd make her rich and famous. She definitely didn't fit in with the other clubgoers. This blond was more mainstream and never would have stepped foot into The Coven if it weren't for Moriarty. Many humans were easily swayed by money and power. Moriarty had both.

"I'd be doin' a lot better if you'd come here and sit with me."

The girl next to him made a noise of disgust, shoved his hand away, grabbed her purse, and stomped off. He shrugged and snickered as she stalked through the crowd toward the door.

"It seems you've upset your date, Mr. Moriarty." Olivia watched the foolish girl run from the club. She probably expected him to chase her. Not likely. "Looks like she's leaving."

"She's not my date," he spat. "Just some bimbo

hanger-on—you know how it is. She should know better than to do that." His lip curled in disgust as he watched her leave, and the smile faded. Olivia felt the anger roll off him as he stared after her. "I don't give second chances. One and done. Know what I mean?"

"Yes, of course." Olivia smiled tightly and looked at him like the black-haired little bug he was. "Well, *gentlemen*, I hope you'll let me buy the final round here. It's almost last call."

She motioned to the waitress who covered the three VIP tables opposite the bar. Suzie, one of only two humans who worked at The Coven, came over quickly, but Olivia sensed her anxiety long before she arrived at the table.

"Sure, baby." He leered. "You can buy me a drink."

Olivia wanted nothing more than to glamour this guy into dancing naked in the middle of the club with only his socks on, but the image alone would have to be enough.

"Suzie. Please get our guests their last round." She flicked her gaze back to Moriarty. "On the house, of course."

"Yes, ma'am." She looked like a skittish lamb surrounded by wolves. She almost hadn't hired Suzie due to her naive nature, but Olivia was a sucker for hard-luck cases. Suzie was straight from the farm and as green as the fields. By hiring her, she figured she could at least keep an eye on her.

Olivia nodded and said a brief good-bye before working her way to the front door. The place was starting to thin out, since it was just about last call. The tension in her shoulders eased as soon as she set eyes on the only other human who worked at the club—their bouncer Damien.

Damien, unlike Suzie, knew what Olivia and the others were. He was what some referred to as a *familiar*, but Olivia hated that term. It seemed like a dirty word, laced with innuendo and ill intent. Most humans who worked with vampires did it out of love and friendship.

However, Damien wasn't just a friend—he was more like family. He was the only human who knew what Olivia was and kept her secret, and not because he had to, but because he genuinely cared for her. She'd met him when he was a boy, spending most of his time on the streets and clearly heading down a bad path.

She'd heard his cries one night, and even though it was against Presidium rules to interfere with humans and their problems, she couldn't help it. That cry of a young boy in the dark overrode any rules she was supposed to follow, and before she knew it, she was plucking him from what was sure to be a deadly situation.

She planned to rescue him from the local drug dealer and send him on his way. Yet the second she looked into those soulful, brown eyes, she was hooked. At first, she told herself that she would only check on him for a few nights to be sure he was safe, but those few nights turned into weeks, and then years. Since vampires couldn't have children, Damien was the closest she'd ever have to a child, and she loved him as if he was her own.

"Hey there, handsome," Olivia said. She walked through the vestibule crowded with folks leaving for the night. "How's it going out here?"

"Hey there, boss," Damien said in his deep baritone. He gave her his trademark toothy, white smile, the one that completely changed the perception of who he was. He was a wall of solid muscle, stood over six feet tall, and had lovely olive skin. One look from this hulking fellow would send most people running, but in reality, Damien was a giant teddy bear.

"So is everything okay on your end tonight? Nothing, um, out of the ordinary?" Olivia asked as she scanned the exiting crowd warily. Damien raised one eyebrow at her skeptically. "You know, out of the ordinary for us?" she clarified.

"Just the usual fare and a few drunken idiots. I did have one crier though, just a little while ago," he said as he pulled the velvet ropes in for the night. "She looked pretty upset. I tried to stop her, but she ran away, down toward Sixth Ave."

"Mmm." Olivia rolled her eyes. "That was Moriarty's date."

"Moriarty's still here?" Damien had barely finished the question, when Michael appeared in the vestibule with his posse.

"We were just leaving, big guy." Michael gave him a smack on the back as he walked to the enormous stretch limo waiting at the curb. Olivia put her hand on Damien to keep him at bay. She couldn't blame him for wanting to go after him, because she wanted to punch the little bastard's lights out too.

"You know, Olivia, one day that guy is gonna get what's coming to him," Damien said quietly as the limo pulled away. "I just hope I get to see it."

"You know what they say, babe," she said quietly. "Be careful what you wish for. Besides, his money is as green as anyone's."

"I realize you're not into live feeds like most of your *crowd*, but boy, does that guy deserve to be dinner or what? I know you can handle yourself, but I don't like the way he speaks to Suzie or any other woman for that matter."

"I know." Olivia smiled and rubbed his arm reassuringly. She knew he had a crush on Suzie but would never admit it. "Suzie is tougher than you think, and you know I've always got her back. Besides," she said in a weary voice, "Moriarty's not worth the trouble."

"Hey, you okay?" He looked at her worriedly with his arms folded across his massive chest. "Did you feed today?"

"Yeah, well, not a live feed, obviously," she quickly added. "Just from my microwaveable stock, which reminds me, we need to place another order with the Presidium's blood bank."

She rubbed her temples absently as various patrons pushed past as they left. Live feeds were always best, but Olivia tried to avoid them. While the live feed was most rejuvenating, it was also the most dangerous. Live feeds were like a drug. The more she did it, the more she wanted it, and each time it got harder and harder to stop. Besides, blood memories came with it, and she wasn't interested in anyone else's baggage. She had quite enough of her own shit to deal with.

"This incident with Maya earlier really rattled me. She's got to learn not to feed in or near the club," she said with frustration. "I don't want any trouble. I mean, it's not just my place of business. We live here too."

"What happened exactly?" Damien asked quietly. He leaned down and looked around to make sure no one would overhear. "I saw her leave with him last night after closing, so how'd she end up back here? I got some of the dirt from Trixie, but then Suzie came around, and well, you know." He shrugged and smiled sheepishly.

He knew Olivia wanted to keep Suzie in the dark about the vamps because it was bad enough she'd let Damien in on their world. It took years for the Presidium to accept him, and *accept* would be a generous description of their feelings on humans in the know. *Tolerate* was a more appropriate word.

"I saw her leave with that meathead last night after closing. I figured she'd ditch him before sunrise, so I locked up and went downstairs to sleep. Then tonight, right after sundown, I go run an errand, and when I come back, I find her in the middle of the club with her boy toy." Olivia looked past him and through the door at Maya, who was cleaning up the bar. "She obviously brought him back here just before sunrise and messed with him all day long. I'm not sure why she'd do that," she murmured.

"My guess is that she wanted to get a rise out of you. Want me to talk to her?"

"No." She shook her head. "I'll speak to her again before she leaves tonight. She's my…"

"Responsibility," Damien finished for her. He sighed and shook his head. "Not everyone is your responsibility, you know."

"No, but *she* is." Olivia patted his shoulder wearily. "I hear the last song of the night." Sadie always played The Strike Nineteens's "Forever in Darkness" as the final tune, and the irony was never lost on Olivia. "Time to go inside and clear out the stragglers."

As she turned to go back inside, an oddly familiar voice floated over, and the scent of the ocean filled her head.

"Excuse me. Can you tell me where I can find Ms. Olivia Hollingsworth?"

Olivia stopped dead in her tracks, and the tattoo on the nape of her neck burned. Her fangs erupted, and little licks of fire skittered up her spine, as one note of that smooth, velvety voice banished all self-control. She closed her eyes and willed her quaking body to settle.

It can't be.

Terrified and hopeful, Olivia steeled herself with courage she'd forgotten she had. She turned around, excruciatingly slowly, and found herself face-to-face with the man of her dreams and the love of her life.

The problem was he'd been dead for almost three hundred years.

Viking Warrior Rising

by Asa Maria Bradley

—◆—

Immortal Vikings are among us

Leif Skarsganger and his elite band of immortal warriors have been charged to protect humanity from the evil Norse god Loki.

Under attack from Loki's minions, Leif is shocked to encounter a dark-haired beauty who fights like a warrior herself. Wounded and feverish, the Viking kisses her, inadvertently triggering an ancient Norse bond. But when Naya Brisbane breaks away and disappears before the bond is completed, Leif's warrior spirit goes berserk. If Leif doesn't find her fast, he's going to lose himself to permanent battle fury.

But Naya doesn't want to be found…and he'll do anything to find her. Because they're both running out of time.

—◆—

"Bradley is a new force to be reckoned with in the paranormal genre! Move over Highlanders…the Vikings are coming!" —Rebecca Zanetti, *New York Times* bestselling author of the Dark Protector series

For more Asa Maria Bradley, visit:

www.sourcebooks.com

In the Company of Wolves

by Paige Tyler

New York Times and *USA Today* bestselling author

—⁓—

The new gang of thugs in town is ruthless to the extreme—and a pack of wolf shifters. Special Wolf Alpha Team discovers this in the middle of a shootout. When Eric Becker comes face to face with a female werewolf, shooting her isn't an option, but neither is arresting her. She's the most beautiful woman he's ever seen—or smelled. Becker hides her and leaves the crime scene with the rest of his team.

Jayna Winston has no idea why that SWAT guy hid her, but she's sure glad he did. Now what's a street-savvy thief going to do with a hot alpha-wolf SWAT officer?

—⁓—

Praise for Paige Tyler's SWAT series:

"Bring on the growling, possessive alpha male… A fast-paced and super-exciting read that grabbed my attention. I loved it." —*Night Owl Reviews* Top Pick, 5 Stars

For more Paige Tyler, visit:

www.sourcebooks.com

SEAL Wolf in Too Deep

by Terry Spear

USA Today bestselling author

His love is dangerous

As a Navy SEAL and police diver, alpha wolf shifter Allan Rappaport knows how to handle tough situations, but the arrival of a human diving partner—especially one as attractive as Debbie Renaud—is a whole new challenge. Getting involved is dangerous, but Debbie's offers are hard to resist. As the heat between them rises and a murder plot thickens, Allan is on the brink of exposing his biggest secret.

But she's diving in headfirst

For Debbie, working with another top-notch diver like Allan is too good to be true, and their mutual attraction is hotter than she could have dreamed. Debbie suspects he's hiding something, though, and she's set on figuring it out—one off-duty rendezvous at a time. But when Debbie gets between a werewolf hunter and his intended victim, suddenly she is plunged straight into the heart of Allan's world—a world she never knew existed.

Praise for Terry Spear:

"Terry Spear delivers the action and steamy romance expected by fans of her shifter stories." —*Paranormal Haven*

"Spear takes readers on a pulse-pounding ride... There's plenty of action." —*Publishers Weekly*

For more Terry Spear, visit:
www.sourcebooks.com

About the Author

Sara Humphreys is the award-winning author of the Amoveo Legend series. The third book in the series, *Untamed*, won two PRISM awards: Dark Paranormal and Best of the Best. The first two novels from her Dead in the City series have been nominated for the National Readers' Choice Award. Sara was also a professional actress. Some of her television credits include, A&E's *Biography*, *Guiding Light*, *Another World*, *As the World Turns*, and *Rescue Me*.

She loves writing hot heroes and heroines with moxie, but above all, Sara adores a satisfying happily ever after. She lives in New York with Mr. H., their four amazing sons, and two adorable pups. When she's not writing or hanging out with the men in her life, she can be found working out with Shaun T in her living room or chatting with readers on Facebook.

For a full list of Sara's books, please visit her website.